OBSESSIVE UNION

MADE
BOOK 9

BROOKE SUMMERS

First Edition published in 2023

Text Copyright © Brooke Summers

Edits by Farrant Editing

All rights reserved.

The moral right of the author has been asserted. No part of this publication may be reproduced, stored in or introduced into a retrieval system, or transmitted, in any form or by any means (electronic, mechanical, photocopying, recording or otherwise), nor be otherwise circulated in any form of binding or cover other than that in which it is published without the prior written permission of the author. Any person who does any unauthorized act in relation to this publication may be liable to criminal prosecution and civil claims for damages.

All characters in this publication are fictitious and any resemblance to real persons, living or dead, is purely coincidental.

BOOKS BY BROOKE:

The Kingpin Series:
Forbidden Lust
Dangerous Secrets
Forever Love

The Made Series:
Bloody Union
Unexpected Union
Fragile Union
Shattered Union
Hateful Union
Vengeful Union
Explosive Union
Cherished Union
Obsessive Union

Gallo Famiglia:
Ruthless Arrangement
Ruthless Betrayal
Ruthless Passion

The Fury Vipers MC Series:

Stag

Mayhem

Digger

Ace

Pyro

Shadow

Wrath

Reaper

Standalones:

Saving Reli

Taken By Nikolai

A Love So Wrong

Other pen names

Stella Bella

(A forbidden Steamy Pen name)

Taboo Temptations:

Wicked With the Professor

Snowed in with Daddy

Wooed by Daddy

Loving Daddy's Best Friend

Brother's Glory

Daddy's Curvy Girl

Daddy's Intern

His Curvy Brat

Taboo Teachings:

Royally Taught

Extra Curricular with Mr. Abbot

Private Seduction:

Seduced by Daddy's Best Friend

Stepbrother Seduction

His Curvy Seduction

Never worry about what could have been...
Always dream of what can be...

CONTENT
PLEASE READ CAREFULLY.

There are elements and themes within this book that some readers might find extremely upsetting.

Please click here for that list of potentially harmful topics. Please heed these as this book contains some heavy topics that some readers could find damaging.

OR GO TO WWW.BROOKESUMMERSBOOKS.COM/CONTENT-WARNINGS

PROLOGUE
ALESSIO

Eight years ago
Aged 16

I'm on the floor, blood pouring from my lip and eye.

Fucker caught me good.

Never again. No more after today.

"You'll learn," my father sneers at me. "You'll learn to have some fucking respect."

I don't answer him. He's a monster. My own personal monster. He lives to hurt me, and feasts on my pain.

I learned by the age of six not to cry, if I did he would laugh in my face and call me a pussy; tell me I'm weak, useless, and would never amount to anything. If I shouted out in pain, he'd tell me I wasn't worthy of the Bianchi name.

I've been Matteo Bianchi's personal punching bag since I could walk. Maybe even before that.

"One day, Alessio, you'll understand what it's like to have three useless children. All of you are disappointments. I work my ass off to ensure this family, our name, is feared, and then I have three bastard children who are useless and will bring down the Bianchi name. I will not stand for it," he snarls. His foot collides with my ribs, and pain erupts, stealing my breath .

Fucking bastard.

The older I've got, the less abuse I have suffered at his hands. I was beaten, starved. Anything the fucker could conjure up to cause me pain, he would.

Nothing was as bad as watching him rape and beat women. Something he saw as a sport, a past time he and his fucking asshole friends could join in on.

The worst one happened mere weeks ago. I was tied to a chair in the basement, and I watched as my father, his consigliere, and an underboss took turns raping the girl I was dating. That girl had her throat slit and was dumped on the outskirts of the city. Her family have no idea what happened to her, and they've yet to find her body.

My father laughed as she begged for him to stop and pleaded with me to help her. Bile crept up my throat. It was like acid burning a hole inside of me. I was powerless, unable to do anything but watch. I paid the penance for dating her—a woman outside of the famiglia—a woman who wasn't assigned to me. I kept my eyes on her as she cried, begged, and pleaded, until the knife slit across her throat and the life left her eyes. I didn't once turn my gaze. I couldn't.

If I could kill the cunt, I would. I'd do it gladly and would take whatever punishment comes with it.

"If for one second you think you'll be anything but a soldier in my ranks, you've got another thing coming."

Everyone says being the son of Matteo is a privilege, how they'd love it if their father was the capo of the famiglia. I always have to pretend he's God's gift to our family, when in fact, the man's the fucking Devil reincarnate. I gave up trying to please everyone a long time ago, but it sure as fuck feels good not to have to walk on eggshells around anyone but Matteo.

His foot connects with my side once again. It has enough force behind it that I end up on my side. I grit my teeth and push to my feet. I'm just as tall as the asshole now, and the fucker only hits me when we're alone. I see the fear seep into his eyes whenever I'm around. Hell, it's the same look he gets when both of my brothers are around too.

Dante and Romero have no idea about the abuse I've suffered at the hands of my father, and that's the way it needs to be kept. If they did, I know my brothers would end his miserable life, and that's a huge fucking no-no in our world. You take out the Capo, you've just handed yourself a death sentence.

But one day, Matteo will get his just desserts, and

I for one will be standing there smiling when the bastard does.

"You're a fucking bastard, Alessio," he growls, his eyes wild as he stares at me. "You have a fucking job to do, and you had better start doing it right. I don't care what you have to do; fuck that cunt's granddaughter if you must. Just get me the goddamn information I need."

I grit my teeth. Fucking ass. He's in bed with the Russians, a fucking huge mistake if you ask me. The man believes he's invincible. He's running drugs, women, and guns. All of which will get his ass killed if anyone in the famiglia found out. But the man doesn't care about anyone but himself, and that's why my ass is now on the line, as I'm having to get close to the Russians.

Matteo is getting paranoid. He believes someone's stealing drugs from him. The asshole doesn't know if he can trust the Russians—even though he's working with them—or if it's the Latinos who are taking the product and making waves.

"Fuck that," I hiss, annoyed as hell that he's putting this shit on me.

He gets in my face—a huge fucking mistake—and glares at me. "You'll do as I fucking say. If not, Alessio, you'll be taken care of."

I laugh. "Keep threatening me, old man, you'll not like what happens when I start to open my mouth."

His nostrils flare as he pulls his hand back.

"You will not speak a word of this to anyone, Alessio. You wouldn't dare." His fist smashes into my cheek. He's going to need to have a harder fucking punch than that. Christ, the man's a fucking bastard.

Hell fucking no, I'm not letting this shit slide anymore. I'm done with this fucker.

I don't hesitate in swinging back. My fist connects with the asshole's jaw, and he hits the ground like a fucking ragdoll.

"Touch me again, asshole, and you'll be six-feet-under. I don't give a fuck if that means I'll be joining you; at least your ass won't be Capo anymore."

I don't let him answer, nor do I help him to his feet. I walk past him and out the door.

"There you are," Rome says as I exit the house. His eyes narrow as he takes in my bloodied face. "Fuck, who have you been fighting with now?"

I shrug it off, not wanting to get into the ins and outs of what's been going on. "Where's Dante?"

"He's looking for our father," he replies.

The man in question walks out of the house, his strides purposeful as he moves toward me. "You seen Father?"

I shake my head. "No, why?"

"The fucker's up to something, I know he is. I want to find out what."

"He's a bastard. The sooner he dies the better," I snarl, my anger still palpable.

Romero nods. "I agree. We should take him out now and get it over and done with."

Dante rolls his eyes. "We have to wait," he says quietly so only we can hear. "You both know what'll happen if we take him out without a plan."

"I don't give a fuck," I reply. "Plan, no plan, it doesn't really matter."

"We need to make sure Dante's in the position to take over," Rome sighs. "Once we have that, then we can do it."

I just hope the cunt dies sooner rather than later.

ONE
ALESSIO

"Alessio," Dante says as we enter his office. "I need you to go to Denver."

I blink. "What the fuck's in Denver?"

He grins widely at me. "A new pipeline that'll make us rich. I need you to go down there and check it out."

"What pipeline?" I ask, knowing damn well my ass will be on a plane before the end of the day and landing in the Centennial State, where it's no doubt going to be hotter than Hades.

"Your brother," Makenna, Dante's wife, says as she breezes into the office, her son on her hip, "has a new contact that is supplying guns. It's cheaper than who we use already, but we need you to go to Denver and check to ensure he's not trying to play us."

I chuckle. "Hell, anyone who does that has a fucking death wish."

My brother married Makenna Gallagher—whom

we all thought was the princess of the Irish Mafia. Turns out, she was the fucking boss. She is the boss of the entire East Coast, and she's one of the most—if not *the* most—powerful criminal bosses in the world. She is a force to be reckoned with, and being married to Dante has only further enforced the power she has. That they have.

Makenna nods in concession. "That may be so, Ales, but we all know that where money is concerned, people get stupid, and stupid people make stupid moves."

She's not wrong there.

"Not to mention, I'm not sure how much we can trust Joe Ranieri, no matter what Malcolm says."

Makenna's family is beyond ridiculous. She has four brothers, one being a half-brother, and she has four nephews and four nieces—not to mention all the damn grand-nieces and nephews she has. And then there's her cousins, who are in Chicago. All the Gallagher family are powerful, whether they have the name or if they're working for the family. It's a wonder anyone can keep things straight. I'm lost once I get past her oldest nieces and nephews.

Makenna recruited my brother, Romero, to become one of her underbosses when she and Dante got married. In doing so, Romero agreed to an arranged marriage with her niece, Holly. The red-haired Irish beauty is smart as a whip and has brought the Gallagher and Bianchi family a hell of a lot of money with the investments she's made on our behalf. She's made us richer than Midas.

"Malcolm's usually very good at judging people," I say. I may not know much about all her family, but her nephews, Danny and Malcolm, are the head of the Irish Mafia in the UK and Spain respectively. Both men are shrewd businessmen and are just as deadly as their aunt when they want to be. It's a Gallagher trait.

Makenna nods. "He is, hence why we're going to scope him out."

I glance over at Dante and see him smirking. Makenna has a little trouble with relinquishing power, and whenever Dante and I have a meeting about the Famiglia, she is always present.

"Babe," Dante says, trying to hide his laughter.

She growls at him. "Don't," she warns him. "I do not want to hear that shit right now. This isn't just a Famiglia matter, this is a Gallagher-Bianchi matter."

He sits back in his chair and raises his hands in mock surrender. "You are the one who said only yesterday that you understood the difference between being my wife as the capo and being the boss for the Irish."

"I also understand that you need a bullet in your head. Doesn't mean I'm the one to pull the trigger now, does it?"

I can't help but laugh at their antics. These two never fail to make me laugh, but they also know how to piss me off.

"The plane leaves in three hours, Ales," Dante tells me. "You're good at getting information. I need everything you can find on him and the operations he's running there."

I rise to my feet and nod. "I'll dig deep," I assure him.

"You're the only one I trust to do this," he says, and I know this is him giving me a chance to prove myself.

"I'll do it," I promise him as I leave the office.

Over the years, I've made mistakes. I've let my family down because I didn't tell them about the job my father sent me to do. I had to look into the Russians and get as close as possible so I could uncover what they were doing. It took me a while, but I finally did it. I infiltrated the Russians and got close to Yelena, the granddaughter of the Maksim—the head of the Russian Bratva.

What Yelena and I had was different. I thought it was love, but looking back, it was infatuation and lust. The woman was gorgeous, sexy, and confident. She knew her worth and wouldn't let anyone say otherwise. We grew closer each day, and feelings started to develop–something I couldn't handle—so I made one of the biggest mistakes of my life. I fucked up and slept with another woman. In doing so, Yelena left. Since then, I have seen her only once, about six months after things ended. She looked happy. She told me she forgave me, but that she would never be with me again. I knew I had wrecked what we had and there was no way back. Hell, had she done what I did to her, I'd have snapped her neck and been done with it. Yelena is a skilled assassin. She could have easily taken me out, but she didn't. Instead, she walked away and hasn't looked back since.

After my father died, my brothers found their feet instantly. Dante with Makenna, and Romero as an underboss and then as Holly's husband. All I had was my mission—my job: to find out what the Russian's were doing. I didn't tell my brothers about the mission, not even after he died. I kept it to myself, knowing I could help Dante in the future with my findings. I found out the way the Bratva was run, I discovered their sources and spies, and I also found out who has been playing both sides. But when my brothers found out, they were furious. My father was dead, and the business alliance he had with the Russians was over. Everything I had worked hard for was gone, and in the end, I almost lost everything.

Being in deep with the Russians and almost losing my family as a result, I learned a fuck of a lot of lessons. Now, I know what I want: to be Dante's Consigliere.

My cell buzzes with an incoming message as I board the plane. Once I have taken my seat, I reach into my pocket and pull out my cell phone. My heart stutters as the message opens.

Thomas: I've found her. She's living in Texas.

Christ. That's not a message I thought I'd ever get. My investigator, Thomas. I told him to stop with the search. After Yelena and I spoke, there was a part of me that wanted to check on her, to ensure she was doing okay, so I hired Thomas. It took me eight months to tell him to stop, that I didn't need him any longer. I had come to realize that Yelena and I were never meant to be. Now she's someone from my past. Someone I hurt. I know better than to dredge up the past. She's better off without me in her life.

I'VE BEEN in Denver for three days, and I've uncovered a lot about Joe Ranieri's operations. I have to admit, he runs a tight ship, just like Makenna and my brother. He doesn't take any crap from anyone, and his men are loyal; they respect him because he respects them.

Going into business with him is a smart move and a great opportunity. It's a smart thing to have Joe as an ally.

I have one more bit of business to do: go to the bar where his men hang out and listen to what they say while they're drunk as fucking skunks.

Christ, this heat is like being in a sauna. It's almost eight in the evening and it's hotter than

Hades. This is why I prefer the East Coast. Every step I take, it just brings more sweat pumping from me.

I hear a deep, feminine laugh—a familiar one. I glance across the street, and my gut tightens.

Yelena.

What the fuck is she doing here? She lives in Texas, that much I know for sure, it's where her mom is. But why is she here all of a sudden?

Her eyes widen when she notices me, and her hand moves to her stomach. I clench my teeth. Fuck. It's hard to miss the protruding bump or the flashy diamond she's wearing on her left hand. She's married and pregnant.

I'm happy for her. She deserves to be with someone she loves, and who can offer the same in return.

She says something to the man she's with, and he turns to look at me, his eyes narrowing. He's familiar to me, but I can't pinpoint where I know him from. It doesn't matter. I'm happy she's moved on and I wish her well. I give them a chin lift and carry on walking.

Christ, I need a beer. Fuck that, I need ten of them.

Entering the bar, I see it's busy, and there's hardly any seats available. All I want is to perch my ass and listen to the people around me, get a better understanding of the dynamics of Joe Ranieri and his men. The perfect way to do that is to listen to the drunk, over-the-top assholes who have nothing better to do than spend their evening in this bar and drink, then go home and argue with their wives.

Hours pass, and all I hear is how great of a man Joe Ranieri is. The man's like a freaking saint. Not a bad word has been said about him, not even by the blithering drunks singing loudly and off tune.

The barman passes me another drink. Once I've finished this, I'm going to call it a night. There's nothing else for me to do here.

My gaze drifts to the beautiful, tanned brunette sitting at a table with three other women. As if she can feel me watching her, she turns her head and gives me a shy smile, before returning to her conversation with her friends. The woman is gorgeous. She has long hair that falls in waves down her back, is petite, and from what I can tell, has a fantastic body. But I'm here on a job, not to fuck a random woman, no matter how much I'd like to.

Finishing the beer, I call it a night and make my way outside. The sidewalk is empty when I step out. It's a little after midnight. There should be people milling about, this area is the place to be. There's more bars and restaurants on this strip than any other. Yet, there's no one around. Something about this doesn't sit right. My gut is going crazy.

I feel a hardness pushing into my back, I hear the snick of a gun being cocked, as I'm surrounded by three men. Fucking Russians.

"The boss doesn't like you," one of the men says,

his accent heavy, his eyes narrowed as he gets into my face.

"Like I give a fuck. I don't even know who your boss is." As far as I recall, there was no Russian presence here in Denver. Hell, from what I heard, Ranieri and his men have full reign of the city.

"Nikolai Vasiliev," he spits at me, his lips turned up in disgust.

It clicks. The man I saw with Yelena was Vasiliev, the head of the Russian Bratva in Texas. I laugh. God, what the fuck is that prick doing in Denver?

"Does Ranieri know he's got Russians in his city?" I question with a raised brow as these fuckers move toward the alleyway. The gun in my back is lodged there, and I'm dying to get my hands on all three of these fuckers. "I'd say not. Imagine what he'll do when he finds out not only did Nikolai enter his territory unannounced, but he also brought his men."

The air around us intensifies. The three men's stances change, and stupidly, the asshole behind me removes the gun from my back.

"You threaten us?" the asshole asks. It seems as though he's the only one who can talk.

"Threaten?" I ask with a chuckle. "Me? Never. I'm just stating a fact."

"Oh, and Ranieri knows an Italian bastard is in town?" the fucker from behind me says as he moves to my side. "Oh, don't tell me, you're in business together?"

I don't answer. This is only going to go down one way. Someone is dying. I'm going to ensure it's not me who loses their life tonight.

I whip out my knife from its sheath at my side and stab it into the asshole who held a gun to me. It sinks into the flesh just below his ribs on his left side. Before he can react, I pull it out and sink it into his chest.

"*Sukin,*" one rages.

I dodge the fist aiming for my face, just as I pull my knife out of the first Russian cunt's chest. Blood spurts everywhere, and he drops to the floor. One down, two to go.

Both men advance on me, and I know I need to take out the stronger of the two first. I kick my foot out and connect with the smaller guy's kneecap, causing him to drop to the ground and I fight back the urge to groan. Something sharp slides into my side, and pain erupts from it. I grit my teeth and push through it. I'm still outnumbered and need to end these cunts lives before they take me out.

I slice my knife across the taller guy's face, and he steps back, his hands reaching up to block my next attack. I advance on him, and just as with the first fucker, I drive my knife into his chest, right where the bastard's heart should be. His eyes widen, and he gasps.

I don't stop. Fuck no. I've seen the movies. These

fuckers are practically invincible. They always seem to come back to life. The moment he drops to the floor, I slide my knife along his throat, opening it up and letting him bleed out.

A war cry sounds from behind me. Before I'm able to react, a gun sounds and white hot pain slices through me. Fuck. The cunt shot me.

Within seconds, the bastard is on me, pushing me to the ground. His hands wrap around my neck. Fuck no. Does this bastard think I'm going to go this easily? Jesus, he's never been around an Italian. We're stubborn, ruthless, and in this life, killers.

I draw my head back and bring it forward. My forehead connects with his nose with a satisfying crunch. He loosens his hold on my neck, and I push him off me and flip us over. My anger is palpable as I lay into him. Punch after punch, blow after blow, all to his head. Within minutes, the fucker is limp on the ground with his head caved in.

I get to my feet, wincing as the pain from my side hits me. Putting my hand to the wound, all I feel is wetness. Fuck, I'm bleeding. I stagger toward the alleyway entrance, toward the bright lights of the street, and that's when I see the gorgeous brunette from the bar, looking like a fucking angel, standing there. Her eyes are wide as she takes in my bloodied state, before her gaze moves behind me, to the three dead men on the ground.

She doesn't scream. She doesn't run. She doesn't cry. She just stays still.

I'm confused. Any sane person would have either screamed their head off or ran, but not her. No, she's staring at me with a blank expression on her face.

I continue to stagger toward her. My head begins spinning as dizziness hits me, and weakness floods my limbs.

Her lips part as she watches me, her gaze fixated on me as I start to go down.

My body's giving out and darkness starts to seep in.

The last thing I remember is small hands holding me before I hit the ground.

"Oh no, you've been shot," her words are soft, and I realize she's British. "You're going to be okay," she tells me.

The darkness comes, and I sink into the abyss.

TWO
GABRIELLA

The handsome guy leaves, and I can't help but feel a little sad. Things are different here than they are back in the UK, or even Spain. Usually, if a guy keeps glancing over at me, and I smile at him, he'll come over and sit with me and talk. Not the handsome mystery guy.

No, I smile at him, and he finishes his drink and leaves.

"Bummer," Megan says as she watches him leave. "He looked like he'd give you a good time."

Tonight is the end of my first week working in the art gallery here in Denver. I love art. It's something I have always been passionate about. My dream is to own my own gallery and feature up and coming artists as well as established ones, so landing this job was amazing. There are five of us working in the gallery, and we all get along—except for Karen. She doesn't like anyone. She certainly doesn't like me.

She's bitchy on her good days. God help us all when she's having a bad day.

I laugh. He has an air of dangerousness about him, something I love in a guy.

"He did, but oh well." I'm not one to dwell on things that aren't meant to be. If it's meant for me, it will be; if not, then that's okay. It's the way I've always thought about things in life.

Growing up without having my father in my life, I learned at a young age that things aren't as black and white as people believe. My father is a married man who had an affair with my mother. I'm a result of that affair. What I didn't know was that my father was pulling the strings in every aspect of my life. What he wants, he gets. Including dictating my life along with my mothers. Something I don't agree with.

"So," Karen begins, and I brace myself. This woman took an instant dislike to me, and I have no idea why. Sure, we all make instant judgments on people, but I'm not someone who'll dislike them for no reason. "This friend of yours, Ryan... where is she?"

I grit my teeth. "Her name is Raylee, and she lives in Spain."

She looks me up and down and turns her nose up. "So why did you move here? You're from London, aren't you?"

I sigh heavily. "No," I snap harder than intended, and she looks taken aback by my tone. I'm not someone who usually gets upset, but damn, this woman is working my last damn nerve. "London is a city in England. It doesn't mean every English person is from there. I'm from Manchester. That's four hours north of London. I moved here because my dad lives here."

I didn't plan on moving to America. I lived happily in Spain with my mum and Raylee, but when shit went down with Raylee's family, my father decided it was safer for me to be here in America with him rather than where I wanted to be—with my best friend.

"It must have been difficult," Megan says, reaching out and touching my hand. "Moving away from your mom and best friend."

I nod. "It was at the beginning, but I'm slowly getting used to it."

Karen pipes up yet again. "You said your dad lives here. What's his name?"

"Joseph," I reply instantly, saying it in a Spanish accent, hoping they don't connect Joe Ranieri to being the Joseph I'm talking about. I want to keep my relationship with my father under wraps. Being the daughter of the biggest criminal underboss in Denver will give me a huge target on my back. Something Joe and I don't want. There are only a handful of people who know Joe is my father, and that's the way I want to keep it.

Things between Joe and I aren't like your normal father-daughter relationships. Since moving to the States, I'm slowly but surely forging some sort of relationship with him, but it doesn't erase the years of hurt I have felt, nor the way he abandoned me because of his wife—a woman who hates me because I'm the result of her husband's infidelity.

"Don't know him," Karen says dismissively, as though my father isn't worth her time, and as a result, neither am I.

"That's okay, love," I say sarcastically. "You don't have to know him."

Megan laughs softly as Jenna and Emily rejoin our table. Both ladies also dislike Karen. The woman's a total bitch who thinks everyone is beneath her.

"Shall we go?" Jenna asks. "I need to relieve my babysitter."

I get to my feet and nod. "Yeah, I think that may be best."

Megan gets up behind me and links her arm through mine as we leave the bar. "It was so good to finally get to know you, Gabby," Meg says as she pulls me into her arms for a hug. Even though I've been here for only a week, I feel as though she and I could be great friends.

"Thank you for being so sweet. I really appreciate you taking me under your wing."

Jenna nudges me with her elbow. "Girl, you're one of us now. We take care of our own. Ignore the bitch. She's like that with everyone."

I feel relieved the girls are on my side and agree Karen is a bitch.

"I'll see you all on Tuesday," I say as I wave them goodbye.

My car is parked a little up the street, while Jenna is giving both Megan and Emily a ride home. I watch as the women get into Jenna's car, and I wave them goodbye. I make my way toward my vehicle, but a grunting noise stops me in my tracks. I glance into the alleyway, but it's dark and I can't see anything. I chalk up the sound to an animal and start to walk away, but then I hear another sound; something definitely made by a human and not an animal.

I'm rooted to the spot, just watching, waiting to see what happens and who exits.

A shadow forms as a mass gets closer to me. The glow from the streetlights shines dimly toward the alleyway. That's when I see him. The handsome man from the bar. He staggers toward me. His hand brushes along the wall, the other is holding his side. My heart races as he continues to stagger toward me.

I know I should run, that I should get away from here as quickly as possible, but I'm unable to move. It's as though my body is made of lead. I can only watch as he steps closer.

A car passes by, the headlights shining brightly, and I'm able to see his face, hands, and clothes are soaked in blood. His eyes are wild, his face pale, and a sheen of sweet covers him. God, what on earth happened to him?

I make the mistake of glancing behind him. My stomach rolls and nausea rises when I see three men on the ground. God, please don't tell me they're dead. *Please no.* But none of them are moving. Did he kill them? Did he do this?

A glint of silver catches my eye, and I glance at the knife on the floor.

I swallow harshly. Fuck. I should be scared. Society dictates that I should be fearful of this man—a man who has obviously just killed three men. But I'm not. There's something about this man that has me acting crazy.

The man's brown eyes slowly start to fade, and I know he's sinking. He's losing consciousness, his body sagging with every step he takes. I know that if I don't help him, he's going to die here. I should call the cops. I should call an ambulance. Run for help. Something, anything, to draw attention to the massacre in front of me. But I don't.

In a split-second judgment, I moved toward him, fully intending on helping him. I manage to catch him before his head hits the ground. His weight hits me, and it takes everything in me not to fall to the ground with him. His hand falls from his side, and that's when I see the gunshot wound.

"Oh no, you've been shot," I cry, completely shocked that nobody heard the gun going off. Had they, maybe none of this would have happened. "You're going to be okay," I promise him, needing to let him know that he's not alone. "You're going to be okay,"

I try my hardest to pull him from the dark, dingy alleyway and toward my car. A sickening feeling hits me when I realize just how empty the street is. Where the hell is everyone? Surely it's never this quiet. It's eerily quiet. The distrustful side of me is wondering if this is a setup; if at any moment someone is going to come out and harm me. I can't help but glance around, surveying everything around me, carefully watching in case someone jumps out.

By the time I reach my vehicle, I'm covered in sweat, my hair is clinging to my neck, and I'm breathing hard. I climb into the car and lift him in. I'm panting and out of breath, but I don't give up. I need to get him inside and get us out of here. It takes me about twenty minutes, but thankfully, I manage to get him laid across the backseat. His eyes are closed, his skin damn, and blood soaks through his crisp white shirt. I'm shocked and scared that not one person has passed me in the time I've been wrangling him. There's something going on, and I need to get the hell out of here, before whatever is about to go down, does.

I know that if my father finds out what I have done, he's going to be so angry. He's kept me from the world, hiding my identity. For his faults, he's managed to protect me in that aspect. He'll call me stupid because I've put a target on my back.

Once I have the man secured in the car, I jump

into the front seat and put my car into drive. I need to get out of here, and I need to ensure no one sees me. At the end of the street, I turn left. Just as I do, sirens sound behind me in the distance. Someone's coming. I should stop and wait for them.

But I can't. I'm in too deep right now.

I have no idea why I'm doing this. I don't know why I'm helping this man. All I know is that there's something in my soul driving me to help him. To ensure he's safe. Thankfully, my house is outside of the city, so no one can see me dragging a man inside.

It takes me a while to get him out of the car and onto the bed. Once I lie him on the bed, I'm stumped as to how to help him next.

Fuck... What do I do now?

I call the only man I trust, my father's doctor. He's the man on call to help my father and his men whenever they need it.

He tells me to apply pressure on the wound and that he's on his way. I breathe a sigh of relief. Someone is going to help me with him.

It takes Monty less than fifteen minutes to get to my house. He wastes no time in getting to work. I sit back and wait for him as he stitches up the man and gives him antibiotics and other medication.

"Gabriella, this was a very stupid idea. Do you know who this man is? Do you understand the gravity of this situation?"

I swallow hard and nod. "I didn't know what else to do, Monty. I had to help him." I don't tell him I was compelled to do so and that I'm unsure as to what that means.

"Gabriella, this man is Alessio Bianchi. He is the youngest brother of Dante Bianchi."

I stare at him. I know that name. Bianchi. How do I know it? It hits me. Dante Bianchi is the head of the Italian Mafia. Shit. I am in so much trouble.

"Alessio was here under your father's orders. I'm going to have to tell him. I'm sorry, Gabriella, but I have to."

I shake my head. "Please, Monty, please don't. If you tell my father, he'll be furious."

Monty nods, and a soft look enters his eyes. "I will keep your name out of this, Gabriella. I have to tell your father that I have Alessio hidden away. But I do not need to tell you about that."

I breathe a sigh of relief. Thank God.

Monty exits the room Alessio is currently in, and I follow him out. I listen in on the conversation he has with my father. He tells him about the condition Alessio is in and that it was a call he received from an informant of theirs; that he knows Alessio is under my father's orders to be here, and how the informant called him and told him where Alessio was.

I'm so very grateful that Monty won't tell my father I was the one who took Alessio, but I cannot begin to understand why I was so, so stupid—to bring a man I don't even know into my home, and save him, after discovering he killed three men.

Monty tells my father about the men and how

they're lying in the alleyway. My father assures Monty his men are on route as they speak.

I sigh heavily, relieved my father's going to sort this out. I move away from Monty and back into the room Alessio is in. He's still unconscious and very, very pale. He looks peaceful. I have a feeling it's very rare to see this man like this. I don't know what is wrong with me. Why I'm so connected to this man. I hate it. I hate that I put myself in danger. For years I've managed to keep myself out of the world my father lives in and now my anonymity could be gone in the blink of an eye.

The door opens, and Monty walks in. "Gabriella, I have to tell you," Monty begins, and I brace myself. The look of fear in Monty's eyes is scaring me. "The men Alessio killed were Russian Bratva soldiers. They belonged to Nikolai Vasiliev."

Oh God, this isn't good.

"The man is dangerous, Gabriella. He sent three of his best men to kill Alessio."

I stare at the man I consider a friend in shock. If this Nikolai sent his best men to kill Alessio, and he was the only one to leave the alleyway alive, that means this isn't the first time Alessio has done this. He's trained for this.

I stare at the man on the bed, wondering just how fucked I truly am.

THREE
GABRIELLA

I glance at the cell phone on the table. This is the seventy-eighth time someone has called in the past four days.

I'm too scared to answer. I see the name *Dante* flashing on the screen, and my blood runs cold. This isn't good. They already know Alessio has been injured and that he killed three men, but they haven't heard from their brother. They're worried. I get that. I would be too.

A part of me wants to answer the call, to tell them he survived and is getting better but needs more time to heal. I want them to know that, but at the same time, I've already put myself in a precarious situation. I cannot out myself because no one in their right mind would have done what I did. No sane person would take a man they knew killed three people home with them to get him fixed up. But someone in their world would do that. And I know that if I answer the phone to Dante, he'll demand to know who I am, and then he'll do some digging, and it won't take long for someone like him to realize I'm the illegitimate daughter of Joe Ranieri. So, I just sit here, listening as the cell rings.

If Dante ever found out my identity, I know my dad would have my back. He'll always protect me. It'll mean a war, and that's not something I want. I'm a lover, not a fighter. I don't take after my father and all the people in this criminal underworld. I prefer my life to be Zen and happy. I don't want to hurt anyone, nor do I want to cause harm to anyone. Hell, the thought of my words making someone cry, hurts me. Whereas my father kills people for a living, then he has people murdered for his own satisfaction. That's not someone I could ever be.

It's been four days since I brought Alessio home. He's woken up once with a delirious fever. His wound is healing nicely—so the doctor says. Monty doesn't seem to be too worried about him. He said he's healing and will be back on his feet in no time.

But I can't help but wonder why he was hurt in the first place. What did he do to the Russians to make them come after him?

I'm curious by nature. I always love to dig deep into mysteries and find out what's going on. It's why Raylee and I ended up in so much trouble a few years ago. Her father was trafficking women, along with his best friend, Ashton Banks, and they got on the wrong side of Malcolm Gallagher—who is now

Raylee's husband—the Irish Mafia boss in Spain. In doing so, Raylee and I lost our best friend, the man who meant the world to us, who was a brother to us. We watched as he was beaten to death, and there was absolutely nothing we could do to save him. I think seeing Alessio bleeding, and those three dead men, brought back a lot of memories. It was like I was back in Spain, being held back as men pounded into my best friend. They wouldn't stop until he was lying on the floor, unmoving. That day haunts me. And it will haunt me for the rest of my life.

A part of me will always dislike Malcolm and his right-hand man, Christian, for holding me and Raylee back and letting those men kill Mayer. But the bigger part of me will always be grateful they did, because if they hadn't, I may have lost more than Mayer. I could have lost Raylee too.

The cell stops ringing, and I breathe a sigh of relief. One more day that I don't have to talk to Dante, Romero, or even to someone called Makenna. Whenever her name flashes on the screen, jealousy hits me like the green-eyed monster. Is she his girlfriend? Wife? Fiancée? From everything I have learned, Dante and Romero are Alessio's two brothers. All three are the sons of Matteo Bianchi, a man who raped, killed, and hurt so many women just for the fun of it.

I glance down at Alessio's sleeping form and I can't help but wonder what he did for those men to come after him. I spot the white bandage covering his wound and find myself glad when I see no blood seeping through. My eyes once again drift to an old wound so similar to the one he has now. It's located on the other side of his body. He's been shot before, and from what Monty said, it was quite bad. I can't help but feel that this man lives for the danger he thrives on.

There's no way anyone should have been able to survive being attacked by three Russian Bratva soldiers. Yet Alessio lies in bed, having done so. There's just so many questions on my mind. I'm not one to just brush things under the carpet. I have to know why, how, and what of the situation. Poor Alessio. Once he wakes up, he is going to be bombarded with all the questions I have. But then, in return, I know he'll have questions for me. Ones I don't know how to answer.

How do you tell a man you don't know that you're the reason he's still alive? That you saved him, when in fact you should have run and called the cops. Hell, I should have just left him there like a normal person would have done.

I know the reason I'm not a normal person. I never have been because the blood of my father runs through my veins, and as much as I pretend otherwise, I don't see the world in black and white. I do know right from wrong, but I also know that some people can't control who they are. They were born to do this job, like my father and Alessio were. Some people were born to rule the underworld and be rich and powerful. You have to be both of those things to be able to rule so many men and women. Their way of life is unthinkable to most. It takes a certain person to be able to do it. It also takes a certain person to be able to take someone's life, and Alessio is one of those people, as is my father.

I don't judge people on their past, future, or present. I don't judge them on their job or what they have done. I judge them on who they truly are beneath the bloodshed, demons, and killings. I always judge people by their hearts. Because if I didn't, no one in my life would be here. Not Raylee, her family, her husband, Malcolm, and not my father. Raylee isn't a killer; she loves a man who is, as well as all her brothers, who are killers too.

I'm no one to judge anyone, because my father is one of the meanest sons of bitches in this world. And I love him. What does that say about me? I guess I'll never know. But I am loyal to a fault. And I am loyal to my father, because he helped me when my life was at its lowest. And I know no matter what, he'll always help me, whether I like it or not. And that is the reason why I will never judge anyone by what they have done, what they are doing, or what they will do, and only judge them by who they truly are.

Alessio's cell starts to ring once again, and this time, it's Romero calling him.

The bedsheets rustle as a low guttural moan fills the air. I turn and see that Alessio's awake and is watching me. "God, turn that fucking thing off," he growls.

I roll my eyes. It seems as though he's better.

"That is your brother calling you. Again," I reply softly.

Our gazes collide, and my cheeks heat as he focuses those deep amber eyes on me. They look as though they're seeing through me. It's unnerving. I hate being made to feel as though I'm being judged, and that's exactly what Alessio is doing right now.

"Answer it then," he snaps.

My temper flares. Hell fucking no.

"I'm not your maid, and I'm certainly not a dog. Don't bark commands at me. You're well enough to growl, you're well enough to answer the damn phone and leave."

Instantly, his dark gaze changes, and he begins to chuckle, but then winces in pain.

"Yeah, I wouldn't do that," I say dryly. "You've been shot, not to mention stabbed. You're lucky to be alive."

He looks unfazed by my words. "It's not the first time. I doubt it'll be the last."

"Obviously," I snap, annoyed that he's getting to me. Usually, I'm not this bitchy, but he gets to me in a way no one has before.

"Listen, little girl, if I could answer it, I would. But as you can see, I'm a little tied up."

I roll my eyes. God, he is an ass. Why are men such pigs?

I get to my feet, reach for the cell, and throw it onto the bed, just far enough away from him that he'll have to move. I walk out of the room without looking back. If he wants to be an asshole, then he can do shit for himself.

I busy myself in the kitchen, cooking bacon, eggs, and sausages. Trying my hardest to take my mind off the man in the bedroom. I'm grateful there's space between us, because not only is he hot and gorgeous, but he's also a jerk.

I can't believe I let him get to me. Something that never happens. Usually, I'm very laid back and controlled. It takes a certain situation to get me fired up. But Alessio managed to get to me with just a smirk and a few words.

"Something smells nice," I hear from behind me.

I jump around to face him, releasing a squeal. My heart beats a mile a minute.

"God, you scared me," I say as I press a hand to my chest. "Someone really needs to put a bell on you. How did you sneak up on me like that?"

I didn't hear him end his call, let alone walk around my house. God, he has me so out of sorts that I'm not even paying attention to things around me. I was so focused on cooking and deep in thought that I was distracted.

I see he's standing before me, his white shirt stained with blood. How did he go from lying in bed, looking like he's at death's door, to standing in front of me, looking like he's about to walk on the set of a GQ shoot?

"What are you cooking?" he questions, his gaze firmly on me.

"Food," I reply sarcastically.

My words are met with a darkened look, and his eyes narrow. Why the hell do I feel as though he's reprimanding me without saying a bloody word?

"I understand that you need time to heal, but you're able to walk around now. I think it's best if you just leave."

The dark look disappears, but instead, a smug smile forms on his lips. Why the hell does that make butterflies hit my stomach? Why do I react this way to him?

"You're cute, babe," he says.

My blood boils.

"It's not up for debate, but I ain't leaving yet. You're cooking and I'm hungry. Besides, we need to talk."

I grit my teeth. God, he's insufferable. I stare at him, hoping I can find a way out of talking, but the determination on his face says it all. There's no way out of this.

"Fine," I grumble. "You can eat, and we can talk. Once you're finished, you're gone. You killed three men, Alessio. Three," I remind him. I may be a lot of things, but I'm not stupid. Him staying here is only going to lead trouble to my door. "Those men were part of the Russian Bratva. They don't just let shit like that slide. The Russians are going to want revenge, and I would very much like not to be part of that equation."

That smug smile seems to be etched on his face. "Yeah, I understand that, and I will get out of your hair, but I need to know how you know the men I killed were Russian?"

Fuck. I really need to think before I speak. I can't do this shit. I can't be careless anymore. If he finds out who Joe is to me, then it could be leverage for him to have Joe do shit. Or even for him to try and take Joe's territory.

"The doctor who patched you up, he told me they were Russian. He wanted to make sure I knew just who you were. So, what did you do to piss them off?"

My words don't seem to faze him. He carelessly shrugs. "I was dating the Russian boss's wife years ago, long before they were together. I cheated on her, and now Nikolai's out for revenge."

I shake my head. God this man is such a prick.

"Okay, so you're a wanker. What's new? I've barely spoken to you, and I already know how much of a prick you are. That doesn't mean someone should kill you."

He crosses his arms over his chest, looking every bit the gorgeous asshole he is.

"I don't get it. You said you cheated on this woman years ago, so why now?"

I hate things that don't make sense. I always have

to know the why's and the how's. It's just the way I am.

He shrugs, seemingly uncaring that someone is out for his blood. "That's the thing about the Bratva, they're unpredictable. They just love violence and blood."

I can't help the giggle that escapes me.

"They can't help it?" I question. "Coming from the man who killed three men singlehandedly; the one who's walking around like he's ready to go ten rounds in a boxing ring, even though he's still injured."

He shrugs. "Look, little girl, things happen, and you just have to deal with them. I was shot and stabbed. It's not the end of the world. I'm still alive. I'm gonna be fine. You, on the other hand..." he says as he glares at me.

My blood goes cold at his words. Fuck, what the hell have I done?

"You have so much to answer for. Firstly, why did you help me?"

I'm as truthful as I can be without exposing myself. "I honestly don't know why I helped you. It's a question I've been asking myself ever since I dragged you into my car. I knew the moment I did that, it was a mistake. By then, things had gone too far. I had to do it." I take a deep breath and continue. "I couldn't let you die, knowing you were injured. That's not who I am."

He tilts his head as he stares at me. "Why don't I believe you?"

Anger swiftly rises through me. "That sounds like a *you* problem," I tell him heatedly. "You don't believe me? There's nothing I can do about it. I'm telling you what happened. I can't let someone die. That's just who I am. You're okay with taking a life? I'm not."

I turn my back to him and continue cooking. "You were injured. If I had left you in that alleyway bleeding out, you would have died. The street was empty, Alessio. It took me twenty minutes to drag you into my car and not one person or car came down that street. Something was going to happen, and I couldn't let it, okay?" I release a huff, annoyed that he's questioning me. "So how about instead of asking all these questions, you just say thank you?"

"Thank you," he says, and it actually sounds as though he means it. "You know my name, it'd be nice to know yours."

"Gabriella," I tell him, instantly wishing I had given him a fake name. "My name is Gabriella Sanchez, and you are Alessio Bianchi, youngest brother of Dante Bianchi—the head of the Italian Mafia. So do you understand why I want you out of here?"

He comes to stand beside me, and I really wish he didn't.

"I understand why you'd want me gone,

Gabriella. But you should know a man like me takes orders from no one."

"Except for your brother," I say. Christ, I really need a bloody filter.

His chuckle is deep and husky, and my chest warms at the sound. "You really let your mouth run wild, don't you?"

I nod. "I can't help it. I always say things I shouldn't. Besides, you'll be gone soon, so it really doesn't matter."

The look that enters those amber eyes of his tells me he's planning something. Alessio is a dangerous mystery, one I should steer clear of, but there's just something about him that makes me want to uncover just who he is.

"Hmm," he says as he moves away from me. "Seems you're in the know of a lot that goes on in my world." I glance over my shoulder, fear gripping my throat in a chokehold. What's he getting at? I watch as he takes a seat, not even a fucking wince out of him as he does so.

"So, tell me what you know about Joe Ranieri. What's he like?"

I freeze at the stovetop. Does he know I'm Joe's daughter? He can't, there's no way he knows that. No freakin' way. If he did, I'd be a target, one he could use to his advantage. He could use me to take over Joe's territory. Gain Denver and everything that Joe has.

"I don't know him," I say calmly, trying to keep

the fear from my voice. "I've heard stories about him. I've heard what he does, but other than that, not much."

"What have you heard?"

I breathe a sigh of relief. He doesn't know. Thank God.

"I've heard Joe's a fair boss, that he has the loyalty of the men and women of this city. But just like the rest of you, he's a killer." It's something I'll never agree with. Taking someone's life just because you can doesn't sit right with me, but it's something I have to accept as Joe is my father.

Alessio makes a non-committal noise. "Again, little girl, why do I get the feeling there's so much more to you?"

I plate up the food and put it down in front of him, then take a seat opposite.

"There's much more to everyone once you delve under the surface. Everyone has a side they show the world, and then there's the side very little see. I have a feeling that annoying smirk you have is a way to hide who you truly are." I grin at him when his eyes narrow. "You push everyone away and act like a complete wanker to the whole world, just so no one can get close to you." I take a bite of food and watch him. His gaze hasn't left me once since I sat down, and it's unnerving. "Like the woman you cheated on. She was getting too close, wasn't she? You couldn't deal with her getting to the real you, so you cheated on her just to push her away."

His eyes narrow, and his lips thin. Seems as though I've hit the nail on the head.

"Alessio, if you don't want people prying into your life, how about you stay the hell out of mine?"

Thankfully, he doesn't say a word and instead begins to eat.

Silence spreads between us as the minutes tick by. Alessio seems quite content on eating, while ignoring his phone buzzing every other minute. No doubt everyone is checking in on him now they know that he's awake. When he's finished, he gets to his feet, and I follow suit. He faces me.

"Gabriella," he says, and the way my name rolls off his tongue has heat pooling between my thighs. "Thank you. You didn't need to do what you did, but I am really grateful you did."

I swallow hard at the sincerity in his voice. "As I said, I couldn't let you die. I really hope you get better soon, and I'm glad your family knows you're okay. I didn't want to answer it because I didn't want to be involved. Yeah, I know, I was already too deep, but I hope you understand?"

He nods but doesn't say anything.

We walk toward the front door. My chest is heavy, and my stomach is in knots. It's as though I'm losing something, losing a part of me. I have no idea what to do. I push through it because I know that no matter what, I'll be okay, and having him walk away is the right thing to do.

I open the door for him. "Take care of yourself, Alessio," I say.

He smiles at me, and this time, it's not smug. It's a genuine, bright smile.

"You too, Gabriella." his words are thick and gravelly.

He steps closer to me, his hand brushing along my chin, his breath hot against my skin. My hand braces against the door, and I pray he doesn't do what I think he's about to do.

He does. His lips slam against mine, and he kisses me hard. His kiss is rough but oh so good. He sweeps his tongue into my mouth and makes me weak at the knees.

When he pulls back, I'm breathless and clinging to him. This should never have happened. God, what is wrong with me? Why did I let that happen? My legs are wobbly, my chest heaving as I try to suck in some much-needed oxygen.

"I'll be seeing you soon, Gabriella. Be good," he says as he walks out of my house.

I pray this is the last time I see him, but I have a gut feeling it won't be.

FOUR
ALESSIO

One week later

"You good?" Dante asks when I answer his call.

"I'm fine," I reply, having had this same conversation with not just him but everyone else in the family, even those who aren't immediate family. I'm sick to death of having everyone ask if I'm doing okay and questioning if I should come home.

"You're pissed that we keep asking, I get it, but Ales, you were shot and almost died. You're going to get questioned a lot."

"From Holly, and even the other women, I expect it, but you, Rome, and Makenna, I don't. I'm fine, I'm alive, and I'm healing. I don't need to be checked up on like I'm a fucking kid."

"You're right," he responds, and I blink in

surprise. "You're not a kid, you're Alessio Bianchi, one of the toughest sons of bitches alive."

"Yeah," I hear Makenna shout in the background. "This is the second time someone's shot him and he's still alive. So much for praying for an alternative outcome."

I chuckle at her words. It's one of the many things I love about my sister-in-law; she always jokes and lightens the mood—hell, half the time, I'm not even sure if she's joking or not.

"Nikolai is back in Texas," Dante tells me, and I grit my teeth. That motherfucker left Denver the day after I was shot.

"What's the plan?" I ask, wondering if he's going to start a war or if he's going to sit back and let it lie.

"We've sent a message," he tells me cryptically. "His right-hand man is missing a couple of fingers, and his bodyguard is nowhere to be seen."

I smile. He's gone for the people closest to him. He's letting Nikolai know that we can get to him and Yelena whenever the fuck we want.

"He called. He's offered a truce."

Ah, hence the phone call today. "And what are you saying to that?"

"I want to tell the bastard, fuck no. He sent three men to try and kill you. That's something I'm not willing to let slide."

I hear a fucking *but* in there somewhere.

"Makenna believes we should take the truce. If

some asshole did what you did to Makenna, I'd have killed them without blinking."

"So, you're taking the truce?" I ask, completely fucking confused as to why he's doing this.

"Kind of. I've told Nikolai that as long as he stays the fuck in Texas and doesn't come into any of our territories, then he's safe. But the second he does, or his wife does, they're fair game."

"Yelena has nothing to do with this," I remind him.

"Alessio, she has every-fucking-thing to do with this. You fucked up and cheated. You didn't kill her, for crying out loud," Makenna says. "She set in motion this entire thing. It happened years ago, a fucking lifetime ago. There was no need for Nikolai to send men. He married her, not you. So yes, she's fair fucking game, and everyone thinks so."

"You're the bosses," I reply, knowing that no matter what I say, they've made up their minds.

"They won't come to New York or anywhere else that's owned by a Bianchi or Gallagher. Not a fucking chance," Makenna fumes. "They fucked up, Alessio. They went after family, and that's something we'll never forget. Hell fucking no."

"Aww, you love me," I joke.

"Shut up," Dante growls. "Now, when the fuck are you coming home?"

I glance across the street, watching the beautiful brunette close the gallery.

"Soon," I assure him. "I've got some business I need to take care of here."

"Alright, but Alessio, you do not go looking for Nikolai or Yelena—hell, any of the Vasiliev men."

"Is that an order?" I ask, my temper rising as I grit my teeth.

"Yes, that's a fucking order," he snarls. "I mean it, Ales, don't go looking for trouble."

I chuckle. "Trouble always finds me," I tell him, my gaze firmly on the beautiful woman who's making her way toward her car.

"Ain't that the fucking truth. Stay safe, Ales, I expect your ass home by Monday."

That gives me four days to get what I need to do, done. "Monday," I assure him and end the call.

I climb into my rental car and follow Gabriella home. Just as I have done every day for the past week. I've learned a fuck of a lot about the woman. She has a routine while working, one she doesn't change. She leads a very simple life. There's no man in her life, nor is there any family. A background check I had my investigator do, told me her mom is in Spain, however there's no father listed on the birth certificate. She's been living here in Denver for almost a year now, although she spent six months here two years ago. From what I've gathered, she's been finishing her degree. She must have liked it enough for her to move. Other than that, there's very little else to uncover about Gabriella Sanchez—yet I have a feeling there's more to her than meets the eye.

She's hiding something, and I fully intend to uncover what it is.

As usual, Gabriella has no idea she's being followed. She's oblivious to her surroundings, and that pisses me off. Someone could snatch her at any moment, and she'd been unaware.

She drives into her garage, and the door closes behind the vehicle. The lights in the house switch on as she makes her way through the rooms. I sit tight and wait.

THE LIGHTS ARE FINALLY OUT. She's asleep. I climb out of my vehicle and make my way inside. I know this house like the back of my hand now. Every night it's the same routine.

Entering the house is easy. The woman needs a damn security system. Any fucker could walk into her house and kill her. Fuck. This woman drives me fucking crazy. I've not managed to get her off my mind since I left her house. She's my constant thought. I'm intrigued by how this beautiful young woman has managed to captivate me. Every night since I left her, I've returned to her house. I'm losing my mind, and I don't care. I need to be close to her, but I also need to ensure I don't fuck up. I enter through the back door, making my way up the stairs, toward her bedroom.

Opening the door, I wait silently, ensuring she's

sleeping deeply. Only when I'm sure she's fully asleep do I step into the room. God, she's fucking beautiful. She looks peaceful.

I don't understand why she saved me. How did someone so pure help me? No one has ever done that before. I think that's why I'm so drawn to her. Sure, my family helped me when I was shot before, but they're family. They have to. Gabby could have left me for dead, but she didn't.

I'm intrigued. Fuck, some would even say obsessed.

I stand over her, watching as she sleeps. Never have I seen something so serene as her. Christ. I'm losing my mind over a woman. Something that's never happened before.

I reach out and caress her cheek, loving the softness of her skin.

"Tomorrow," I whisper.

Tomorrow, I finally make my move.

Tomorrow, she's mine.

HER ROUTINE IS THE SAME. Does she not understand how stupid that is? How easily someone could use it to harm her? Gabriella Sanchez is a fucking mystery. How can a woman who helped me, a man she knew killed three men, be so normal? It doesn't make sense. There's something about her that

I'm missing. But it doesn't matter, because tonight, I finally make her mine.

For a week I have watched and waited; got to know everything there is to know about her. In that time, I've come to realize just how fucking depraved I truly am. I'm stalking a woman who helped me. My repayment should be leaving her the hell alone, just as she asked. But I can't. I don't know why, but I can't walk away from her.

I make my way through her home and up the stairs. The house is encased in darkness. She went to bed three hours ago, watched TV for forty minutes, before the lights went completely out. I creep into her bedroom, not making a sound. Her breathing is light as she lies in her bed, on her side, facing away from the door. The bedsheets are strewn about her body, and a thin ray of light from the outside shines into her room, showcasing her beautiful, naked skin.

Fuck me. She is sleeping naked.

My cock thickens instantly. From the moment I saw her, I wanted her, and tonight, that's exactly what I'm going to have. I undo my tie, pulling it off me as I pad toward her sleeping form. I wrap the tie around her eyes, making sure she can't see. The woman is so deeply asleep that she doesn't even stir.

Once I have the blindfold secure, I run my finger along her cheek, down her neck, and toward her breast. Her nipple pebbles as I drag my knuckle over it.

A light moan escapes her, and she turns onto her back, her legs parting slightly. As much as I want to sink my fingers deep into her cunt, I don't. I'm going to take my time, savor this, enjoy everything I'm about to do to her. Everything I've fantasized about since I saw her.

My fingers play with her nipples, pulling, pinching, and massaging them. Her moans get louder, encouraging me.

"So good," she moans when my mouth covers the erected bud.

"You like that?" I ask her, as I brush my hand along her pussy.

Her body tightens and she starts to shake. "Wh—" she cries as she twists to get rid of me. Not happening, I push my finger in deeper and she stills.

"Ssh, little girl," I growls. "It's only me."

"Alessio?" she questions. There's a slight tremble in her words.

"So fucking wet, I'm going to fuck you, now little girl," I hiss as I once again cover her nipple.

The tension leaves her body. I press my finger deeper into her tight wet pussy, she grinds her hot pussy against my finger.

"You want me to finger that cunt?" I ask her.

"Yes," she cries, once again grinding down on my finger.

I push a digit into her tight heat and almost swallow my fucking tongue at how snug it feels. "You've wanted this, haven't you?"

She throws her head back as I finger-fuck her. "Yes. God, have you seen you?"

I chuckle. I love that she's not afraid to say what she's feeling. "What do you want, little girl?"

She growls at me. "For you to stop calling me that shit."

I smile. She's fucking ferocious. "What do you want me to do to you, babe?"

"Eat me," she says without hesitation. "Eat me, and I'll suck you."

Fuck yes.

I withdraw my fingers and strip out of my clothes. My cock springs to attention the moment I take my pants off.

"Up," I tell her as I move closer to the bed.

She's a good girl and does as I ask. She sits up on her knees and waits for instruction. I climb onto the bed behind her and get situated. I lift her onto me, her back to my front.

"Have at it," I tell her as I drag her pussy to my lips.

She practically comes undone at the first swipe of my tongue.

"Alessio," she cries.

"You want me to eat you, babe?" I growl, and she nods. "Then suck."

I grit my teeth as her petite hand wraps around my aching cock. When her lips encase it, it takes everything in me not to thrust into her mouth.

She's fucking good at this, twisting and pumping

her hand as she sucks me deep into her throat. I shove my face into her pussy and go to town on the sweetness of her juices. I spear her with my tongue, and she grinds down on my face. I smile, loving how much she gives in to her needs and doesn't care. I tongue-fuck her hard and fast, knowing that with the way she's working my cock, I'm not going to last much longer.

"Alessio," she cries. "I'm so close."

I slap her ass, and she bucks against me, crying out in pleasure. I repeat the action, and it sends her spiraling. Her orgasm washes over her, and she floods my mouth with her juices as she practically swallows my cock. I thrust deep into her mouth, loving the way she gags. The tightness of her throat is enough to send me over the edge. I release stream after stream of thick cum down her throat, and she keeps still, taking every last fucking drop.

I pull her off my softening cock and lie her down on the bed.

"I'm nowhere near finished with you," I snarl as I push my finger back inside her pussy.

"Alessio," she whines. "What are you doing?"

"You really want to have this conversation now?" I ask as I push another finger inside of her, stretching her pretty pussy.

"Yes," she moans. "How did you get in?" she asks as she grinds down against my hand.

Fuck it, if she wants to ask while I'm finger-fucking her, then so be it.

"I've wanted to fuck you since the moment I saw you. I couldn't deny myself any longer, so I'm taking what's mine. As for how I got in, it was easy, especially since you don't have a fucking security system."

She cries out as I add yet another finger. "Too much?"

She shakes her head. "So good." She sucks in a deep breath. "So what happens after today?"

Ah, that's the million-dollar question. "I have a feeling that once with you won't be enough. I'm only here for a few more days. Once I'm gone, Gabriella, I'm not coming back."

She gives me a blinding smile.

"I can deal with that," she says, as her hand reaches down for my cock.

She starts to jack me off as I finger-fuck her, and it doesn't take long until my cock starts to rise.

"Fuck me, Alessio," she pleads.

I lift off of her and position myself at the entrance of her pussy. Her legs open wider. She's ready for me; her pussy is glistening with her juices and need.

I thrust into her and release a long groan. Fucking nothing feels better than being balls deep inside of her tight, wet pussy.

"You on the pill?" I ask, needing to make sure she is. The fucking last thing I need is a mini me running around.

"Yes," she tells me. "Been on the pill since I was fifteen."

What the fuck?

"Are you going to stay like this all night or are you going to fuck me?" she asks in a bored tone.

I withdraw slowly and thrust deep inside of her—hard. "Why have you been on the pill for so long?"

She releases a harsh sigh. "Not everything is for a sexual reason, wanker. I have awful periods and the pill helps regulate them. Not that it's any of your business."

I move, my thrusts are hard, fast, and hit deep every fucking time. "That's where you're wrong. I'm fucking you, so it is my business."

She moans loudly, her fingers tightening around my nape. "Just because you're fucking me, it doesn't give you the right to question what I do with my body. It's mine, Alessio, and I can do whatever the hell I want with it."

I grit my teeth and fuck her harder. Her moans get longer and louder, her body tightens, and I know it's not going to take much more for her to come.

"When I'm fucking you, Gabriella, it's only me."

"Yes," she hisses as she grinds against my cock. "Same goes for you. I won't fuck you if I'm not the only one."

I take her mouth, sliding my tongue inside, needing to taste her.

"Only you," I assure her. She's the only one I've felt this way about. The only one who has me breaking into their home just to fuck them.

She kisses me back as we fuck hard, fast, and frenzied. My spine tingles and my balls tighten.

"Come for me, babe," I grunt as my hands move from her hips to her asscheeks. My fingers dig into the skin there, and I have a feeling I'm about to leave bruises. The thought of marking her has my cock thickening.

I release her mouth and move to her neck, and waste no time in leaving my mark there, sucking and biting until I know it's going to bruise.

"God," she cries, her pussy clenching around my cock. "Alessio."

Once I'm satisfied the mark is big enough, I move to her breast and do the same thing there.

That's all it takes for her to detonate. Her back bows, and she calls out my name as her pussy suffocates my cock, drawing my cum from my balls. I grunt as I thrust deep, burying myself to the hilt.

We're both breathing heavily. She's limp beneath me, and I'm completely spent. My balls are empty. I climb off her and reach for my clothes.

"Goodnight, Alessio," she says sleepily as she turns over as though she's going back to sleep.

Did I just get dismissed?

What the fuck?

"Babe?"

"Lock up when you leave, yeah?" she says as I pull on my shirt.

"Whatever," I say, pissed that she's acting as though she doesn't give a fuck.

Once I'm dressed, I move to the bed and see she's actually asleep. Damn, this woman is a fucking blow to the ego. I untie my tie and shove it into my pocket. Reaching for the bedsheets, I pull them over her body and press a kiss against her lips.

I soundlessly leave the bedroom and make my way out of her house. Once I'm at my car, I wonder what the fuck just happened. Never have I ever been dismissed by a woman after sex. It's usually the other way around.

Fucking Gabriella.

I knew she was different. But never did I think she'd have me wanting more.

FIVE
GABRIELLA

Feather kisses make their way down my spine, and I groan with pleasure at the feeling.

"Mmm," I groan, as Alessio continues to make his way down my body. I love waking up to him touching me.

His lips continue to press kisses against my back, and I grind my ass against his rock-hard erection. I love how greedy he is. He always wants it. He's the biggest guy I have been with and he's the most experienced also. I love that he knows what he's doing and always ensures I come first.

"So, you want me?" I ask as I reach down to wrap my hand around his thickness.

His chuckle is deep and throaty. "Like you even have to ask."

He flips me over. My hand releases his cock, and I pout. My pussy is soaked from the sensory overload of him trailing kisses over my body. God, I have never had a man fuck me the way he does. He stretches me in a deliciously sore way, and it's something I know I'll remember forever.

I spring upwards. Over the past four days, he's taken me missionary. Today, I want to be in charge. I take him by surprise and push him onto his back. A cheeky smile forms on his lips as he gets into position. I straddle him, my wet pussy is against his stomach. I press my lips against the scar on his body. He's still got a white bandage covering his latest wound.

I slide down onto his cock, loving the way he fills me up.

"Oh, Alessio," I gasp. "You're so much thicker this way."

His fingers sink into the flesh at my hips as he thrusts into me. "Fuck me, Gabriella. Fuck me until your juices flood my cock."

I throw my head back and begin to slowly ride him. His words spur me on. The man is a dirty talker, and I fucking love it. He revs my engine in more ways than one, and he can have me panting for more with just his dirty talk.

He wraps his hand around my throat and he pulls me into him. I gasp, I'm so needy with want, I grind my pussy down against his cock, his mouth touches mine. He takes the breath from me as his tongue sweeps in and kisses me. This isn't just a kiss. This is him dominating me. The man is power and sexiness rolled into one. He takes whatever the hell he wants. But I'm only here for the ride. Alessio is a man who knows what he wants and somehow knows what I want. He reaches into my darkest fantasies and brings them to life.

I continue to move, and all the while, his hand stays wrapped around my neck. He squeezes a little, and I gasp. My gaze flies to his, and I see darkness in his eyes. He's loving this just as much as I am.

My hips move in a hypnotic rhythm. I'm unable to control myself. My fingers claw into his chest as my orgasm starts to build.

"I can feel your pussy clenching," he grinds out, thrusting deep inside of me. "Do not come. Not until I say."

I stare at him in disbelief. How the hell am I going to do that?

In one slick, fluid movement, he has me on my back and he's driving into me like a man possessed.

"Tonight," he growls. "You come when I say you can."

I gasp and nod. I want that too. God, I want this man in ways I never thought possible.

He grits his teeth and fucks me until I'm unable to do anything but lie here and pant. My orgasm building inside of me, ready to explode like a raging inferno. He tilts his hips and thrusts into me, his strokes hard, fast, and powerful. His hand on my neck tightens, and he drags me toward him, his mouth once again claiming mine.

"Come for me," he growls.

I detonate, absolutely shatter into a million pieces.

"Christ," he grunts as he thrusts deep inside of me and releases his cum into me. "So fucking good, baby. You're pussy is fucking amazing. I love the way your body responds to me."

His chest heaves as he holds his weight off me, his gaze firmly on mine. This is when he usually pulls out and gets off me. Instead, he slants his mouth against mine and kisses the hell out of me. I wrap my arms around his neck and pull him closer. He comes willingly, and the kiss heats up. My pussy is still convulsing around his softening cock. I want him again. There's just something about Alessio that makes me feel alive, makes me feel wanted, beautiful, and special.

I wince as he pulls out of me, his cock soaked in our juices. He glances down to see what I'm looking at, and smiles when he sees how soaked his cock is.

"I love how wet you get, baby."

I chuckle as I lie back against the bed. Tonight has been different. Every time with Alessio has been amazing, but something about how he was this evening was different. He treated me differently. We got closer. I can't help but wonder what this means?

I'm basking in the glorious afterglow of sex, when I hear him move. The sound of his belt clinks as he starts to dress. Instantly, that afterglow begins to leave my body, God, I hate this. Every day for the past four days, it's been the same. He breaks in, enters my room—we fuck, and it's without a doubt the best sex I have ever had, but as soon as it's over, he leaves. I know I shouldn't care. Getting involved with a man who is deeply ingrained in a world I want no part in should have been a huge no-no. Instead, I let my heart lead my head, and I've gotten into a situation I'm not sure I can get out of.

Alessio Bianchi is a man who seems to only want one thing—sex. I could be anyone, and he'd get his rocks off. I'm okay with that. I've got into the mindset that this is just fun and nothing else. I'm praying he'll end this soon. If this continues, I could start to fall for him, and that's something I can never let happen. I'm screwed. I know I am. I can't end this myself. There's something about Alessio I'm drawn to. I'm slightly more addicted every day. I wait for him to arrive, praying I'll see him. It's crazy. I'm losing my mind.

"I've got to go back to New York," he tells me, his words soft and regretful.

I blink into the darkness. My heart racing as pain spreads across my chest. This is what I wanted—what I needed—him to sever ties. I need him to end this craziness. So why the hell do I feel as though I'm losing a piece of me?

I take a deep breath and strive for nonchalant. "Okay?"

"I'll be back," he assures me.

"Okay, Alessio, whatever you say. Have a safe flight," I say, as I sink further into the bed, wishing he'd leave already because my bastard eyes are watering. "Don't forget to lock up as you leave." I sound like an uncaring bitch, something I'm not. My heart feels as though it's splitting in two, but I need to do this. I need a clean break.

"Christ," he growls. He stalks toward me, flipping on the switch. Light illuminates my bedroom from the lamp beside me. He bends low so that his face inches from my own. "Get this," he snarls. "You and me, we're far from over. This shit you do when I leave, making it seem like I'm your fuck buddy, stops."

I raise a brow as I stare into his deep amber eyes. "Oh, really? And what do you think we are?"

His lips slam against mine, his tongue sweeping into my mouth. I'm putty in his hands within seconds. This man can control my body in ways I never knew possible. He's a fucking magician. He knows the right ways to get me to submit to him.

His hand circles my neck, and he holds me there, as he takes everything he wants from me.

When he pulls back, I'm breathless, and his eyes are heated. He wants me again; of that I have no doubt. The man is a machine and can go again and again.

"You're mine," he growls. "If you weren't, I wouldn't be here. Knew from the moment I saw you there was something about you, and then you fucked up. You let me fuck you, baby, and let me tell you, no one has lit up for me the way you do. No one takes my cock like you. You're mine, and that's never going to change."

I sigh. He's saying all the right words, but I can't believe them. I choose not to. In the world he lives in, things happen, and people change. I know what it's like to have someone promise me something, only to renege on it in the end. I've been broken-hearted more times than I can count waiting on my father, but I won't do it again.

"I've got business I have to attend to, but I'll be back. In less than a week, I'll be back, and Gabriella, your ass better be here when I return."

He doesn't let me say a word. He kisses me once again, until I'm clinging to him and breathless. Heat pools between my legs, and I'm squirming, wanting more.

"A week," he promises me.

"A week," I reply, unsure of what's going to happen; if I'll let him back or not. I have a week to figure out what the hell I want in my life, and if it's to be dragged into the criminal world or not.

"See you soon, baby," he says as he walks out of my room.

I watch him go. "Don't forget to lock up," I shout out to him, knowing he'll be cursing me a blue streak as he heads for the front door.

"Pushing it," he snarls as I hear the front door opening.

I flip the lamp off, flop back against the mattress, and sink into my bed with a smile. God, he makes me giddy, but even though I'm happy with the words he's said and the promise he's made me, I also know my gut is screaming that this is a bad idea.

My mind is spinning, wondering what the hell I should do, and I fall asleep, my inner turmoil at its highest. I feel as though whatever decision I make is going to be the wrong one.

I GROAN as my cell rings. I turn over on the bed and reach blindly for it.

"Hello?" I answer groggily.

"Hey, Gab," my best friend, Raylee, says happily. "I'm so sorry, did I wake you up?"

I glance at my nightstand and see it's almost midday. Damn, I slept deep once Alessio left. "It's okay."

"I just wanted to call you because I knew you'd worry," she says, and I sit up in the bed and wonder what the hell is going on. "Mal and I are heading to the States. There's some crap going on with his family and he needs to be there."

"Is everything okay?" I ask, my heart pounding a mile a minute.

Raylee is my best friend, my sister. I'd be lost without her. We grew up together. I was with her through her toughest times, and she with mine. In the past six months we've not been able to see each other much, but we still call at least four times a week, and have a weekly video call so I can see my nieces and nephews.

"Yeah, just Makenna's husband having a little trouble with some work."

Makenna is Raylee's aunt-in-law. The Gallagher family is a weird dynamic. There's aunts, cousins, and nieces and nephews the same age. It's crazy, but they love each other very much. I have only met Malcolm and his father, Denis, who both are sweet as pie, even though they're gangsters.

"Know that feeling. Dad's having some trouble here too." When Alessio was hurt, Dad was furious. He wants Nikolai's head on a platter. No one comes into Denver and takes out a hit on a guest of his. He's furious, but Alessio's brother has said that things between them have been settled. There's a compromise, and Dad's not happy.

"Guess it's a bad week all around. Makenna's brother-in-law was shot while he was in Denver. Did you hear?"

My blood runs cold at her words. "What was his name?"

"He's still alive," Raylee tells me. "Alessio was badly injured, but he's home now."

"Whoa," I say, unable to breathe. "Is Alessio Bianchi related to you?"

She makes a humming noise. "Yes. He's Makenna's husband's brother. Dante is really close with both his brothers, and with Holly marrying Romero, they're all pretty close. They have a bond that's something even I'm jealous of, and I have a great relationship with my brothers."

I go silent, unable to comprehend what she's saying. How the hell did I not know that the Bianchi family and the Gallagher's were related? I've heard stories from Ray-Ray about the antics Makenna's brother-in-law got up to. But they always called him Ales, not Alessio. I never made the connection.

"Gab, is everything okay?"

I wipe my eyes when I feel the wetness coating my cheek. Why the hell am I crying? "Yeah, sorry, I haven't been feeling well lately and I'm tired."

"Oh no, I should have texted before I called. Go get some rest and I'll talk to you later. I'm hoping that while we're in the States, Mal and I can make a pitstop in Denver."

I smile, happy that I may be able to spend time with her. "That would be great."

"Awesome," she breathes. "I'll talk to Mal, and we'll get it sorted. Feel better soon, Gab. I love you."

I close my eyes as my heart fills with warmth. "I love you too. Give the kids a kiss from me. I'll talk to you later, bye."

The call ends, and I stare at the wall, trying to process everything I've just learned. Alessio Bianchi isn't just a dangerous man, he's one of the most dangerous men in the world. He has more connections than most of the bosses put together.

I have no idea what the hell I'm going to do now. I want the man, my body craves him, but I don't know if I can handle the life he lives—the disappointments—and the broken promises.

I have a week. One week to think-out my options and decide what I should do next.

Do I try with Alessio, or do I walk away?

SIX
ALESSIO

Six weeks later

I walk through our club, Dynamite. My shoes are soaked with the blood that flows like a fucking river from the bodies that litter the ground. Rage pulses through my body as I take in the innocent faces of the ones who lost their lives. Tonight was one of our busier nights. A Friday night is always good for people to come out and unwind after a week of work or college. They wanted time to chill and have fun—now they're lying on the dirty club floor. Dead.

I scan the room for survivors, listening for a sound, a mumble, a groan, a cry for help. But it's no use, they're all dead. Anyone who was alive, has already gone. As soon as the gunmen opened fire, they ran for their lives—something no one would ever blame them for. Had they stayed, they'd be just like all the others who are scattered across the floor.

I turn on my heels and reach for my cell, then hit Dante's number. My brother is going to be pissed.

"What?" he snarls as he answers my call. No doubt I'm taking his time away from his wife—something he hates anyone doing.

"We've got a problem," I inform him on a growl. "The club was hit. The cops should be here any minute."

I hear movement and the sound of an angry voice. No doubt Makenna's awake, and just as I am, she'll be pissed. A hit against us, is a hit against everyone.

"You know what this means, don't you, Dante?" I snarl as I exit the club.

"This means fucking war, Alessio. Fucking war. Those Serbians aren't going to know what's hit them by the time we're finished."

I smile as the call ends. It's about fucking time we took care of these bastards. Six weeks I've been back here in New York, and these fucking pricks have tried to infiltrate our turf. The shitshow the Serbs are doing is laughable. They're trying to make moves, trying to make their mark by coming after us. Fucking idiots.

Up until today, it had been stupid, small, shitty things, like moving into our turf, trying to undercut our drugs, and trying to poach our men. Things we have let slide but dealt with in a clear warning. The last thing we need is a full-on war on the streets of New York. Over the years, we learned the hard way about what a war will do. We've lost so many people. Too many good men have died at the hands of wars. Both Dante and I know that sometimes violence is needed, but we also understand there are other ways to take care of business. Silently but deadly. Do it in a way that not all eyes are on you. The world doesn't know that we're the monsters our father was.

These Serbs have no warning lights. They've just kept coming for us. Losing all their customers when we let it be known that we price matched them with their drugs. Instead of realizing how fucked they were, they've done this tonight. There's no coming back for them. They brought the war, and something that the Serbians didn't realize is they're not just going up against us. This club may be an Italian Familiga owned club, but with us Italians comes the Irish. Over the years, we've built up a lot of alliances, a fuck of a lot of them.

Dante and I have learned the many reasons as to why our father wanted the alliance between Dante and Makenna. He knew that the Irish were making moves. He knew that when the time came, and a war broke out, he wanted to be surrounded by people who could protect him.

He was a fucking cunt, but he was a smart bastard. Something no one can deny him. But as the years went on, the alliances between the Italians and Irish have only strengthened. There's so many

Gallaghers—most of whom are married now—each one of them has married into a powerful family. A threat against one of us, is a threat against us all. If the Serbs come for our turf, next, they'll go for the Irish. It's not going to work. They fucked up, and they're going to realize by the end of the night exactly how they've done so.

The sound of sirens reaches me. I've only got a few minutes until the cops start storming the place and barking orders like they own it. My rage is palpable. In the year since my father died, Dante has prided himself on being an old-school mafia don. Yes, we kill people—only those who have slighted or wronged us—but our communities, the streets we own, they do not know or feel the death and destruction of our world anymore. All they know is peace and harmony and that's the way we want it kept. In one night, the Serbians have fucked up completely. And for that, they will pay.

I wait at the entrance of the club, knowing the cops are going to want to question me.

Not only am I angry that I'm here, stuck in a stupid fucking war, but the woman I want to see is hundreds of miles away, no doubt thinking I'm never coming back. Gabriella Sanchez is the woman who has been on my mind since the very beginning. I knew as soon as I saw her there was something special about her. And every time I've been with her, she's proven that to me one way or another. The moment I fucked her, I knew I wasn't letting her go.

No matter how she might just dismiss me afterwards. Something that not only pisses me off but makes me smile. I know it's her way of protecting herself. But she has to know there's no way she can protect herself from me. Not anymore.

She had her chance that night those Russian bastards got me. That was her one chance to walk away. But she didn't. She chose to stay, and now I'm addicted. I get hard just thinking about my woman and how effortlessly sexy she is. I know my family thinks I was fucking around while I was down in Denver. They have no idea just how serious things got. Makenna has made a few comments, ones that make me chuckle. She thinks I'm going after Yelena. That's laughable. Especially after her old man tried to take me out.

Something I've learned over the past six weeks is that what Yelena and I had was merely attraction. I was young, dumb, and stupid. I needed a way to break through my father's hold on me. And Yelena was there. It was my act of rebound. Feelings did start to form, but they weren't love. I don't know if I'm even capable of feeling that emotion. But I did care for the girl. Her leaving was the best thing that ever happened to me.

I got my head on straight, I was more focused on what needed to be done, and I became the man I was destined to be. The Consigliere for the Famiglia.

Dante arrives not even twenty minutes later, while I'm still talking to the cops. His expression is calm and relaxed, but the swirling anger in his eyes tells me this isn't the end. No one gets away with doing this to us. Revenge is going to start, and it's going to start soon.

He does pretty much what I did. Just walks straight into the club. The cops try to stop him, not wanting him to contaminate their crime scene, but Dante doesn't give a fuck, he doesn't listen to them. He needs to see for himself the damage that these Serbians have done. He needs to see the savageness they wrought. He will let that rage simmer beneath his body just like I am. One way or another we're going to unleash that rage we have built and those cunts that did this are going to feel our wrath. Nobody comes after us and gets away with it.

Once I'm finished with the cops, they move on to Dante, wanting to question him about what happened tonight. Fuck, they all saw him arrive after the fact, yet these cops will do anything to try and pin shit on us.

I reach for my cell again and call Romero. My brother is on alert letting me know that Dante has already spoken to him. Good. The more people that are awake and in the know the fucking better.

"Holly and I are on our way," he tells me. "We should be in New York in about an hour."

Knowing Rome, it'll be a fuck of a lot less than an hour. He and his wife Holly live in Connecticut. Most of the time, he travels to and from New York. He is the underboss for the Clann. He's one of

Makenna's right-hand men. But as much as he is the underboss of the Irish Mafia, he is still very much ingrained in the Famiglia.

"It's fucking carnage here, bro," I say, letting him know just what to expect. "The cops are here and taking statements. They've pulled out twenty-five dead bodies from the club." Most of them are barely out of their teenage years, finally able to have fun.

"Fucking bastards," he growls. "I'll meet you and Dante at the house."

I grind my jaw. God, it's going to be a long fucking night.

"I'll see you there," I say. "Prepare yourself, Rome, the war is coming." I end the call, my gaze firmly on the door to the club, where the emergency services are rushing in and out.

It's another hour before Dante and I are able to leave. Eleven more dead bodies have been brought out. I counted every single body bag that left the club. I know they're still hopeful there are survivors, but I know there won't be. This day will sit in the hearts of those emergency workers and in the community for years to come. It's time for the Famiglia to act, and to do so with the full extent of our arsenal.

My gut is screaming as Dante and I walk toward my car. His is currently blocked in by the emergency services. He'll get one of our men to get it for him tomorrow. I glance back at the club, and it hits me. How the fuck did those cunts get into the club with fucking guns and open fire? How were they allowed into the club with guns at all?

It's something we're going to have to find out.

"Talk to me," he demands as soon as I start the engine. "I can tell by your face that you're thinking hard about something, so what is it?"

I pull out into the light New York traffic. "How the fuck does this happen?" I growl. My anger simmering along the surface. "How do five gunmen walk into our club with fucking guns and kill this many people?" I glance at my brother. "Where were the men on the door, Dante? Where the fuck were the bouncers?"

It's something that has been niggling at me since the moment I walked into that club. None of our men were on the door, none of their bodies have been found. Not fucking one. So where the fuck are they? My jaw tightens. Either our men have been taken or they're working against us.

"That, Alessio, is something we are going to find out," he snarls, his fists curling into balls. "The war is about to begin."

I direct my grin at the windshield. Fuck yes. It's time to end these motherfuckers once and for all. God fucking help them because no one else can.

SEVEN
GABRIELLA

Nausea rolls through my body once again as bile empties out of me. This has been going on for over a week, and I know there's no denying it anymore. My boobs are tender and bigger, I've been getting sick in the mornings, and my period is late—something that it never is.

I'm pretty sure I'm pregnant.

I rest my head against the toilet seat and ponder what I'm going to do if I am pregnant. Do I wait for Alessio to return—something he may never do—or do what I've been wanting to do for the past six weeks and run? Things between Alessio and I were never meant to be the way they were. It was just meant to be one night of fun. The first night he came to my room, I got a taste of him. I became love-drunk. I was intoxicated on him.

Having the space between us made me realize just how stupid I had been. He's dangerous. His family is dangerous. I want out of this world. I don't want to be dragged further into it. My father has managed to keep me out of the limelight, making sure nobody knows who I am. If Alessio and I are together, everyone will know that I'm part of the life. They'll dig further into my life and uncover who I am. That's not something I want. It's not something I crave. I don't want that power. I don't want that accolade of being a woman of a powerful man. It's not something I have ever wanted for myself.

Growing up, I learned from a very young age that the criminal world takes precedence over everything, including children. I lived with the heartache of my father putting his world first and it broke me. It's not something I want for my child.

Once I finally finish throwing up, I sit back and wonder how the hell I got to this position. I'm always so careful. I take my pill every day like clockwork. I've never forgotten to take them. I always have an alarm to remind me. The time Alessio and I were together was crazy. Between the beating and shooting he took, along with the fear I felt as I brought him home, not to mention us being together, it was lunacy. But I still believe I took my pill.

How the hell could I be pregnant?

I shower and get ready for the day, my mind in overdrive as I think about what my future could be like with a child. I'm so thankful that I am not working today but I do need to buy a pregnancy test. I need a definitive answer on whether or not I am pregnant. Once I know for sure, I can make a decision on what I need to do next.

Two hours later, and I'm looking at two pink lines.

Positive.

I'm having Alessio Bianchi's baby.

What the hell am I gonna do? This is not what I wanted, not what I envisioned for myself. I had so many plans. So many things I wanted to do, to achieve. I just can't believe this is happening to me.

As I stare at the two pink lines, I think about the life that's growing inside of me. I think about the baby that is mine, and I know that no matter what happens, I'll always protect him or her. But that means I can't have Alessio finding out about him or her. I know in my soul that if he finds out, he'll demand that I be with him. And that's not something I can do. I cannot live that life. I will not put myself in that position, and I definitely won't put my child into it either.

My panic starts to rise as I begin to wonder how I'm going to get out of this situation. I know there's only one person who can help me; a man I don't tend to go to for help. But someone who will help me no matter what. My dad. Our situation isn't normal, and our relationship isn't what others have, but I trust him, and I know that if there's one person who'll not judge me nor try to force me to do something, it's him.

It takes me a little over thirty minutes to get to my father's house.

When I arrive, his wife, Christina, opens the door. She's dressed head-to-toe in designer outfits, and gold jewelry coats her neck, wrists, and fingers. She looks every bit like she just walked off the runway.

She glares at me. The woman knows who I am, and she absolutely hates me. I am a reminder that my father cheated on her.

"Is Joe here?" I ask, keeping my head held high. As much as the woman despises me, I won't let her make me cower beneath the darkening looks she gives me.

She opens the door further for me to come in but doesn't speak a word to me—something that isn't out of the ordinary. If she could, she'd pretend I don't exist.

I follow behind her as her heels click against the marble floor. This house is huge. It's almost as though it's a museum. There's art and sculptures everywhere. Every shelf is filled with innate objects, things Christina loves, all of which cost more than a normal person's mortgage. I dutifully follow her as she weaves through the house, toward my father's office. It's so huge, it's a wonder no one has gotten lost in this place. There's only Joe and Christina who live here. I know Joe buys everything Christina wants in a bid to keep her happy.

"Joe," her nasally voice calls out. "*That* woman is

here to see you," she says with as much disdain as possible.

My father walks out of his office, his brows narrowing as he glances at his wife. They widen ever so slightly when he sees me. The smile he gives me is bright and welcoming. As bad as things have been between us in the past, he's always shown me that he cares. I just don't come above his work. His empire comes first, and that's something I have come to live with, even though it still hurts me to this day.

He directs me into his office, just as his wife tells him she's leaving. I know it's because I'm in her house and she doesn't like me. Christina doesn't like what I represent: what she doesn't have. And my heart hurts for her because if the tables were turned, I don't think I could stay with a man who cheated on me and impregnated another woman.

I take a seat and wait for my father to close the door. "Hey, Gab, is everything okay?"

I can't hold back the tears any longer. I've been holding my emotions in check for almost three hours, and right now, I don't have the energy to hold them back any longer. My body wracks with sobs as the tears slowly cascade down my face.

"I messed up," I tell him. "I made a huge mistake, Dad. I need your help."

He's instantly crouching down in front of me, framing in my face with his hands. "Talk to me, sweetheart. What happened?"

I gasp for some air, my body trembling. "I'm

pregnant, Dad," I whisper, and hear him pull in a sharp breath. "I'm not gonna tell you who the father is. But I cannot stay in Denver anymore. I just don't want him to know about the baby."

He releases a harsh breath as he gets to his feet.

"Are you sure about this?" he questions, and I know he's not asking about the baby. He's asking about my decision to leave.

"It's all I've thought about all morning. Dad, he's in the same world you are. I can't put my baby through what I went through with you. Being second best, hurt. Knowing that no matter what happens, I will never come first... I want my baby to have an amazing life. I want him or her to be happy and feel loved," I tell him as the tears continue to tumble down my face. "I don't want them to feel the way I did. Unloved. So yes, I am sure."

His eyes narrow, but he doesn't say anything. And I know he's feeling what I said. I hate that I may have hurt him with my words, but I need him to understand my decision.

"I need some way to build a life, Dad. I need to be able to live happily with my baby without having to worry about yours or my baby's father's enemies coming for me." I give him a weak, wobbly smile. "I know you've done a great job keeping me hidden from everyone, but that's only gonna last for so long. I need to be out of Denver."

He doesn't even hesitate. He nods instantly. "Whatever you want, Gabby. I'm here for you, no matter what. Find a place, tell me what you want, and we'll get it done."

The relief that washes through me is unlike anything I have ever felt before. Gratitude, love, and acceptance. That's all I felt from him. He may not have been the best dad, maybe not have been the world's greatest father, but he's trying. He's doing everything he can for me. I love him, I always have, but what he's doing for me, for my baby—for his grandchild... it's something I'll never forget, and can never repay.

We spend the next hour or so figuring out the perfect place for me to settle down and make a life for my baby. It takes a while, but we finally settle on Indianapolis. It's hours away from Denver, and it's someplace I know I can blend in. I hope that by being so far away, Alessio will never be able to find me.

Why would I be there? If Alessio does come to find me—something I doubt he'll do since it's been six weeks and I've not heard a single thing—he may think I've gone back to Spain or England.

I'll always know there's a slight chance he could come looking for me, but I'm hoping that being somewhere as inconspicuous as Indianapolis will help me stay hidden.

Joe immediately starts looking for houses and properties for me to open a gallery and have a place to live. He knows what I want and love. I don't even have to tell him. He's obviously paid attention to my life, something I never thought of before. But it's so nice to know that while I was thinking I was second best, he was making sure he knew everything about me. He may not have been at all my important things, but he's here now.

"Are you okay?" he questions after he gets off the phone to a realtor.

I swallow hard. Maybe now is the time to be completely honest with him. I want him to know that no matter what, I'm glad he's my dad, and I love him so much.

"I know my existence hasn't been easy for you. It's caused you a lot of heartache, especially with your wife, and it's caused you a lot of fear that one day your enemies would uncover our relationship." I give him a soft smile. "We started off rocky, Dad, we really did, but we've worked through everything, and I can honestly say you are the best man I know." It's true, even though some things may not be what I like or expect, he's still the greatest man I know. "I love you, Dad, and I'm so thankful you're here with me. I couldn't ask for a better person to help." I know that if my mum found out that Dad knew about my pregnancy before her, she'd hit the roof, but I can't deal with Carmella right now. She's overbearing, and she'll demand I move back to Spain. Something I don't want to happen.

He pulls me into his arms, and I begin to cry again. God, I hope I'm not this emotional all the time.

"No matter what, Gabby, I'm always gonna be here for you," he promises me.

I look up at him and see the sincere smile on his face.

"You're gonna be a grandpa," I tell him, finally seeing the goodness in this. I feel happy and relieved to be starting again. I'm going to ensure that me and my baby have the best life I can give us.

He straightens. "Oh, my God. I'm going to be a granddad," he says, his words filled with pride and joy. I watch as his face falls and his expression hardens. He shakes his head. "I promise you now, Gabby, I'm going straight." I freeze at his words, unable to believe he's actually saying them.

"I may not have been the best father to you. I'm going to try, and I'm gonna be the best grandfather there is. Just as I should have been the best man I could be for you."

I don't say anything. I don't believe him. I've listened to one too many empty promises before. But I do see that he truly believes he can do this. And for that alone, I just smile.

I won't be in Denver when the baby's born, which means my father will be able to visit without the worry of us being hurt. And that is all I care about.

My child being safe and us being happy.

EIGHT
ALESSIO

"So, not only have these fucks gunned down innocent people, their drugs are sending people to the hospital," Romero growls as he paces Makenna and Dante's office.

Once again, when shit hits the fan, everyone turns up at the Gallagher compound. The house used to belong to Makenna's father, Seamus, but the old man was gunned down outside while trying to protect my sister-in-law, his granddaughter, Holly. Now it's the headquarters for all things Famiglia and Clann. Whenever there's family meetings or any planning, it goes down here. It's become a place of foreboding. Nothing good ever comes from being here anymore.

"How many?" Makenna asks, just as her brother Finn steps into the office with a scowl on his face.

"Seventeen so far, three dead, four in ICU. It's going to have the cops on red alert, which means if we're going to hit the Serbians, we're going to need to do something soon," Rome answers as he shakes Finn's hand.

Both men are Makenna's right-hand men. She trusts them above everyone else in her organization. They're family. Finn is her brother, the man who would go above everyone else to protect her. He's proven his loyalty to her in ways many wouldn't, including almost losing his woman over not going against his sister.

"How the fuck has this been happening and we've not known until it's too late?" Dante demands. He's furious. Not that anyone can blame him. This shit has been happening in our city, on our turf. It's a bad fucking look for not only us, but the entire criminal underworld.

"It's too neat," Stefan says as he glances around the room. The man has been promoted to Dante's most trusted soldier. He's proven his loyalty to not only the Famiglia but also to the Clann. For that, he's been given the biggest honor he can receive: being promoted above everyone else.

"What do you mean?" Finn grunts. "How is it too fucking neat? The bastards have killed people."

"Exactly. They've been selling drugs laced with fuck knows what, and then they waltzed into Dynamite without a care in the world, killed over twenty people, and walked away without anyone getting a good look at their faces. No, this is way too neat. It reeks of planning, organizing."

Dante scrubs a hand along his jaw. "They've had this in the works for a while," he concludes. "Which means they no doubt have more planned."

"They'll have gone to ground," I say. "There's no way you can be that organized and not have a plan in place to disappear until the heat dies down."

Makenna nods in agreement. "Finn, call Danny. We're going to need Melissa to find out as much as she can about the cunts who hit Dynamite and anywhere they could be hiding."

Finn walks out of the office, his cell to his ear. Within the next twenty-four hours, every Gallagher is going to be in New York. Danny is Finn and Makenna's nephew. He's the head of the Irish Mafia in the United Kingdom. He's a fucking beast who'd take anyone out who would ever try and harm his family. Come after his wife, and he'll kill you without a second thought. He's proven it once already. He was kidnapped, and his wife was threatened. Danny boy beat the ever-loving shit out of the guy who took him and killed him without breaking a sweat. Lucky for us, his wife, Melissa, is a fucking genius when it comes to hacking and technology. She can get us any information we may need. She's the best in the business.

Everyone is in deep thought, trying to figure out how we can find a way to track these bastards down, but there's something about this situation that doesn't sit right with me. Hell, why on earth would the Serbians come after us? It's a fucking death sentence.

No matter what, you'll end up dead. Coming after the Familiga means you tangle with everyone we're associated with, and that's a fuck of a lot of people. No, something about this all has my gut screaming.

"What if they're not working alone?" I muse out loud.

The air in the room goes static. Dante's jaw clenches, Makenna sits forward in her seat, and Romero looks as though he's about to go hunting. I guess I've hit the nail on the head.

"Who?" Dante growls. "Who'd be stupid enough to come after us?"

"Who wouldn't?" I retort with a snort. "I mean, whoever it is, they're working behind the scenes, getting the Serbs to do their dirty work. Whoever it is, they're sneaky as fuck."

"Which means they've had this in the works for a while, maybe even years," Mac says as his gaze moves around the room. Liam 'Mac' McCarthy has shot up the ranks within the Clann and is now Makenna's right hand man. He's as close to her as her brother and Romero are. He's earned that loyalty from her. He's the man who went against his boss—Makenna's underboss—and told the truth regarding the missing drug shipment. From that moment on, Mac was regarded as a straight talker and a man who could maybe be trusted. Instead of being made Underboss, he became Makenna's guard, and in turn, her closest man.

I grit my teeth as one organization comes to

mind. The Bratva. We fucked them over in more ways than one over the years. As the Famiglia and the Clann grew to prominence, the Bratva slowly disappeared, but their men are still out there. They're rebuilding, I just know they are. The question is, who's at the helm these days? Is it still Maksim?

Dante and I share a look. It seems I'm not the only one to jump to the Russians for this. "Given what's happened in recent weeks, I wouldn't say it's out of the realm of impossible."

Romero snorts. "Yeah, especially when we took out most of their men when Holly was missing."

The anger in his voice is clear for us to hear. My brother still thinks a lot about what happened to his wife, and I know it haunts him even to this day. With this shit happening now, it's probably going to send him into overdrive to protect her.

When my sister-in-law went missing, Dante and Romero opened fire on the Russian boxing gym, killing the majority of the Russian fighters. It turned out the Russians had nothing to do with Holly's disappearance. That was all down to Georgia, Romero's ex—also the woman I cheated on Yelena with. It's been years since that shit went down and the Russian's haven't made a move. It's the only thing that makes sense. No one else has the motive to come after us.

Dante rises to his feet. "It's time to have a meeting with Maksim," he announces, and I smile.

Fuck yes, it's time to get this shit sorted once and for all.

ENTERING the restaurant brings back a lot of memories. This is the base for the Bratva. They all meet here and plan their shit. It's easy to spot outsiders, and whenever someone who doesn't belong to the Bratva turns up, everyone leaves. It's one of the many reasons the cops can't get dirt on them. They can't send anyone in to get information. The moment they enter, they're under suspicion.

"You have a lot of nerve," I hear the heavily accented, feminine voice say, her tone full of disdain. "I'd leave if I were you."

"Annika," I respond dryly. She's Yelena's cousin. The woman doesn't give a fuck about her cousin as she tried to get me to fuck her on more than one occasion. I was never that desperate, though. She dislikes me for no other reason than I preferred her cousin to her. My gaze moves to her finger, and I see the flash of a gold band. "I see you're married. Condolences to your husband."

Her cheeks heat, and she narrows her eyes. "What is it that you want?"

"To speak with your grandfather," I say as I take a seat, both Dante and Stefan following suit.

I had thought Dante would have taken the lead, but while we were on our way here, he told me he was going to let me do so. I have more of a relationship with Maksim than he does, and I never killed any of his men—as of yet. That could all change, depending on how this meeting goes.

For Dante to give me that trust, it tells me that he's put to bed the past and has fully given me a second chance, something many others would not have done had the tables been turned.

My cell buzzes in my pocket. Reaching for it, I see it's a text from Thomas. I once again have tasked the man with a job. I should really employ him full-time with the amount of money he charges me. As I'm busy here in New York, I have tasked Thomas to keep tabs on Gabriella. With this shit show going down, not to mention what happened while I was in Denver, it wouldn't take a genius to find out who helped me out of that alleyway—even though Melissa worked her magic and got the security tapes erased. It wouldn't be impossible for someone to find out she's the reason I'm alive.

She's gone. The house is empty. Looks as though she left in a rush.

I stare at the message, my heart fucking stopping. There's no fucking way she's gone. Hell fucking no. I can't believe this shit. I'm hundreds of miles away and can't do anything about this. Right now, my family needs me to be here and be present. My hands are tied. I'm going to have to wait until this shit with the Serbians is cleared up before I can make my way to Denver to find her.

"Alessio," Maksim greets me as he steps up to the table.

I rise to my feet and shake the old man's hand. It's been a few years since I last saw him. He's aged a lot in that time, and I'm truly wondering if this man is the same one who's running things. Surely not.

"Maksim, it's been a while," I reply politely but all the while I want to scream. Everything is falling to shit. But yet all I can think is, *where the fuck is Gabriella?*

He nods solemnly. "It has," he responds as he takes a seat. "What is it that I can do for you?"

Dante raises a brow at the tone.

"I'm not stupid, Mr. Bianchi. I'm pretty sure we've been through this before. You wouldn't show up here unless you wanted something, so what is it?"

"Information," I reply, knowing he's right. He's not stupid, and neither are we. There's no point in wasting our time. "I'm guessing you've heard about what happened last night?"

"I did. Can't say I'm all that sorry. What goes around comes around."

Bastard. "Have you heard about the new wave of heroin?"

His brows knit together. "No," he grunts.

"Three dead, four in ICU, and fuck knows how many more," Dante says as he sits back in his seat. "Want to hazard a guess at what's causing it?"

The old man shakes his head. He doesn't look too interested.

"Cocaine laced with fentanyl. It's a lethal concoction. They're selling it just a fraction lower than what heroine costs, and the people are buying them like they're going out of fashion. I mean, who can blame them?"

Darkness seeps into his eyes. "Who?" he questions, glancing from me to Dante and back again. "Who's doing this?"

Ah, seems to have hit a nerve. Now I'm wondering what could have happened for him to be this wound up.

"The Serbians," Dante tells him. "But we have a feeling they're not working alone. Whoever they're working with is trying to take us down, and the way we see it, there's only one person who has a grudge against us."

Maksim grins. "Me."

"Bingo," Dante snarls. "So, Maksim, are you using the Serbs to do your dirty work?"

The utter contempt that forms on the old man's face makes me wonder just what the fuck is going on.

"Never," he spits. "I would never work with those bastards."

"Damn," Stefan chuckles. "Seems as though he hates someone more than us."

"You," Maksim grunts. "You killed many of my men. But then Dante, we made a deal," he says, and I slide my eyes to my brother. That's fucking news to me. "You gave us the women. The way I see it, I'd have made more money off the whores than the fighters. We're even. If I were to go after you, I wouldn't hide behind the Serbians."

"Fuck," Dante snarls. "Then who?"

I watch as Annika moves from behind the counter and over to a man who's way too comfortable standing back and watching this play out. If it were any of our men, they'd be on edge, wondering what could happen, especially given the past, but not this guy. No, he's laid back and smiling, something that doesn't fit.

"Who's the guy in the cheap suit?" I ask him, making sure I'm not overheard.

Maksim laughs. "That, Alessio, is Annika's husband, Taras. He thinks of himself as something."

Dante glances over at the man in question and rises to his feet. "Thank you for meeting with us, Maksim, but I'd watch your back if I were you. That asshole is waiting for the perfect time to try and take over."

Maksim and Dante shake hands. "I always sleep with one eye open," he tells us. "I suggest you do the same. Whoever this is, Mr. Bianchi, they're not going to stop until they get what they want."

The smile that comes across my brother's face is sinister. "Better men have tried, Maksim, and those men have failed. We're ready for them. They think the war has started, but they haven't seen anything yet."

I don't say anything as we leave the restaurant. My anger about the situation is palpable, but I'm also pissed that Gabriella has disappeared.

"What was that about?" I question my brother once we're in the car.

"My wife knew about the deal. We agreed we didn't want the women. We're not into running stables, Ales, you know that. It was the perfect way to ensure there were no throwbacks after the fiasco at the boxing hall."

"Why didn't I know about this?"

My brother spears me a glance. "Back then, Ales, I didn't know if I could trust you."

Fuck.

NINE
GABRIELLA

"Are you sure about this, sweetheart?" Dad asks as I enter my new home.

I turn and look at him. He's been amazing. How he's managed to make everything happen in less than thirty hours is beyond me, and yet here we are.

"I'm sure," I promise him.

I take a couple more steps into the house, and I feel a sense of peace, something I haven't felt before. I've always been on edge, knowing that at any moment something could go wrong—and usually it does—but right here and now, I'm calm and collected. I feel good, and it feels right that I'm here.

"Alright," he says as he carries my bag into the house. "How about we have a look around?"

Yesterday, I flew into Indianapolis on a fake passport, something I never before imagined doing, but my dad insisted that it would be for the best. I trust him, so I did as he asked, and everything went off smoothly. I landed early yesterday morning and spent the day scoping out properties for my gallery. There's a few I've found that are ideal. I just need to look at the locations and do a bit of research before settling on one.

While I was looking over real estate, my dad was in Denver doing what he does best and bossing people around. While I had my clothes packed and ready to go, my dad hired movers to pack up the rest of my stuff and drive it out to me. I'm not sure how much he paid them, but as of right now, everything except for my clothes and kitchen stuff is all unboxed and set up. I'm in awe of how easy this move was. When I left Spain to come live here in the States, it was a nightmare trying to get everything over here. In the end, I had to leave some of my stuff behind.

I'm like a giddy schoolgirl as I check out the house, looking around every room, scoping out every little nook and cranny. I can't believe how big this house is.

There's nothing that could ever repay everything Joe has done for me. I've thanked him a hundred times and he always grunts at me, telling me I'm his daughter, that he'd do anything for me.

"Okay, kiddo," he says as I enter the master bedroom. I turn to face him. "I'm going to leave you be and let you get settled in. We'll have dinner later?"

I blink, my heart sinking. "Um, yeah, sure," I reply. "Do you have somewhere to be?"

He glances away, and I instantly know that

means yes. It's the same thing he does whenever I ask about his plans and it involves a woman. He feels guilty—as he should. He's cheating on Christina. Not that I like the woman, but she doesn't deserve the heartache of what my father's doing to her.

"Dinner?" he asks again.

"Sure," I reply. "Let me know when." I turn my back on him, trying my hardest to quell the disappointment. I shouldn't feel this way. He's helped me so much already. But I can't help it. It just brings up a lot of memories and none of them are good.

"Sweetheart," he begins, but I don't turn around. I don't want him to feel guilty for this. It's his life. He's able to live it how he wants.

"Call me later, yeah?" I say as I reach for my duffle bag on the floor. "Hopefully, I'll be unpacked by then." I release a little laugh. It's humorless, but it seems to do the trick.

"Alright then, have fun. Love you, Gabby."

I sigh. No matter what, he's my dad and he's trying. "Love you too, Dad."

UNPACKING TAKES me the best part of the day. By the time I'm finished, darkness has descended. But my house is now a home. Everything has been unpacked and is in its perfect place. I had to move some things—I'm a perfectionist when it comes to my home—as I like to have things tidy and neat.

I collapse onto the couch and sigh. I'm tired. I could sleep for a week right now, but first, I need food. I reach for my cell that's sitting on the coffee table and see I have two missed calls and a text from my dad. I hit dial on his number and call him back.

"Sweetheart, is everything okay?" he asks as soon as he answers. "I tried to call but there was no answer."

"Sorry, Dad, I was busy. I didn't hear my cell ring."

I hear the long release of breath, and I hate that I had him worried. "Good. Are you still on for dinner?"

I curl up more on my couch and pull the blanket down on top of me. "Any chance of us getting a takeout?"

"Absolutely," he responds instantly, and I giggle. "Pizza?"

I laugh. "You read my mind," I tell him, glad I don't have to get dressed up and go out and face the world. All I want to do is shower, get into my ratty sweats, and chill for the night. "Dad, I'm not sure what your plans are, but I want you to know that there's a room here for you whenever you want." I need him to know that I want him in my life. I want him to know that he's not just someone I expect to help out when times are rough. I want him around always. I missed out on spending time with him when I was younger, but since I moved to the States, I've learned a lot about him. Some things I love, others I don't, but it's him, and I love him because he's my dad. I just haven't been able to show how much he means to me.

"Alright, sweetheart, I'll order the pizzas, get some beers, then I'll swing by. Is there anything you want?"

"Ice-cream," I reply, knowing I'll probably eat the entire pint myself.

He chuckles. "Should have known. I won't be long. I'll see you soon."

Once the call ends, I drag myself upstairs to the shower. There's nothing better than sleeping on fresh sheets when you're all clean and snug.

"Gab?" I hear my dad call out almost thirty minutes later.

"I'm upstairs, Dad. I'll be down in a second," I yell back. I pull on my sweatpants and hoodie and make my way toward the smell of food. My stomach rumbles as I enter the kitchen. "Hey, Dad," I say as I walk up to him. "You okay?"

He presses a kiss against my head. "I'm good. You've done a great job, Gab, the place looks amazing."

I smile at his praise. "Thanks. I'm about ready for bed," I laugh. "But first, food."

He shakes his head. "A child after my own heart."

I roll my eyes and reach for the boxes of pizzas. He's in great shape for a man in his late fifties, but he sure as hell eats a lot. I've never seen anyone eat or drink as much as my dad. He's like a human garbage disposal.

We sit down and Dad puts a movie on. It's the latest action blockbuster. I sit back all snug in my blanket and sweats as I set about eating my pizza.

An hour later, we're both finished eating, and my dad's cell rings. I watch as he glances down at the screen and scowls. He gets to his feet and walks out of the room. He doesn't even hit pause on the movie, and we're getting to the good bit.

I groan as I reach for the TV remote. Ugh, I've eaten so much that I'm bloated, but damn, it was the best pizza I've ever had. I now have a new place to eat at, and I couldn't be more excited.

"Sweetheart," my dad says as he walks back into the room.

"Yeah?" I say as I look up at him. I swallow hard as I see the sorrow in his eyes. I know that look. I've seen it before. It's the look everyone gave me when my best friend, Mayer, died. It's one I wished I'd never have to see again. "Dad?" I whisper, my heart racing.

He crouches down in front of me and takes my hands into his. "I'm so sorry, sweetheart," he begins, and a lump forms in my throat. *No.* "Your mom—"

"No," I snarl. No, this can't be happening.

"I'm so sorry, Gabby, but she was in a car accident. She didn't make it."

His words hit me, and I hear a loud shriek rent the air. I realize it's me. I'm screaming and crying.

The pain I feel is like no other. I'm lost, utterly lost, like I'm out at sea floating.

My dad holds me, whispering reassurances that I'll be okay, that no matter what he'll be here with me. My sobs wrack through my body, my heart explodes with pain. I'm broken, my heart is shattered.

"Why her?" I ask, needing to know why she's gone.

He gently brushes my hair with his hand. "I don't know, sweetheart. I'm so sorry."

"But I never got to tell her," I wail. "She never found out she was going to be a grandma."

"She'll watch over you both, Gabby. She'll get to watch you both grow. She'll be so proud of you, just as I am."

His words are comforting but painful. The thought of her not being with me throughout this experience is heart-wrenching. It never crossed my mind that I'd have to live without her, that my child would be without her.

Mum... God, I can't even remember the last conversation we had, nor can I remember the last time I saw her. I feel like such a bad daughter. I should have done better, should have made the effort to call her more, spent more time with her. Now I'll never be able to get that time back.

I just want to call her, to hear her voice, and for all this to be a bad dream, but it's not. I know it's not. My heart feels as though something heavy is sitting on it. God, what am I going to do? How can I go on without her? The sobs flow through my body, but my dad doesn't let go. He holds me tight and promises to hold on.

"I'll arrange for our flights in the morning, Gabby. Once we're there, we'll organize the funeral."

At his words, my body buckles and I collapse against him.

"I can't," I breathe. The thought of burying her is abhorrent. I can't do it. I can't be without her.

"I know, baby girl, I know, but we'll get through it."

I sob against him, hating that such an amazing day has turned out this way. I've lost one of the most important people in my life.

"You'll be okay," he promises me.

I don't know if that's true. When Mayer died, I lost a piece of myself. I watched the man I considered a brother be beaten to death. I never recovered from it. I don't think I'll ever recover from losing my mum either.

TEN
ALESSIO

A week later

"We've got our window," Stefan says as he strides into the office. "The Serbs have set a meeting. It's taking place in two hours."

It's been a week since the shooting at our club. Everything since then has been full tilt. Every member of the Clann is now in New York. We've been planning, watching, and waiting. Melissa managed to find out which motherfuckers shot up the club and has been able to pinpoint their location. For the past week, we've been sitting on that location as we watch what happens next.

"And this information has come from...?" Denis asks. His Irish accent is thick and sometimes unintelligible.

"Maksim," Stefan responds as he takes a seat.

Dante and Makenna share a look. Neither of them have told anyone about the deal they made with Maksim a year ago, but I think their time's up. This family wants answers, and they're all as fucking stubborn as each other. Both Danny and Malcolm are glaring at their aunt, while Denis crosses his arms over his chest and waits his sister out.

"Fucking assholes," she hisses as she glares right back at them. "Sit down. You're making the place look untidy."

I hide my smirk as she takes her seat behind the desk, Dante standing behind her, as always. Ever present and protective. As much as we all know that the people in this room would never harm Makenna, Dante still feels the anger and fear he had when Makenna's other brothers tried to make a move and take over while I was in Denver. Lucky for us, they're now dead, and we don't have to deal with their brand of fucking crazy.

"When the shit went down when Da died," she begins, "we all know the Bratva got dragged into this shit."

Denis slides his gaze to me. I glare at him. Only my family knows why I was with the Russians, and I don't owe anyone else an answer. They don't like me, I don't give a fuck.

"Anyway, Alessio had been working for Matteo. He had to infiltrate the Russians as Matteo and Maksim were running guns, selling drugs, and selling women. As you know, I don't want a stable full of women. I have no problem if that's what the girls want to do, but I'll not have any of them forced into that life."

Dante stretches his legs out as he leans against the wall behind his wife, his arms crossed over his chest as he looks to Makenna's family. "When my father died and I took over, I was left with the deal Matteo and Maksim had made. With the relationship between us and the Russians at an all-time low, we decided to do what we thought best—"

"You gave the Russians the stable," Danny surmises. "Okay, so they've got a business that is no doubt worth millions now, so it would make sense that they wouldn't hold a grudge, but we're talking about the Russians. They're not exactly known for their tact."

"True," Dante agrees. "But after speaking with Maksim, I believe he has nothing to do with this. He hates the Serbians more than we do."

"So the meeting is legit?" Denis asks. "Maksim knows for sure they're all meeting?"

Stefan nods as he fights his smile. "Yes. They think they're untouchable, that we have no idea who hit the club."

"Waiting a week for revenge is unlike us," I say. "We're not the type to sit back and wait. We hit hard and we make them pay."

Makenna smiles. "That's true, which is why they think they have gotten away with it. But don't worry, those fuckers are going to get their comeuppance."

The sound of pipes roar in the distance, and I turn to my sister-in-law. "Really?" I ask. "You've got the Fury Vipers coming along for the ride?"

She merely grins. "What? Ace wanted to help. He heard about the shooting, and he says he owes us." She shrugs. "The more the merrier."

I shake my head. The Fury Vipers are the local motorcycle club. The president of the New York chapter happens to be Makenna's best friend's brother. Over the past two years, they've had a fuck of a lot to deal with. When the shit hit the fan and Ace's woman was in danger, Ace turned to Makenna, and as he's family, she didn't hesitate to step up to the plate. Now he's here to help us.

"While we're all practically congratulating ourselves for pulling this off—" I begin as I take in all the smiles around me. "We still haven't uncovered who's pulling the Serbian's strings. They're not doing this alone, and if we take out the Serbians, we won't find out who's actually gunning for us."

The look that's shared between Dante and Makenna tells me they've also thought about this.

"Ales," Dante sighs. "Kenna and I have spoken about this. We either take out the Serbs now and then dig deep into who they've been working with, or we miss this opportunity and have to go after them individually, meaning they'd catch on to what's going on and we could lose men."

Fuck, but he's right. Today is the best chance we have. If we're going to limit the casualties on our side, taking the Serbs out when they least expect it is the right way to go.

I nod. "Alright," I say as I get to my feet. Today's the day to get our revenge. "Your women, are they here?" I direct my question to the Gallagher men. Romero's wife is at Dante and Makenna's home under more guards than anyone can count while she looks after my nephew.

"No," Malcolm says. "Melissa is at home with the kids, but she's on standby if we need her. Callie is in Ireland, and Raylee's in Spain. Her best friend lost her mother, so Raylee's with her."

"Good," Dante says. "It means there are less targets for them to go for. Those that are here are protected."

We will never make the same mistakes we did in the past. The women have been targeted one too many times as a result of who they're married to. This time we've got them protected, just as it should always be.

Ace walks into the office, a grin on his face. "Are we ready?"

Makenna laughs. "Bored are we, Ace?" she asks with a raised brow.

"Pyro wants to make something go boom," he chuckles.

I turn to the guy in question. The fucker has no teeth in his mouth but still manages to give everyone a fucking bright smile. Christ, where the fuck did they find this dude?

"You all know the plan," Dante says as he moves toward the door. "No one survives."

The darkness in his tone sets the mood. Everyone has been told what to do, the Fury Vipers are here to help. Their guy, Pyro, is going to rig the compound the Serbs are in to explode. Any one lucky enough to survive will be gunned down as they scramble out of the wreckage.

"ARE YOU READY FOR THIS?" Romero asks as he stands beside me.

Cold air wraps around us as we wait for the signal from Pyro. Our men, along with the Gallaghers and Vipers, are situated around the compound. We're ready to finish this shit. Once it's done, we can find out who's behind it all.

"Why wouldn't I be?" I ask with a frown.

He shakes his head, not wanting to answer, and I grit my teeth. This is the shit I've had to put up with since I got back from Denver. My family has been watching me, whispering about me.

"Spit it out, Rome," I growl. I'm far from breakable.

He heaves a heavy sigh. "The women are worried. You were shot and you've not mentioned anything about it."

I shake my head. "Don't want to talk about it," I grunt.

"That may be so, but, Ales, you and I both know more than what you're letting on happened down in Denver. Are you going to finally tell me what you've been holding back?"

I pause as I look into the darkness. Do I tell him?

"I met a woman. She's the one who helped me. She saved my life."

I feel his sharp gaze on me. "What?" he grunts. The word that got back to Dante was that one of Joe Ranieri's men helped me and brought me to a safe house where the doctor was called. I've kept the same story as I don't want anything happening to Gabriella.

"She was in the bar that night. She was on her way home. She should have fucking walked away, Rome. Instead, she stayed and dragged my unconscious ass to her car and got me the fuck out of there."

Silence spreads between us. My gaze firmly on the compound in front of me, I watch as Pyro and a guy called Shadow move silently through the night, setting the explosives.

"You and this woman—" he begins carefully. "—is it just gratitude?"

"Fuck no," I hiss. "If it were, I wouldn't be losing my fucking mind over the fact she's gone."

"What do you mean, gone?" he asks, and there's no anger or malice in his voice. He's merely curious.

"She was skittish. She didn't want this. Didn't

want anything to do with me. But fuck, Rome, I tried staying away, but I couldn't. She's not like anyone else. I promised her I'd be back, that I'd return to her in a week, and now it's been almost two months since I was back there. I had Thomas check up on her." I grit my teeth, my anger at the situation raw and explosive. I should have known she'd run. I should have prepared for that possibility.

"What happened?"

"She left," I tell him. The anger in my voice is filled with bitterness. "She packed up her shit and left."

"You have no idea where she is?"

I shake my head. "Right now, my focus is on this family. I've let you all down before. I'm not about to do the same again. So when this situation with these fucking Serbs is done, I'm making my way to Denver and finding out what the fuck happened."

"I'm coming with," he tells me, and I turn to look at him. "You're different," he says. "Since you came back, everyone was worried because you were more focused, more energized. I get it now. Your woman—that's why you changed. It happens. You find the one you want, the woman who means the fucking most, and you become more focused, so you can be with her. She saved you, Ales. That means I owe her. So I'm going to help you find her."

I heave in a deep breath, letting the air fill my lungs. For the first time since I found out Gabriella was gone, I finally feel relief. "I doubt Dante and Makenna will feel the same."

He shrugs. "They don't have to know. Not right now."

I smile. My brother is the fucking shit.

"Once these fuckers are dealt with, me, you, and Holly are taking a trip to Denver."

I chuckle. He thinks I'm stupid. Him bringing Holly will be his way of trying to get more information from me. Holly is tenacious at the best of times, but once she gets a bee in her bonnet, she won't stop until she has every scrap of information.

A low whistle goes through the air, the breeze carrying it toward us. I reach for my gun, Romero doing the same. Pyro and Shadow move through the night, into position. I hold my ground, keeping my gaze firmly on the compound exit.

Three.

I straighten my shoulders. We're almost there.

Two.

Get this done and go find Gabriella.

One.

I raise my gun, my finger hovering over the trigger.

Boom.

The ground beneath my feet shakes with the force of the explosion. The compound explodes, and shards of glass and debris skyrocket through the air as smoke and fire bellow from the building. Screams fill the silence, and I smile. There are people alive.

Good. They're about to find out what we've got planned for them.

A shadow emerges from the rubble, and I don't hesitate. My finger squeezes the trigger. My bullet sails through the air and sinks into the fucker's head. The bastard thought he tasted freedom. Unfortunately for him, it was short-lived.

I hear gun after gun sound as the rest of the family picks off the survivors.

"Ready?" Rome asks with a grin.

I nod and we step out of the shadows and move toward the compound. It's time to ensure there's no one else alive. Although, judging by how much this building is burning, I highly doubt anyone is. Pyro did his job—hence his name. The man's a fucking pyromaniac. He loves playing with fire. If there are any survivors, they'll be heavily burnt and may not even survive the night.

There's not an ounce of sorrow for any of those who lost their lives here tonight, just as they didn't have any for those innocent people they killed in our club. If you're going to come after us—do that. Don't direct your anger at innocent bystanders. It's the coward's way out.

The heat of the inferno is hot against my skin, but I grin and bear it as I move around the fallen compound, my gun trained, ready for me to fire if anyone should happen to be alive.

"I think we're good," Dante says as he steps up to Rome and me. "No one is getting out of here alive, and if they are, they won't be in much shape to fuck with us."

"Time to go home and party," Ace shouts. The rest of his brothers hoot and holler. Those guys love any excuse to throw a damn party. "If anyone is alive, there'll be only a few. They can't do anything. We'll take them out before they can even blink."

It's true. Melissa will keep tabs on the hospital reports of anyone admitted with serious burns. If it's one of these fuckers, we'll have them killed before they can speak about what happened.

Now this is over, it's time to focus on finding my woman.

"MR BIANCHI," the woman says with a smile. "We have a deal."

I nod, glaring at her outstretched hand. "Good, make sure it's taken off the market today."

She blusters at my abruptness. "Of course," she says, trying to continue acting professionally. "The owner is looking for a fast sale. With you paying cash, this shouldn't take too long."

"Good," I grunt, and I turn on my heels and move up the stairs.

Even though everything is gone, I can still smell her. Gabriella's scent lingers in the air and that fucking bitch downstairs has been flirting with me non-stop since I came to view the house. Hell, I didn't even let her get her over-rehearsed speech out. I told her I'd take it, full asking price, in cash. It was an offer no one could refuse.

I move to the bedroom, the last place I saw her. My hands ball into fists. How the fuck did this happen? How the fuck did I lose my woman?

I scrub my hands down my face. Fuck.

"Mr. Bianchi," the bitch of a realtor purrs as she comes up the stairs.

"Out," I snap as I turn and face her.

The smile falls from her face. "What?" she breathes.

"Get the fuck out. Your services are no longer needed. Now get the fuck out."

She swallows hard and scurries away from me.

I take another steadying breath. This isn't over. Gabriella can only hide for so long.

"Don't worry, Gabriella, I'll find you, and when I do, I'm making you mine."

ELEVEN
GABRIELLA

"Hey, Gabby," Raylee whispers as she crawls onto the bed beside me. Her arm curls around my side and she holds me tight. "Are you doing okay?"

"Yeah," I whisper, even though it's a bold-faced lie.

I'm numb. I still have that sense of loss, that I'm drifting away at sea. Sometimes it's as though I'm having an outer body experience and watching it happen. Everyone has been amazing and supportive, especially my dad and Raylee. They have been with me every step of the way. My dad organized the funeral the way I wanted it, but I didn't have to do anything except tell him how I wanted it. He had to return to the States today, and having him gone, hurts, but Raylee is here and she's helping me through it.

"You always were a bad liar," she says with a soft

laugh. "God, remember the last time we were like this?"

I swallow back the sob. The last time Raylee and I were lying in bed holding one another was the day of Mayer's funeral, something neither of us will ever forget. His death will always be with us.

"If he were here, he'd tell me to get up and stop crying."

Ray laughs. "He'd tell you to stop being a girl."

I smile. It was totally like May to say that. Even though we were his best friends, there were pieces of himself he never gave to us. He wanted to hide the darkness he had inside of him. Little did he know that Ray and I would have never judged him. We knew he held back but we let him do what he needed. He was protective of us both. He'd do whatever he could to ensure we were safe, and he died protecting Raylee—something she cries about even to this day. But Mayer died due to being betrayed by the one man who should have protected him.

"How are you really, Gabs?" she asks, and I turn over so I'm lying on my back. "You've lost so much weight since the last time I saw you. Are you eating?"

"I'm okay," I promise her. "I'm tired, I'm numb. It doesn't feel real. I expect to get a call from her at any moment."

Raylee's hand grips mine. "I'm so sorry, Gabby," she whispers. "So, so sorry."

I swallow past the lump in my throat. I can't speak. I don't even know what to say. It's been a week and it still feels surreal. How am I meant to go on without her?

"Malcolm and I have been speaking. We want you to move back here. We would like you to be close to us."

I rest my head against her shoulder. "I love that you both want that, but I've made a home in the States now, Ray-Ray. I finally feel as though I'm home. That doesn't mean that we won't visit each other." I slide a hand down to my stomach, where my baby is currently growing. God, everything is so different now. Never did I plan on any of this happening.

"Gab?" she questions.

"I'm pregnant," I whisper. "I never got to tell her."

She chokes on a sob. "Oh, Gabby," she cries. "Why didn't you tell me?"

I shrug. "I'm not that far along. Only seven weeks or so." I wasn't even sure if I was going to tell Raylee, but I need my girl. I need my best friend.

"Are you sure you won't move back? You'll always have a place to stay with us. You know that. Not to mention, my brothers adore you and they'll be happy to have you back."

She's right, her brothers do adore me. I consider them my own. Coming back to Spain would be the best option. I'd be surrounded by people I love and who love me. But it's not what I want. I don't feel at home here. There are too many memories. My heart and soul hurt just thinking about the past.

"My life is in America now, as much as I hate to admit it." I crack a smile. "Besides, Dad's there, and he's trying," I tell her. "He's been amazing since he found out about the baby, and then Mum."

She nods. "He really was amazing. I was in awe of how he took charge of everything."

"I wouldn't have gotten through the last week without him."

"So," she begins carefully, and I instantly know where this is going: the father of my baby. "I didn't know you were dating anyone. The last guy I knew you were with was Christian."

I sigh. My love life has always been a subject I rarely talk about. Raylee and I know what it means to be the daughters of powerful men. Thankfully, most don't know about my father, but they know about my connection to Raylee Silver, and in turn her father. It led to a lot of heartache growing up, as the majority of boys we dated were only with us in the hopes of joining the Silver gang. I learned the best thing to do was keep who I was dating, quiet. Only when I'd date them longer than a month would I tell Raylee about them. Most never even hit that mark, they'd show their true colors before that. It's been a while since I have been dating.

"Christian and I weren't dating," I remind her.

"I don't get it," she whines. "You both are

awesome, hot, and single. You're similar, and you love me."

I laugh. No matter how much Raylee pushed Christian and I together, it wasn't ever going to happen. That's not to say we didn't hookup—we did. Anytime Christian was in the States or I came back to Spain, we'd get together. He's a great lover, we're just not compatible for more than a casual fling. "Isn't Christian dating someone now?"

Her lips turn up at the corners. Raylee is extremely territorial when it comes to those she cares about. She wants the best for them, and judging by the disdain on her face, Christian's new woman isn't what she'd like for him.

"Yes," she grunts. "But both Mal and I thought you and Chris would have gotten out of the friends zone."

"You just want that because if Christian and I did get together, I'd move back here, and you'd be happy."

She throws her hands up. "Is that so wrong?"

I shake my head. "No, you want everyone you love around you, Ray, and I get that. If it were only me, I may have come back, but my baby is going to need his or her granddad."

Her eyes fill with tears. "He's really trying, isn't he?"

When I moved to America, Ray was worried Joe wouldn't change and that he'd continue to put me second best, but he's tried to mend our relationship and he's worked damn hard to keep me in his life, even if it meant going against his wife. Christina made it known she didn't want him and I to have a relationship. She'd have preferred if I wasn't anywhere near Joe, but my dad put his foot down and gave her an ultimatum. She either accepted that I was in his life, or he'd file for divorce. She chose to accept it, but it doesn't mean she likes it, and I can't blame her for it either.

"He really is. He's told me he wants to be active in the baby's life. He's talking about going straight."

She sits up and stares at me, her eyes wide and filled with disbelief. "Fuck off," she gasps.

I laugh and sit up next to her. "Right?" I ask, still unable to believe what he said.

"Wait, so is he saying this as a way to try and get you to stay in America or is he saying it because he means it?"

"He seems to be determined. I'm not getting my hopes up—I've been let down too many times by him to accept his words. We both know that actions speak louder than words."

"Our parents are trying," she whispers. "We just have to know when to walk away."

I don't say anything. Raylee's still trying to figure out what's happening with her mum. When the truth came out about her dad and how he and his organization would steal women and put them into a whorehouse, Raylee's world crumbled around her. Harry Silver was her idol, the man treated her like a princess, and she never had any idea who her father truly was.

It was then revealed that her mother went missing as a young teenager and showed up years later married to Harry Silver. Raylee's mum was one of the earliest women Harry Silver took, but when he saw her, he kept her. Now that Harry is dead, Raylee's mum is able to work through the trauma. She left mainland Spain and moved back to the island where she was born. She's surrounded by her family. Raylee's happy her mum's healing, but she's angry and upset because her mum walked away from Raylee and her brothers without a second thought. Now their relationship is strained as neither knows how to ease the pain that was caused by Harry and his selfishness.

"So, the father?" she asks. "Who is he?"

I shake my head. "He was a guy I had a couple of great nights with," I tell her. I may not tell Raylee everything, but I never lie to her. We've both had enough lies in our lives, so I try to tell her the truth without telling her every detail.

"Okay, and what does he think about the baby?"

"He doesn't know, Ray. He promised me he would be back, but it's been almost two months and I haven't seen him. We both know he's not coming back, and he only said he would so he wouldn't come across as a prick."

She crosses her arms over her chest and hmmfs.

"God, what a bastard. If I ever see him, I'll have his balls. No one treats my sister like that."

I smile at her words. God, I love her so much.

"This doesn't change anything," I say, needing to know that no matter what, she's going to stay ever present in my life.

"You know it," she replies without missing a beat. "You may not be my blood, Gabby, but you are my sister, and I love you. Nothing could ever stop that. Mal and I will be with you whenever you need us. You want me in the delivery room, I'm there. You want me to stay with you for a while after you have my beautiful godchild, I'm there."

My emotions get the best of me, and I sob, grateful that I have people in my life who love me and want the best for me. Raylee curls her arms around me and holds me tightly.

"You're not alone, Gabs. You're never alone."

TWELVE
ALESSIO

Four years later

"Ales," Makenna sighs. "Why do you look as though you're about to kill someone?"

I grit my teeth. I'm not in the mood for jokes and shit right now. Once again, Thomas' trail has run cold. Four years we've been searching for Gabriella, and every time we think we're close to her, it turns out to be a dead end. The last sighting we had of her was in Spain nearly two months after the last time I saw her.

Thomas has dug deep into Gabriella's life, and we've since discovered she's Raylee's best friend. The woman that's married to Makenna's nephew, Malcolm. I'd love nothing more than to contact Raylee and find out where her best friend is, but the moment I do that, Makenna and Malcolm are going to be on my ass, demanding to know my business and no doubt want to protect Gabriella from me.

Thing is, she's mine. I knew it from the moment I woke up in that bed, patched up, and alive. I saw her sitting beside me, worrying her lip between her teeth, trying to decide if she should answer my cell or not. I won't listen to anyone who tries to tell me otherwise. She ran away. I fucking knew she would, I could see it in her eyes when I told her I'd be back. But fuck. How has one girl managed to keep hidden for four fucking years?

"Ales?" Makenna says, a brow raised as she looks at me, waiting for an explanation.

"Kenna," Dante says with humor. "That's a permanent look these days."

My sister-in-law sighs. "Please tell me you're still not chasing after Yelena?"

I ignore her. I've let my family think she's the woman I want. It's better this way. They're nosey as fuck and always up in each other's business. I'd rather them stay as far away from mine as possible.

"Leave him be," Holly says softly. My sister-in-law always tries to make peace with everyone. She never wants to have arguments or conflict within the family. She's sweet and kind. The woman never gets on the wrong side of anyone, but if you piss her off, you'll know about it. I'm still getting calls from that BDSM sex group. Holly always gets payback, no matter what you do.

Makenna glares at me, so I smirk at her, knowing damn well it's only going to annoy the ever-loving fuck out of her. She hates not being in the know, and she despises being ignored. She should know by now that I don't have to tell her anything. Unlike my brother's, I'm not under her thumb. Hell, Dante doesn't even ask me what's pissed me off. He knows that if I need to talk to him, I will.

"Has Declan worked out who's working with the Serbians?" Mac asks. Over the past four years, the man has become vital to the Clann, surpassing Romero as Makenna's right-hand man. No one would ever take Finn's place, but if anyone could, it would be Mac.

Makenna shakes her head. "No. Whoever the fuck it is, they're good at hiding their tracks."

"I'm telling you," Stefan says as he crosses his arms over his chest. "It's the damn Russians."

This argument has been ongoing for four years. We took out every Serbian player that was in New York. The stupid fuckers had a meet with every one of their men. It's ridiculous to do that so soon after hitting our club. But nevertheless, we took them all out, avenging everyone who lost their lives that night —including our bounces, who had their throats slit and whose bodies were left in the back alleyway beside the trash. We made our statement, and we did it loud and clear. Anyone who takes aim at the famiglia will do so by paying with their lives.

"If it's the Russians, do you honestly believe

Maksim would be working with us to figure out who?"

I chuckle. "Maksim may be helping us, but the man lost a fuck of a lot of men. That's a blow to the ego no one can recover from. What better way to get back at us than coming after us?"

Stefan nods in agreement. "Exactly. By helping us out, he also gets to know just what we've found out. He could be waiting until we get close to finding out who, and then attack. We'd never see it coming, as he's played the part of being an ally so cleverly."

Dante's eyes darken. "I'm far from stupid. You keep your friends close and enemies closer, Stefan. Maksim isn't going to know anything we find out. I haven't been giving him details on anything we've uncovered."

Makenna nods. "You should know by now, Stefan, that we're distrusting people at the best of times. Just because we handed Maksim a million-dollar business, doesn't mean we're fools. The stables of women aren't something we're interested in. Yes, both Finn and Malcolm think it could be a lucrative business, but it's not what I want. We do not need them."

While I agree with Finn and Malcolm, having a stable of women would mean more ears to the ground. When men get horny and drunk, they spill secrets. It's true. Having a whore house would attract influential clients such as politicians and higher ups in the police department. Whorehouses owned by criminals such as us would give these ass's anonymity, and in doing so, would have them and their asshole friends frequenting the places. Those men get real talkative when they're fucking around on their wives and partners. Pillow talk is never attractive.

"I'll have Declan do a deep dive on every member of the Bratva," Makenna sighs. "It'll take him a while, but he'll get it done."

Declan joined us almost six months ago. The man has been a fucking Godsend. He's a hacker. He's barely an adult, the youngest member of the Clann. Since he joined Makenna's ranks, he's hacked almost every database we're on. Declan's managed to hack the FBI and DEA. Thankfully, they're not any closer to figuring out what we're doing. However, they had a search warrant for the Fury Vipers compound two months ago that Declan managed to uncover, giving Makenna enough time to warn Ace, so when the feds came calling, there was nothing for them to find.

"We're traveling to Indianapolis next week," Makenna announces once the talk of who the hell is after us has died down. At the moment, they're probably trying to rebuild and find another way to come after us. Hopefully, we'll uncover who it is before that. "Every family member is to be in attendance."

I grin, loving that I don't have to go. There are too many Gallaghers, and they're popping kids out like it's a fucking race. I'm not sure how many kids have been born since they all got married off, but Makenna's brother Denis takes the cake. The man has eight kids. That's a small army in itself.

"Ales," Dante chuckles. "You're coming too."

I grit my teeth. "Why?" I don't go to these events. As much as I love my sisters-in-law, I do not need to be around their crazy family.

"Because it's been almost five years, you're family, and that means you're coming," Makenna tells me as she raises her brow, daring me to argue with her. "Adelina has been through hell, Ales, and she's finally celebrating something, so your ass will be on a plane with the rest of us and we'll be going to Hayden and Ade's baby shower."

I grind my jaw. This is bullshit. The fucking last thing I want to do is go to some baby shower. "Isn't that shit for women anyway?" I ask.

Dante and Rome chuckle, but I can see in both of their faces that they'd rather be anywhere than at the celebration. Talk of births, babies, and God knows what, is something I want no participation in.

"You'll enjoy it," Holly assures me. "It'll be fun."

"Doll face," Rome says with a smirk. "Nothing about it will be fun."

I sigh, knowing there's no way in hell I'll be able to get out of this. "Fine, but there had better be alcohol."

Makenna beams at me. She's all about her family and ensuring they're all happy. I still don't understand why the fuck I have to be there. But whatever it takes to keep the boss happy.

"So, what's happened?" Rome asks once we leave the Gallagher mansion. "I can tell by your face that it's something to do with Gabriella, so what is it?"

Ever since I told him about what went down, Romero has done everything in his power to help me find her. Not only do I have an investigator looking for her, but he does also.

"Thomas said he picked up her trail in Louisville, Kentucky, but when he got there, she was gone."

He shakes his head. "How the fuck can one woman disappear? She's evaded both men over the past four years. What the fuck did you do to her?"

I roll my eyes at the fucker. "Nothing," I say, knowing I did a fuck of a lot more than that. I promised her I'd be back, and she thought I was full of shit. Turns out, I was. The Famiglia comes first. The shit we had going on needed my full attention, although, that was something I could never do. The moment I saw Gabriella, I wanted her, but when she saved me, put her neck on the line for me, I knew I'd have her. But the more I fucked her, the more I knew it was more than just lust and want. I became obsessed, and nothing has diminished that obsession over the four years. It's been simmering on the surface as we've tried to find her.

"We're heading to Indianapolis, Ales. That's what... a two-hour drive from Indianapolis to Kentucky? Use the time we're there to find her.

You'll be able to do some digging and see where she was, and maybe, you'll be able to find out where she headed."

A slow smile forms on my lips. Fuck. He's right. Maybe going to this baby shower won't be so bad after all.

THIRTEEN
GABRIELLA

"Sweetheart, are you okay?" my dad asks as I sink down on the sofa. I'm beyond tired. I just want to crawl into bed and sleep. "You've been working nonstop; you need a little break."

I laugh. "Break? What's that?" I have a three-year-old boy who has more energy than should be allowed. He's energetic, funny, and is the double of his father. Every time I look into Anthony's face, I see Alessio.

"Funny," Dad grins. "But you've worked your ass off these past four years and you're an amazing mom. While you're here, take a load off and let me spoil you and the boy."

I smile at him. He's really trying. As much as he was a shitty dad to me while I was growing up, he's been an amazing grandfather to Anthony. The two of them get along like a house on fire. I'm so glad my baby has that relationship.

"That would be nice, but I can't expect you to do that," I say through a yawn. "You're busy too."

My dad has tried his hardest to get away from the business, but it's a lot harder than said. He's bought some legitimate businesses and has moved his base to Kentucky. He lives less than a two-hour drive away from me. Something I'm ever so grateful for. Both Anthony and I can visit him anytime we like without having to plan a vacation.

"Never," he says vehemently. "Never too busy for you or Anthony."

That's another thing that has changed. He's right, no matter when I call, he's never too busy to take it. Whenever we drop by, he'll stop what he's doing to spend time with us. He's been my biggest supporter over the past four years. He's been with me every step of the way.

When I was giving birth to Anthony, I wanted Raylee to be my birthing partner. She was more than happy to be there with me. But so was my dad. He held my hand throughout the entire process, never once letting go.

I think in that moment, I let go of all the anger and resentment I felt over the years and was just so happy to have him with me. Since then, our relationship has become more. He's my father, and I'm proud to call him that, just as I'm proud to call him Anthony's grandfather.

"Dad, we're only here for a few nights," I tell him. It's his birthday tomorrow and I'm taking him out for dinner. "I have to be back in Indianapolis for Adelina's baby shower."

Ade has become one of my best friends. She's sweet, caring, and amazing. Her husband, Hayden Gallagher—who happens to be related to Raylee's husband, Malcolm—owns the club next to my art gallery. Ade took over running it, and the moment we met, we hit it off. It was so nice to have a woman around my age that I could talk to.

That was almost a year ago. Since then, Ade has been through Hell and back. Her husband's enemies planted a bomb in her house, which left Ade with a scar on her cheek and led to the death of her thirteen-year-old sister, Vivianna. It took a while before Ade was able to come to terms with the scar on her face. Her entire life, she was made to believe that she was only wanted for her looks, so having a scar that's so prominent brought about a lot of insecurities. Thankfully, her husband is amazing and has showed his wife that she's more than her looks. But even with the scar, Ade is one of the most beautiful women I have ever come across.

"Ah, how is the lovely Adelina?" my father asks.

I roll my eyes. "Hayden would kill you for calling her lovely," I tell him with a smile. As amazing as her husband is, he's also very protective and possessive.

He smirks. "I know." Silence descends on us, and I wait, knowing by the hesitant look on my father's face that he has something to ask or say. "Dinner tomorrow, would you be okay with Hazel coming?"

I inwardly smile. I knew it. I knew she was the woman he was dating.

"Dad..." I begin. "Is she your woman now?"

Four months ago, my father told me he was getting a divorce from Christina, something she wasn't too happy about. I knew he must have found a woman. It coincided with my father finding an assistant. A young, sexy, funny assistant who treated both Anthony and I like we were family. The second I met Hazel, I liked her. However, she's my age, and the fact that my dad is dating her is a little weird, but I'm not going to make a big deal about it as he seems happy. Probably the happiest I have ever seen.

He sighs as he glares at me. "Yes."

I press my lips together so as not to smile at him. "So does that make her my new mommy?"

"Gabriella," he says sternly.

"You're too easy to wind up, Dad."

He pinches the bridge of his nose. "Look, Gab, I've made mistakes, some I wish I could go back and change and others that are mistakes but also the proudest moments of my life. Like meeting your mom and having you. That wasn't meant to happen, but I wouldn't change it for the world."

I let his words sink in. "Dad, is Hazel pregnant?"

"You always were the smart one," he grumbles. "Yes, and if Christina finds out, she'll hit the roof."

That's something that is going to happen anyway. Christina is a bitch. I understand her husband cheated on her multiple times and his mistress gave birth to his child, but the way she treats Anthony is something I'll never forgive. She screams and shouts at him whenever he's near her. She even pushed him away from her when he was learning to walk. Thankfully, my dad took her out of the room because I was about to rip the hair out of her head.

"Of course she's coming. She's family now."

It's that simple to me. Hazel makes my dad happy and that's all that I want.

He gives me a bright smile, and I know I've made the right choice.

"Have you heard from Anthony's father?" he asks me a little while later.

This is a conversation we have every six weeks. I think it's my father's not so subtle way of telling me I should tell Alessio that he has a son. Even though Anthony looks like his father, my dad hasn't made a comment about it. He either doesn't see the resemblance or he's just not letting on that he knows. Either way, I'm grateful.

"Dad," I say with a deep sigh. I'm sick of having this conversation. "While I appreciate that you're looking out for me, you have to realize that I'm doing what I think is best for my son. I don't want Anthony to go through what I did, always being second best." It's taken over twenty years for me to be at peace with the way I used to feel and to forgive my father for how he treated me. It's not something I would wish on anyone, let alone my son. So I'm doing what I believe is the best thing for him.

"How do you know he'll do what I did?" That's another thing I respect my father for; he's admitted his faults, he's understood how it made me feel, and he takes responsibility for that. He allowed not only his work, but his wife to stand in the way of our relationship, and to me, that was unacceptable.

"Because he told me he'd be back in a week and he never returned." That hurt a hell of a lot more than I'd ever admit to anyone. Alessio Bianchi managed to get inside my walls and make me feel something I never thought possible. Yet even now, when I think of him, my heart melts and all those feelings start to surface.

I don't hate Alessio. I never could. But I don't trust him, and that's something I don't think will ever change.

His eyes soften as he looks at me. "Okay," he says, and I pray that this'll be the end of it.

"Next month, we're doing a local talent exhibition in the gallery," I say proudly. It's something I wanted to do, spread out and open the gallery for local artists to showcase their talent. "I had over three hundred entries. I hate that I could only pick seventy." It's always heartbreaking to send an email telling someone they won't be featured.

"If this is a success, then hold another one and invite those who weren't able to be featured," he tells me, listening with rapt attention.

He's so supportive of my work and what I do. He'll listen to me for hours talking about what I want to do to bring more people to the gallery. Thankfully, I've been lucky and have a steady flow of clients looking to buy pieces. And I have been able to expand my gallery by buying out the store next door. My dad gave me the money to buy my first store, and I paid back the loan, even though he didn't want me to.

"If you're around, I'd love for you to come."

"I'll be there," he promises me.

"Great, and that invitation extends to Hazel, Dad. If you two are together, that means she's family. So next family dinner, she had better be there."

His chuckle is deep and throaty. "I'm proud of you, Gab. The woman you have become is amazing. You're smart, kind, caring, and loving. You could have walked away from me when you moved to Indianapolis, told me you were done. I wouldn't have blamed you. Instead, you gave me the opportunity to repair the damage I caused to our relationship, and you gave me the chance to be a better man. I love you."

Tears fill my eyes as I stare at him. "You're my dad," I tell him simply as I get to my feet and walk into his open arms. "I love you too."

I couldn't be where I am today without him. Losing Mum hurt me so much. It was hard leaving Spain, but I knew I had to. Dad flew back and helped me get home. He was a shoulder to cry on and someone I could talk to. Him and Raylee helped me through my darkest hours. Without them, I would be in a deep state of depression.

Dad's cell rings and I pull away, letting him get it. As much as he's trying to put distance between family and work, work still needs him. His eyes brighten a touch when he sees the screen, and I know it's Hazel calling him. He always gets that spark whenever he speaks to her.

I walk toward the bedrooms and stop at Anthony's. It's hard to believe my little boy is three. He's amazing, and I'm so in love with him. I never knew what people meant when they talked about the love you have for a child is different than that to anyone else until I held Anthony in my arms for the first time. My heart filled with so much emotion, it took everything in me not to cry. I held my boy for hours, just staring at him, visualizing everything about him. I find myself doing it still to this day. I always check on him while he's sleeping. I stare at his peaceful face, making sure I take in every single detail.

Pushing open his bedroom door, my heart warms as I see him fast asleep, his stuffed animal tightly held in his arms. It was a gift from Raylee when he was a baby, and he's never without it. Thankfully, Ray had the foresight to ensure we had a spare, in case anything happened to it. I press a kiss against his head, thankful to have him in my life.

Giving birth to him was hard. It was chaotic, and it was painful. What was meant to be a natural birth went AWOL. I wasn't dilated enough, and Anthony was in distress—as was I. I ended up needing an emergency c-section and lost too much blood. I hemorrhaged. It was touch and go whether or not they'd have to do the drastic measure of taking my womb. But we're both here, we're both happy and healthy, and I couldn't ask for more.

When I was released from hospital and returned home, I was shocked to find Christina waiting at my house, a sweet but fake smile on her face. She congratulated me on the birth of my son and then proceeded to tell me I took the lazy way out by having a cesarean section. I was three days post op, I was tired, sore, and my patience was gone. I informed the stupid cow that as long as my baby was okay, that's all that mattered. Giving birth—no matter how you do it—is an amazing experience, and no one should be shamed for it.

Thankfully, she backed off when my dad walked in with mine and Anthony's bags. He glanced between us, and obviously noticing the tension, told Christina to back off. Which she did for all but a minute. She then had something to say about me not breastfeeding Anthony. Something I tried to do, but ultimately failed. She made me feel like a bad mother, that giving Anthony formula was the worst thing in the world. But Raylee went off on her and made sure I knew that I was doing everything right for me and my baby. It was a stressful week, and I was so glad when Christina returned to Denver and left me the hell alone. There was only so much criticism that I could take, and I was close to losing my mind with her.

"Sweetheart," Dad whispers as he walks into Anthony's room behind me. "Are you okay?"

I turn and look at him. "I'm good, just reminiscing," I say with a smile.

His eyes darken slightly. "Almost lost you that day."

"Hardly," I whisper as we leave Anthony's room. "We're here, Dad, and that's all that matters.'

He nods. "That is true. Hazel's delighted to be coming to dinner. She was a little nervous that you wouldn't accept her."

I raise a brow. "Oh, and why is that?"

He glares at me, his lips twitching. He knows I'm only joking. "Because of her age."

I lift my hands in the air once we're in the kitchen. "I'm not your mother, neither am I hers. What two consenting adults do is none of my business. The only thing I care about, Dad, is that you're happy. I can see that you are with her."

"She's a nice woman. She's family oriented, and she's kind and caring."

"That's all I could want for you. I have no idea what you saw in Christina. She's everything you despise."

He nods. "Sometimes, sweetheart, we have to make a deal with the Devil himself to get what we want, and that's exactly what I did when I married her."

I shiver at the thought. God, I don't think there's anything worse than marrying someone you hate. I guess my dad wanted to be the boss of Denver, and to do so, he had to marry someone in power, which is where Christina came along. The two of them were miserable, and in the end, they ruined countless lives with their affairs.

"I'm going out. I'm not sure if I'll be home tonight," he tells me.

"Dad, you're old enough to do whatever you want. You don't have to tell me. Just make sure you're back here by eleven tomorrow morning. You promised Anthony you'd take him to the soft play."

He smiles as he reaches for his jacket. "I'm looking forward to it. I won't be late. Have a good night, Gabs. I'll see you in the morning." He presses a kiss against my cheek, and I watch him leave. He's got an extra pep in his step. I love that he's so happy, and I really hope Christina doesn't find out about Hazel. I can only imagine what will happen if she does.

Christina is losing everything. Her status as dad's wife, the money, the house, and everything else that goes along with being married to the boss. She's going to be angry, and anger can cause people to do stupid shit. I just pray that when she finds out, she doesn't do anything rash.

FOURTEEN
ALESSIO

"Remind me again," I growl as I climb into the car. "Why am I having to go to this chick party?"

"You're an ass, Ales," Makenna snaps. "You're going because I said."

I glance at Dante and see that he's chuckling to himself. "Babe, ignore him. He doesn't do well with family."

He's right, I don't. The only family I want is those that I trust. Dante, Romero, Makenna, and Holly. Everyone else can fuck off for all I care. I've lived the life of being beaten and tormented by those who are supposedly family. I wouldn't wish it on my worst enemy.

"Well, this is my family and, in turn, yours. You've been with us for so long now, Ales. You should really know better."

I sit back against the seat as Makenna drives us

toward her cousin's house. No matter what I say, they are not going to listen to me. They want what's best for their family. I get it. I just wish it didn't include me.

We arrived in Indianapolis last night. Makenna has managed to find a couple of houses to lease, so we're all under one roof with Romero and Holly, Finn, and Destiny. Then Holly's brothers are staying with their dad in another, along with their wives. Denis' wife Callie is friends with Hayden's wife. The two of them spend a lot of time on the phone talking about business, as Adelina runs Hayden's bar.

"Remember, Ales," Dante says. "This is a family gathering. No need for the snarl."

I roll my eyes. He thinks he's fucking hilarious, whereas he's not. "I know, which is why I left my gun at home."

Makenna laughs. "You may have left one of them there, but you're not unarmed."

Hell fucking no. Of course I'm not. I'm not stupid. I know better than to leave the house without a weapon on me.

"No one is going to be shooting," she says, and I'm sure I hear a little disappointment in her voice. The woman loves violence. I'm sure she suffers from bloodlust, just as my brothers and I do. It's one of the very many reasons that my brother, Dante, is completely besotted with her.

As much shit as they both give me and I give

them, they're family, and I respect and cherish them. Just as I would with Romero and Holly. Sometimes I see the way my brothers are with their wives and want the same thing. Other times, I'm grateful that I don't. If I were to have what they have, I know that the only woman I'd want it with is Gabriella. The woman is someone I want, someone I crave. I've been obsessed with her since I woke up in her bed.

"Who else is going to be here?" I ask, hoping like fuck Hayden's grandmother will be. That woman is a riot and gives her daughter-in-law, Edwina, shit on a daily basis, while her son sits back and tries not to laugh.

"All the family and a friend of Ade's. I'm not sure who, but someone who owns an art gallery next to the bar," Makenna says. "She's helped Ade a lot since Vivianna died, and I know the girl means a lot to Ade, just as Annamarie does."

I press my lips together so as not to laugh at the distaste in Makenna's voice as she mentions her cousin's wife. I'm not really sure what actually went down between the women in the Gallagher family and Hayes' wife, Anna-Marie, but I do know there was a fuck of a lot not told to them and the woman suffered multiple miscarriages that had the Gallagher family constantly asking her when she and Hayes would have another child. The woman apparently snapped and became bitchy—not that anyone could blame her—and that began the dislike.

"You can't kill a pregnant woman," Dante tells his wife.

Makenna sighs. "That's not what I want to do at all."

My brother chuckles. "You're pissed because you have to be nice to her."

Silence descends between them, and I chuckle. My sister-in-law despises being wrong and she hates making nice with people. She either likes you or hates you, there's no in between with her, and the fact that she's hated her cousin's wife for so long and now has to be nice, pisses her the fuck off.

Makenna and Dante start talking about work and what their plans are as they continue to make waves throughout the US. They want to break into the south of the country, along with moving further west. But instead of just having the Gallagher's break into those states and take over, they're talking about having the Bianchi's do the same. Something my brother is on board with. Having our alliance so tightly with the Gallagher's has meant we've had a lot more Italian men sign up to be our soldiers. Since my brothers married into the Gallagher family, our men have tripled in size—something that could also be attributed to Dante taking the helm. We've slowly but surely taken over other states in the west, joining the ever-growing Gallagher family.

Dante has moved into Pennsylvania, New Hampshire, Maine, Ohio, and West Virginia. Making some of his more trusted men, Underbosses, and having even more soldiers in our ranks. We've grown, our Famiglia has expanded, and the men are happy. There's no longer unrest at having Dante marry the Irish woman. Those who were against it are dead and we will continue to eradicate anyone who dislikes what we now stand for. Dante isn't our father; he's the furthest thing from it. He's worked his fucking ass off without harming innocents to grow the Famiglia into something my father could only ever dream of. Dante is a better boss than my father ever was, and now everyone knows it.

We pull up to the house and I see we're one of the last people to arrive. Good, last in, first out. It's the best way to be. Also, with me arriving with Makenna and Dante, I can grab a beer and not have to be welcomed by the fucking entire Clann.

"You're here," I hear cried, and turn to see Edwina Gallagher walk out of the house with a smile on her face.

Standing at the door is Edwina's son Hayden and his wife, Adelina. There's no denying the woman is absolutely gorgeous. She's beautiful. Hayden lucked out by being arranged to marry the Italian beauty, but he also showed everyone that he'd die for her. The man loves his wife, and he's proved it time and time again. The moment Hayden found out his wife was pregnant, he went to kill her father—a man who had beaten her frequently. He also took out the entire family that had his sister sent to prison, who killed his uncle and sister-in-law, and who gave his wife the gnarly scar on her cheek. Hayden will kill anyone who harms her.

"I am," Makenna replies uneasily.

Even with her aunt, Makenna is prickly to say the least. Over the past five years, the Gallagher family have lost a lot of family members. Seamus died first. The man was killed trying to protect his granddaughter—my sister-in-law—Holly. After Seamus came the death of his two youngest sons, Patrick and Cian. Those fuckers deserved a slow and painful death. They betrayed their sister and wanted to take over her job as boss of the Clann. Something that was never going to happen. In their stupidity, Patrick kidnapped Finn's woman, Destiny. Their deaths spread like wildfire around not only the Clann but also the Famiglia—letting them know what'll happen if you go against the family. Then, only months ago, they lost Killian, a man who was an integral part of the family.

Edwina lost both of her brothers. But the woman is standing tall and celebrating the life that's about to happen with her son and daughter-in-law.

Edwina rushes toward Makenna and pulls her into her arms. I glance at my brother and watch as he fights his smile. Damn, Makenna hates being touched, something her aunt knows all too well. "Thank you," she says softly. "For coming."

This will be the first celebration since Killian and Ade's sister, Vivanna, died.

She releases Makenna and then swiftly hugs Dante, before she turns her eyes on me. My smirk falls from my face as she wraps her small arms around me. I freeze as I look down at the small woman and wonder why she's touching me.

"It's been a while, Alessio," she tells me as she beams at me. "I'm so thankful you're here. Come on in, everyone else is already here."

"Hay," Makenna hisses. "Why is your mother being so..." she pauses as though to find the right word. "Nice."

Hayden laughs as Adelina fights her smile. "Not everyone is a bitch, Kenna." Thankfully, his wife stays at his side and hasn't taken after her mother-in-law.

Makenna's lips twitch. "True, but we also don't have to be touchy feely."

"She's your auntie, Kenna. She loves you," Denis chuckles as we enter the house. "Sometimes, people like to show their love by being affectionate."

She flips him off. "That's my affection," she huffs, and I shake my head as everyone around us laughs. This is Makenna. She takes no shit from anyone, but she loves fiercely. Everyone under this roof is family to her, even Anna-Marie. She'll do whatever the hell she can to protect them, and they would do the same for her.

A little while later, I hear arguing and follow the

sound to the backyard, where Jade's arguing with her grandmother. The two of them clash a lot, but their arguments are hilarious.

"Now that we've got the pleasantries out of the way, can my wife and I finally find out what the gender of our baby is?" Hayden says.

Laughter fills the air, and not for the first time since Dante married Makenna, I wonder what the hell our lives would have been like had our mother been alive, but just as quickly as those thoughts come, they vanish. My mother was weak. She let our father get away with whatever the fuck he wanted and let it happen. She knew what he was doing to me when I was a boy, how he'd beat and starve me, but she stood by and let it happen. Once she told me that if only I listened more, it wouldn't happen.

A kid calls out while Adelina and Hayden cut through the cake, and my brows knit together. There are more kids? Cheers and cries fill the air as they pull the slice out and we see the pink frosting. They're having a girl.

"Gabby?" Raylee screeches, and my gut clenches at her words. "Oh, Gabby," she cries.

I turn and see the woman I have been searching for the past four years for. She's even more beautiful than I remember. Her brown hair is shorter than I remember. She's got a bright smile on her face, and my cock begins to tighten, but then she glances around the backyard, her eyes widening and her face paling when she sees me. "Alessio?"

Movement at her feet has me coming to a halt. It's as though a bucket of ice-cold water has been thrown on me.

"You have a son?" I snarl at her. What the fuck? I can't believe this shit.

Staring at the little boy, it's like looking in the mirror. He's my double.

"*My* son?" I hiss.

Fuck. Why the hell did she keep him from me?

There's no excusing what she's done. Fuck. I could strangle her right now.

"I'm sorry," she whispers, reaching for the boy and pulling him into her arms before she rushes back into the house.

I don't hesitate, I follow after her. There's no way in hell I'll let her leave with my son again.

I reach her just as she's putting our son into her vehicle. My hand wraps around her wrist and I pull her to a stop. "You're not fucking leaving," I snap at her.

"Please, Alessio," she breathes, her eyes filled with tears and fear. "Please, not here. Ade doesn't deserve to have her baby shower ruined."

I nod as I release her hand, and she deflates.

"Thank you," she whispers. "Maybe we can catch up later. I know you'll have a lot of questions, and I understand that you're angry. You have every right to be, but you have to understand that Anthony doesn't know who you are."

Wrong fucking thing to say. "And who's fault is that?"

She flinches at the anger in my voice.

"Give me your address," I demand. "I'll swing by in an hour. You're not there, Gabriella, and we're going to have bigger problems than we already do."

She trembles but nods. She rattles off her address, and I grit my teeth.

"We'll be there," she promises me. But her promises mean nothing to me right now. She's kept my child from me for the past four years. That's something I'll never forget.

I watch as she climbs into her vehicle and drives out of the driveaway. I make a mental note of her license plate, something I'll send to Thomas. I'll have him do a deep dive. We have her address, and we have her tags. That should be more than enough for him to dig deep into her life.

A hand clamps down on my shoulder.

"Talk to me, Ales," Rome says. There's a tightness in his voice. He's just as pissed as I am.

"She's got my son, Rome. She disappeared, and she never said a fucking word."

His fingers tighten. "What are you going to do?"

"I'm going to get my family," I tell him. Even after this shit, I still want her. I need to find out why she thought keeping him from me was a good idea. Something she should have never done. But from what I know of Gabriella, she's sweet, caring, and loving. Why the fuck would she do this?

"Yeah?" he asks in disbelief. "The woman kept your kid from you."

I pin my brother with a glare. "I know," I hiss. "I fucking know what she's done, Rome, but we've not spoken properly, and when we do, I'll make a judgement then."

"Alessio?" The gentle voice pulls my attention from my brother. I turn and see Raylee standing with Malcolm at her side. She's wringing her hands together.

"I know what she's done isn't right. Hell, she knows that too. But Gabby's had a pretty hard couple of years. She's not always had the best relationship with her father. She wanted better for her child. She wanted to give Anthony the best life she could, and she made a choice, one that I'm sure she debated a lot over making. But ultimately, she made a choice to protect her son. Something no one can fault her for."

"She kept my son from me, Raylee. There's no justifying that."

She nods, but her lips purse. "She waited for you," she tells me, and I bite back the flinch. "Six weeks, she waited for you. The day she found out she was pregnant, she was done waiting. So how about you take a moment to think about how you two began and what you promised her before you judge?" she snaps, and glares at me. "Do not hurt my best friend again, Alessio."

I smirk. "Is that a threat?"

She shakes her head. "It's a goddamn promise." She turns on her heel and storms back into the house.

Her husband, on the other hand, stays back. "I've known Gabriella for a while now. She's a great ma to your boy, Alessio. What she's done..." he pauses. "It's done. There's nothing that can change it. Just as there's no way to change the way you disappeared and never returned," he says pointedly, and I'm pretty sure he's acting like a big brother right now. "But you have a son. A little boy who'll be fucking delighted he's got his dad."

He's right. Anthony is the most important thing right now.

"If you think you can walk into Gabby's home and dictate what's going to happen, you've got another thing happening. Gabby can and will disappear again, especially if she thinks you're going to take her son away from her."

"Why are you telling him this?" Rome asks, and I'm fucking glad one of us is able to speak right now.

"Because Alessio needs to realize that she owes you nothing. To her, you were a guy she fucked a couple of times, and you left without a trace. No number, nothing. But you've also got to contend with Gabby's father. That man isn't going to take too kindly to you knocking up his daughter."

"Her father?" I echo, wondering what the hell Thomas has missed. The man never uncovered her father's identity. He's a fucking ghost.

"Yes, her father. Just prepare yourself, Alessio.

She's not going to be welcoming to you." He grins at me. "Good luck though. You're going to need it."

"I'll call you once I've spoken to her," I tell Rome, needing to get my shit together and go see her.

He hands me the key to his rental. "I can't wait to meet my nephew," he tells me and slaps me on the back.

I take a deep breath and climb into the car. Fuck, I'm going to see my son.

FIFTEEN
GABRIELLA

My hands tremble as I drive away from Adelina's house. God, I have to call her and apologize. I never meant to cause a scene at her party. That was the last thing I wanted. Hell, I never expected to walk into that backyard and see Alessio standing there, looking sexier than ever.

I quickly call my father, needing someone to talk to.

"Hey, sweetheart. Aren't you going to Adelina's baby shower?"

I pull in a shaky breath. "Anthony's father was there," I say, glancing through the rearview mirror and checking on my son, who's smiling happily with his toy in his hand. He's not paying attention to what I'm saying.

God, this is going to be so bad. Alessio's so angry, not that I can blame him. But shit. I fucked up.

"What?" my dad hisses. "Gabby, tell me you're fucking joking?"

"I wish I were. It's like something out of my worst nightmare, Dad. What am I going to do?" All I want to do is break down and cry. Everything that I have built could be destroyed. Alessio has every right to be angry and upset. He has an amazing son he knew nothing about.

"Start talking," he demands.

So I do. I tell him everything that went down between Alessio and I, leaving out the sex parts. My father does not need to hear about those.

"You and Alessio Bianchi?" he asks. His voice is deceptively calm. "Why did you never tell me?"

"That I slept with a man? I don't need to tell you about my love life, Dad. That's never going to happen. As far as I was concerned, Alessio walked away. He could have called, but he didn't."

"You changed your cell number, Gabs. You didn't give the man a chance, did you?"

The tears slowly begin their descent, and I leave them be as I focus on the road ahead of me.

"I did what I thought was right. Growing up second best hurt, Dad. It fucking shaped me into a mistrusting bitch, okay?" I snap. "So forgive me for thinking that a man who couldn't keep his word, would do the same thing you did." I sigh. "I've got to go. Alessio said he'll be here in an hour."

I end the call, not wanting to hear anything else. I know I fucked up. God, I've made some bad decisions in my life. Most I don't regret, but today, seeing the hurt and anger in Alessio's eyes has made me regret keeping Anthony from him.

Forty minutes later and I've got Anthony settled and playing in the living room while I pace the kitchen floor. My heart beats a mile a minute, and nothing I do is calming it down. I'm getting worked up, dreading what could happen. My mind is running wild. Ultimately, my worst nightmare could happen. Alessio could take Anthony from me. Once again, the tears fall freely as I grip a hold of the countertop.

Would he take my baby from me?

He'd have every right to. It's what I did to him.

I begin to hyperventilate. The thought of being without my baby is almost too much to bear. I was wrong to keep my pregnancy from him, but I honestly believed it was the best thing for us all. My vision is blurry as I struggle to breathe, and tears continue to fall from my eyes. It's like a damn waterfall right now, and there's no off switch.

"Gabriella," I hear a deep voice say. It sounds as though it's in the distance. "Baby, I need you to breathe for me."

Hands touch my face, and I listen to the voice speak. Something about the voice is calming and familiar. Once I'm able to try and regulate my breathing, I blink through the tears and see Alessio staring at me, worry etched in those deep amber eyes of his.

"That's it, Mama, breathe for me."

I sink into him and burst into tears once again. "I'm so sorry," I whimper. "So damn sorry."

His arms tighten around me, and he holds me as I sob against him. "You've got to calm down, Gabriella," he says, and I'm surprised there's no anger in his voice. "Look at me."

I raise my head and look through my teary eyes and see the man who stole a piece of my heart four years ago. The air crackles around us, his eyes darken, and his cock thickens against my stomach.

"Alessio," I whisper, unsure what the hell is going on.

"Gabriella, why did you leave?" he questions, not once letting go of me.

I lick my lips and prepare to bear my soul.

"I was a mistake. My dad had an affair. He slept with my mum, and I was the result of that. He was an American and my mum was British. My dad was absent most of the time. He'd promise that he'd come to see me, and he'd lie. It would be weeks, maybe even months, before he'd be back. I grew up hating him. It hurt being second best to his job, Alessio."

I press my hands against his rock-hard chest, needing to put some space between us. He's too close. Now that I'm able to think and breathe clearer, he's too close, especially when I'm at my most vulnerable.

He doesn't let me go. Instead, he tightens his arms around me even more. "I fucked up by being gone," he says.

I nod. "I waited. I didn't want to. I had my doubts from the very beginning."

"I knew that," he muses. "I knew you doubted me, but Mama..." God, I fucking love that he calls me that. Shivers work their way along my spine as heat pools between my thighs. "I thought you'd realize that what we had was real."

I lift my shoulders in a careless shrug. "I've never had real," I tell him honestly. "I don't let people in."

He reaches for my chin and tilts my head. "Because you don't give them the chance to hurt you."

I swallow hard and nod. "But you got through," I whisper. I hate talking about this. He hurt me without even knowing he did so.

"And I fucked up by not coming to you when I said I would," he surmises. "You kept my son from me, Gabriella. Why?"

"You're in the Mafia, Alessio. Your world is dangerous. Look at how we met? You disappeared after you promised you'd be back. I couldn't—wouldn't—let my child feel the way I did growing up. I made a choice. I'm sorry that it hurt you, but I did what I thought was right for my child."

"Our child," he corrects. "Why did you apologize then?"

I give him a small smile. "I saw how much it hurt you by keeping him from you, and I hate that. I owed you an apology for keeping him from you. I knew the moment I saw the hurt and anger in your eyes that I made the wrong choice. I'm really sorry."

"What happens now?" he questions.

I cling to his shirt. "Please don't take him from me," I plead with him. My breathing starts to deepen at the mere thought.

"Christ," he snarls. "Fuck, Gabriella, I'm an asshole but not that much of one. Anthony is ours, that's the way he's going to stay."

"Really?" I ask, wondering what the hell is going on. From everything I ever heard about Alessio, especially over the last four years, he's ruthless, relentless, and unforgiving. It's what made me keep us hidden for so long. Had he not been at Adelina's party, I would still be hiding.

His thumbs stroke along the base of my jaw. "Really."

I stare at the man who's haunted my dreams for years and wonder what happens from here. He lives in New York while I live here in Indianapolis. This is my home. I've made a good life for me and our son here. I don't want to leave. Before I can ask him another question, his mouth descends on mine. Within seconds, I lose every semblance of reality. My fingers clench around his shirt as our tongues caress one another. His fingers skim along my body until he reaches the hem of my dress.

I whimper low in my throat, loving that he's touching me again. Something I have dreamed about for the past four years. He pushes me back against the countertop, and I hold onto him as he lifts me onto it. He pushes my dress up to my hips and slides my panties down my legs. I'm breathing hard as he deepens our kiss.

The sound of his belt buckle fills the silence in the kitchen. I shiver at the thought of him being inside of me again. I want Alessio. I think I'll always want him. He's always had a hold over me. The years haven't diminished just how much I want him.

Today has been a rollercoaster of emotions, and no doubt I shouldn't be doing this, but neither of us are in a place to think straight.

Our past collides with our future and present as he presses his cock against my folds. I'm soaking wet. I need him.

He slides into me, his thrust hard and deep. I tear my lips away from his, gasping at the sheer size of him.

It's been so long since I've been with a man that it stings as he slides in and out of me. He fucks me hard and fast on the countertop.

"Ahh," I cry out as he picks up his pace.

"Fuck," he growls, his hands on my hips, his fingers digging into my skin.

I'm so close, my body's burning with pleasure. God, nothing has ever felt this good. I want more. I need him.

"Please," I beg breathlessly. "I'm so close."

He slams harder and faster, his hips rotating as he drives into me.

"Come," he growls, his lips pulled back into a snarl as he thrusts deeper and deeper into me. "Come for me, Mama."

"Alessio," I cry out as I shatter, my body shuddering as my orgasm washes over me, my pussy squeezing his cock as I come.

"Christ," he growls. "Fuck, Gabriella, I'm going to come." He thrusts into me once, twice, three times more before he grunts out his release. "Fuck, it's good to have you back in my arms," he growls as he breathes hard.

I drop my head onto his shoulder and breathe. That was amazing, something I hadn't expected nor thought would ever be possible.

"Momma," I hear Anthony call out.

I freeze at the sound of our son's voice. I turn my wide eyes to Alessio, who looks like a deer caught in headlights.

"Fuck," he snarls as he withdraws from my pussy. I wince but push through it and quickly climb off the counter and fix my dress.

"That shouldn't have happened," I say, unable to meet his gaze, because if I do, I know I'll fold. I want Alessio. Hell, I crave him. Have done since the moment we met. But it's different now. Anthony is the most important person in my life. His needs come first, and that means anything that Alessio and I had, is in the past.

"That's not the only time that's going to happen,"

Alessio promises me. "I'm going to want a repeat of that, over and over again."

I don't argue with him, because truth be told, I am too. But it can't happen, and I'm not in the mood to argue about it.

"Want to meet your son?" I ask cautiously.

He fixes his clothes and smiles at me. "Abso-fucking-lutely."

The heat of his stare on my back makes it difficult to move, but with Anthony calling me still, I don't stop. The second I'm in the room, Anthony rushes over to me, his lips pressed into a pout as he shows me his bottle.

"Empty?" I ask.

He nods. "It's gone," he says. "Thirsty."

I smile and take the bottle from his hands. "I'll get you some more, darling. But first, there's someone I want you to meet." I lift him into my arms so he can look at Alessio properly. "Anthony, honey, this is your dad, Alessio."

Anthony's eyes widen, and he gives Alessio a toothy smile. "Dadda," he cries, his arms outstretched, wanting his dad to take him. I fight back the sob as Alessio takes Anthony without hesitation and holds him close to him. His eyes close as he presses his lips against his head.

Emotions well up inside me as I watch this man —this deadly, scary, intimidating man—be so soft and gentle with our son. I quickly mumble that I have to fill his bottle and move out of the room.

I should never have kept them apart. That wasn't fair on Alessio, and it certainly wasn't fair on Anthony. Neither of them deserved to be without the other. I'm just glad they're together now. I messed up huge, and I need to ensure I do everything in my power to let them have a relationship.

Alessio's cell rings, and I quickly fix Anthony's bottle for him. My little man drinks water like we're going through a drought. Once I have his bottle filled, I move back into the living room, where Alessio is currently sitting on the floor watching Anthony play.

"Here you go, honey," I say as I hand him his bottle. I run my hand along his dark brown hair. He smiles up at me, and my heart melts.

"Thank you, Momma."

I press a kiss against his cheek. "You're welcome, honey. Did you show Daddy what you drew this morning?"

His eyes widen dramatically, and he runs out of the room, racing toward his bedroom. I can't help but smile at his enthusiasm.

"He's amazing," Alessio tells me.

I nod. "He really is. He reminds me a lot of you," I say. "Other than looking like your clone, that is. He's got your temperament and smile."

Alessio gets to his feet and moves toward me. He runs his hand along my jaw. "You've done an amazing job, Gabriella. I can't believe we have a son."

I lean into his touch, craving his warmth. "Alessio," I whisper. "I can never apologize enough."

He shakes his head. "I get why you did it, Mama, I do, but I'm so fucking angry. Not only at you, but at myself." He presses closer to me, his lips inches from mine. "We'll get through this, Gabriella, and when we do, your ass is going to be in my bed forever."

I suck in a sharp breath. "What?" I hiss. He can't be serious. "We barely know each other."

"Four years, Mama, that's how long I've been searching for you. You think for one second that now I have you, you're going to be going anywhere?" He raises a brow, daring me to argue. "Your sexy ass is going to be knocked up and in my bed."

I blink, surprised by his words.

"Momma, Dadda, look," Anthony cries as he rushes into the room. I pull away from Alessio, gladly putting distance between us. Right now, he's acting crazy. I turn my attention to my baby, who's happily showing us his drawing.

I hear car doors closing, and my brows knit together. Who could that be? The doorbell rings, and I turn to Alessio, who's already moving toward the door.

"That's my brothers," he says casually.

I stand rooted to the spot. What the fuck? He's brought his brothers to my house? Is he for fucking real?

SIXTEEN
ALESSIO

"What the fuck is wrong with you Bianchis?" Raylee snarls as she pushes past Makenna and toward me. "Since when do you think it's a good idea to barge into someone's house unannounced? This doesn't concern you."

"Um," Makenna says bitchily, no doubt pissed at the disrespect Raylee's just shown her and Dante. "Want to watch your tone? And for your information, this is our business, because Alessio is our business."

Raylee moves so she's standing beside me, crosses her arms over her chest, and glares at my sister-in-law. "Yeah, well, Alessio doesn't own this house. Last time I checked, it was Gabby's name on the deed, so again, not your business."

Malcolm steps forward and draws his wife into his arms. "Raylee's upset. What would you do if it was Kinsley in Gabby's position, Kenna?"

My sister-in-law's shoulders slump slightly. "Fine," she snaps. "But I'm reserving judgment on her. I don't like her right now."

"That's nice," Gabriella says from behind me, a sweet fucking smile on her face. "No one asked you to like me. I sure as fuck don't like you right now."

I press my lips together to stop the laughter from bursting forth. The one thing Makenna respects is strength. Having Gabriella stand up for herself will show my sister-in-law she's not one to be pushed around. Makenna smirks, and I know she's already on her way to winning her round.

"So," Raylee says. "Can we come in?"

Gabriella rolls her eyes. "Like you even have to ask, Ray-Ray." She smiles, and within seconds, the two girls are embracing one another. "How's the kids?" she asks as she leads everyone into the sitting room, where Anthony is currently drawing.

"Good, they're with Kiro," Raylee says, talking about one of her brothers. I haven't met any of Raylee's family as of yet, but from what I've heard, they're okay. Tough as fuck and good bosses.

"Who'd have thought he'd be the one who would look after them," Malcolm says as he pulls Gabriella in for a hug. They're close, from what Makenna and Denis have said about them. When Raylee and Malcolm were going through their shit, Gabriella was right by their side.

"He loves them because he loves his sister."

Mal nods and moves toward my son, scooping

him off the ground and throwing him in the air. Anthony laughs.

"Mal," he giggles. "Again."

"God, it's been a while," Raylee says. "How are you holding up?"

"About as good as expected. Dad's pissed."

"You told him?" Malcolm asks, his brows knitted together. "Fuck, Gabs, is he coming here?"

My woman shrugs. "I don't know. I ended the call before he could speak. That was close to two hours ago now."

"You do that a lot to him," Raylee murmurs. "You get annoyed and end the call."

Gabriella shrugs. "He was angry, and I was an emotional wreck. I couldn't listen to it. I wouldn't listen to it while on speaker in the car. I didn't want Anthony overhearing."

"Better pray, Alessio, that Gabby's da doesn't make an appearance." Malcolm grins as he glances at me. He's uneasy. I get it. Gabriella's his woman's best friend, they're close like sisters, and he considers Gabriella one too. He also knows me and knows what I'm like. His mind must be running wild. No doubt he wants to tell me to leave Gabriella alone, while on the other hand, knowing if he did, I'd knock his teeth down the back of his throat.

"Who's your da?" Makenna questions, still holding that bitchy tone.

I glance at her, but she ignores me and continues

to glare at my woman. Shit. This could go very wrong.

"Not your business," Gabriella replies. Great. Fucking great. The last thing I need is these two at each other's throats constantly.

Makenna's eyes narrow. "Why did you keep his child a secret from him?"

"Because we had—" Gabriella begins and pauses before glancing at our son, who's still in Malcolm's arms, "S-E-X a few times and then he disappeared. What would you have done in my situation? Waited for him to return or got on with your life. I for sure wasn't waiting around. He may never have returned."

I was always going to return, and that's something I need Gabriella to understand. She wasn't just a woman I fucked. She was something a fuck of a lot more than that. She's become my obsession. I wasn't going to stop looking for her.

Makenna doesn't respond. Instead, she nods. She doesn't look happy, but thankfully, she's not pushing the subject.

"Now, I understand that as Alessio's brother," she says to Dante, "you feel as though you deserve answers, and you do. But you don't get to show up at my home and demand them. This is my son's safe place. Having people he doesn't know show up isn't fair on him or me." Her tone is polite, but it has a bite to it.

"I invited them," I lie. I warned them not to come, but of course, my brother has other ideas. You don't tell him or Makenna what to do. They do whatever the fuck they want.

"Wasn't your place to do so," she fires back. "Now that they're here, will there be any more family members turning up?"

No, there fucking shouldn't be. Dante called, wanting to know what the hell happened. He's pissed. I get it. I didn't tell him about Gabriella when it happened and no doubt when we're alone, he'll demand answers, but right now, this ain't the time. A look passes between him and Makenna. I grit my teeth, knowing damn well that means Romero and Holly will be on their way.

"When?"

"Should be outside," Dante replies with a smirk. He knows damn well that I said I'd talk to him later, that right now I need to focus on sorting things out with Gabriella and ensuring we're on the same page before my crazy fucking family descend on her.

Makenna will always be standoffish with everyone. The woman has been burned too many times in the past to be trusting. I get that. Fuck, I respect that. But I won't tolerate the bullshit any longer. Gabriella is the mother of my child, and she's not going anywhere.

"I'll let them in." Malcolm says as he leaves the room with my son in his arms. The man is completely comfortable with my child, and I fucking hate that.

"Other than your brother and Holly, am I

expecting any more family members?" Gabriella asks softly. Gone is her anger. Instead, she looks defeated and tired. I fucking hate that she has that look, and I know she's probably feeling as though I betrayed her by inviting everyone, something I'll be making sure my brothers know was not fucking okay.

"No, Gabriella," I say sternly, giving Dante and Makenna a pointed look, letting them both know I'm beyond pissed.

"He calls you Gabriella?" Raylee questions, her eyes wide and her voice shaky.

"Told you, Ray-Ray, it was just a couple of nights," she responds, her gaze moving past Raylee and toward the door, where Rome and Holly are walking in with Malcolm on their heels.

"But you hate being called that," she points out. "Have you told him that?"

Gabriella shakes her head. "We didn't get much time to talk before I was ganged up on."

Oh, she's pissed. No doubt she'll let me know just how much when everyone is gone.

"Family takes care of family," Makenna snipes. "You kept his child away from him for years. Do you really think we're going to let you walk away again?"

Gabriella stares blankly at Makenna. "You do not have a say in anything I do. You may be the boss in New York and the east of the country, but you're not here. I don't take orders from you, and I sure as fuck don't owe you an explanation for anything I do."

"Okay," Holly says, stepping in, no doubt sensing

her aunt is about to lose her damn mind, and if she goes for Gabriella, I'll be stepping in. "Gabby, I understand there's a lot of people in your house, and you're undoubtedly annoyed about that, but you have to understand that we're Alessio's family and we're trying to figure things out."

Raylee huffs as she crosses her arms over her chest. She, along with Malcolm and Gabriella, are all looking at me expectantly.

"Seeing as Alessio has nothing to say about this matter," Raylee begins, "I think it's best if you all leave."

"Ray, you don't want to do this," Holly implores. "Don't let this cause us to fall out."

"Enough," Gabriella hisses. "Don't you dare try and make my best friend, my sister, feel guilty for sticking up for me. Just because you think Alessio can't make choices for himself, it doesn't give you the right to try and railroad me. Raylee can say and do whatever the hell she likes, just like you all have."

"But—"

"She's right, Hol. You've all pushed your way into her home and demanded answers for something that doesn't involve any of you." Raylee hisses. "Had you listened to Alessio, you'd have found out that he had this under control. But all you've done is made things harder for him. He was getting to know his son, spending time with him and talking with Gabby. Now we're all here and you're acting as though you've never made choices that affected anyone else. What Gabby chose to do four years ago is her damn choice and no one, and I mean no one, other than Alessio has an opinion on it. Do I make myself clear?" My best friend is shaking with anger, her eyes flashing with rage. I don't remember the last time she was this angry.

'Told you Mo Stor, she'd have been better off with Christian," Malcolm says. "At least no one was in her business."

Gabriella presses her lips together, her eyes dancing with laughter.

"He was always much happier when Gabby was around. Those two were perfect together. Hell, he'll be happy to see her," Malcolm says, and I know he's just saying it to piss me off. "Having you home would be great. The kids would be happy."

"You fucked him?" I snarl, pissed that she's been with Malcolm's right-hand man. I can't control my outburst. The thought of her with anyone else sets my blood on fire.

"Not your business," she replies haughtily.

I move so that I'm in her face. "That, Mama," I say quietly, "is where you're wrong. You're my business. Every fucking inch of you. So have you fucked him?"

Her eyes flash with anger and need. "Not since I fucked you," she sighs, her cheeks flaming with redness.

"Keep it that way. You're mine, Gabby. Mine. Anyone else touches you, and they die."

She rolls her eyes at me. God, she thinks I'm joking? Just let them try. "When it comes to you, Mama, I'm possessive, protective, and downright obsessive. It's time for you to catch up."

"Alessio," she whispers. "I don't understand," she says. "After what I did—"

"I get it. I told you that, babe. I get why you did it. I'm angry as fuck that you did but I can forgive it. Just as you can forgive me for not coming back when I said I would."

"Um, Gabs," Raylee says, interrupting us. "You may want to brace."

My woman frowns, her lips pulled into a thin line. "What? Why?"

The front door opens, and I reach for my gun, just as Joe Ranieri walks into the house. What the fuck?

"Put the guns down," the man growls as he glances around the room.

Dante, Makenna, Romero, and I all have our guns drawn. Malcolm has a smirk on his face, and Raylee and Gabby are looking happy but confused.

"Seriously," Gabby snaps. "Put the damn guns away. There's a child present!"

Fuck. I quickly put my gun away, just as the rest of my family do, but I can't help but wonder why the hell Joe Ranieri is walking into my woman's house like he owns the place.

"Dad, what are you doing here?" Gabby asks,

pushing me out of the way and walking over to the fucker.

I do a double take as the two of them embrace. Never. Not fucking ever did I think Gabriella would be Joe's daughter.

"He's your dad?" I ask, still completely fucking stumped at how we never uncovered it.

Gabriella beams at me. "What's wrong, Alessio? You look shocked."

"You," Joe hisses at me. "What the fuck do you think you're doing? Hmm, knocking up my daughter?"

Gabriella and Raylee laugh.

"Dad, stop it. Leave it alone. You can't say anything. At least Alessio wasn't married when he got me pregnant." She pauses as she walks toward me. "Right?"

I glare at her and pull her into my arms. This is where she belongs. "Think if I were married, I'd be making you mine?"

She shrugs. "Have you met my father?" She says it low, so only Raylee and I can hear.

She's got a point. Joe cheated on his wife with a woman that's around Gabriella's age. All reports that have come in are saying she's pregnant and Joe's divorcing Christina so he can be with her. I don't blame him. His wife is a fucking bitch.

"Why didn't you tell me your dad was Joe?" I ask, and she sinks into my body. I fucking love having her next to me.

"Same reason I never told Dad who you were. I knew you'd freak, and he'd flip out. Besides, I've stayed away from your world, Alessio. I've seen firsthand what devastation it can cause. I don't want that."

I grit my teeth. Fuck. That's not what I wanted to hear. The Famiglia is my life, and I won't be leaving it, but I'm not leaving Gabriella behind either.

"Grandpa," Anthony yells as he wiggles out of Malcolm's hold and runs over to Joe, who with practiced ease picks him up and smiles at him.

Fuck. I have missed out on so much. Anthony has made so many memories and connections to other people, ones I don't have with him. It fucking hurts. But I know deep down that had Gabriella and I gotten together four years ago, I'd have been a fucking bastard. I wasn't ready for what I'm ready for now, and a small part of me knows that finding out about Anthony now is a blessing in disguise. Now, I know what I want, what I need, and that's my family. Gabriella and Anthony.

"Gabs, sweetheart, I'm sorry. I was shocked, I shouldn't have snapped at you," Joe says softly as he looks at his daughter with love and adoration.

"It's okay, Dad. I get it," she replies as she leans against me.

Joe glances around the room. "Is there a party I didn't know about?"

Raylee giggles as she moves toward him, and the two embrace. "No, Gabby was ambushed by Alessio's family, who thought they could make her do as they wished."

Joe chuckles. "My Gabby do something she doesn't want to?" He shakes his head. "Better men have tried and failed." His eyes narrow on me, and I see the warning there. The man hasn't yet put two and two together and found out how we met. "Malcolm, it's good to see you again."

Malcolm and Joe shake hands.

"Wait," Makenna says. "You two know each other?"

Joe chuckles again. "Of course we do. Who do you think helped him when Raylee was taken? Makenna, dear, I always know those who are closest to my daughter. She may have been hundreds of miles away from me, but she was always looked after."

"How come you've kept her hidden?" Dante questions. "A man like you, no other children other than Gabriella, surely you'd want to find someone to take over from you?"

"My daughter's safety is more important than that, Dante. Surely you, as a father, would put your child above all else. My enemies find out that I have a daughter, they'd use her for leverage against me. Gabby is my daughter. I'll do anything to protect her, including keeping her under wraps."

Anthony wriggles from his grandfather's arms and moves to his mother, who expertly scoops him up and chats away to him. My boy has too many people in the house and is constantly looking around, he doesn't have the capability to stay in his grandfather's arms.

"So, now that you know about Anthony, what are you going to do?" Joe asks as he takes a seat on the couch.

"She's mine," I say simply. There's no two ways about it. Gabriella Sanchez is mine.

Joe doesn't respond to my proclamation, but he also doesn't object to it.

"Now, how about we order some food in and let Anthony get to know his family?"

Dante agrees, and I'm shocked. Usually, my brother despises small talk, and that's exactly what's going to happen with dinner. I just pray there's no bloodshed with this meal, because the tension in the room could be cut with a knife.

SEVENTEEN
GABRIELLA

Sitting down for dinner is an awkward affair. I'm just glad my dad, Raylee, and Malcolm are here with me. It's been hard since the Bianchi's walked in. I understand why they're upset, and I even understand that they're trying to protect Alessio, but they're not helping matters. They want to ensure the best for their brother and nephew, but all they're doing is trying to railroad me, and that's not something I'm okay with.

Conversation moves smoothly, thanks to my father's ability to speak to everyone and anyone and not annoy them. Something that completely missed me when the genes were being handed out. No, I'm awkward as hell, and I'm more of a loner, whereas my dad is a people person. It's what makes him a great boss.

He hasn't yet demanded answers, something I know is going to happen sooner or later.

Alessio's bitchy sister-in-law has been glaring at me. She thinks that because she's the boss, she can intimidate me. Hell no. I smile sweetly at her. I know that I'm poking the bear, but I can't help it.

"Gabby," Alessio says, and I turn my attention to him. His lips are curled at the end, and his eyes are dancing with humor. He's trying not to laugh. "You doing okay?'

I nod. "I'm good. Are you? Today's been…" I pause, trying to find the right answer, "shocking. But you seem to be taking it well. Hell, better than I could have expected."

He smiles at me. "Not sure if you've been listening or not, Gabby, but I've been searching for you. Told you, baby, I'm fucking obsessed."

My heart batters against my chest at his words. He seems sincere. Everything he's telling me is all the right words, but I have my reservations. I know what I felt waiting on my father to come home. It sucked. It hurt. It shaped me in a way I don't want my son to be shaped.

"I'm so angry," I whisper. "You let all these people into my home, Alessio, and not one of them has even tried to talk to our son."

It's the truth. The entire time they have been here, they've demanded answers and they've wanted explanations. But not once have they thought, fuck it, let me get to know my nephew. I don't want my child around people who don't want him around. I had that with Christina, and never again. I won't allow someone to make my child feel unwanted, and I'm sure as hell not going to let it happen in his own home.

"Trust me, Mama, they're shocked and hurt."

I take a deep breath. "They have no right to be hurt, Alessio. This doesn't concern them right now. Sure, Anthony's their nephew, but until they can be trusted to treat him with love and actually show that he's wanted, they don't get to have my answers or respect."

I'm standing firm by my words. Until his brothers can show that they actually want to forge a relationship with my son, they can fuck off. I'm not afraid of them. I don't care what they think of me. I made a mistake by keeping Anthony's birth from Alessio. I didn't purposely set out to hurt the man. I did what I honestly thought would be best. I know now that it wasn't and I'm not going to stand in the way of Alessio and Anthony having a relationship. I'm not vindictive, nor am I an awful person. Alessio never hurt me or Anthony. He deserves the chance to be a father.

"I'll talk to them," he tells me. "But, Mama, I don't give a fuck what they say. You're mine, no matter what. Your ass is in my bed, you're at my side, and our boy is going to be where we are. Nothing is ever going to change that. I've wanted you every day for the past four years, and I'm going to want you every day until the day I die."

Oh my God. I pull in a shaky breath. His words

mean so much to me, but there's a guard around my heart that has never been opened, and I'm not sure if it ever can be.

"I want to go slow," I say to him, hoping my words don't hurt him. "You and Anthony need to build a relationship before we even think about anything else."

I need to find a way to trust him. To be able to know he'll be there for our son no matter what.

"Slow?" he repeats. "That's not something I'm capable of, Gabriella. I've been fucking waiting, four years of waiting. Now that I've found you, you think I'm going to go slow?" He shakes his head. "Not a fucking chance."

"Gabs, sweetheart," my dad says as he gets to his feet. I take a deep breath and follow him as he moves toward the kitchen. "Talk to me, sweetheart, what's going on?"

I lean against the counter, trying my hardest not to think about what happened here with Alessio earlier. I really need to clean the countertop.

"I don't know, Dad," I say softly as I get my cleaning supplies out. "I'm so confused."

It's true. Alessio is dead set on wanting things between us to be full speed ahead. But that's never been an option. When we were together years ago, it was hot, consuming, and amazing. But it wasn't more than a few nights of fucking. That's it. Alessio's expectations aren't realistic. I can't automatically get into a relationship with him. I can't do what he wants. It's not fair to any of us, and it's definitely not fair to have Anthony believe we're a family and for everything to fall apart. I can't do that.

I scrub the countertop hard, wanting to ensure it's sanitized properly.

"Gabby, talk to me," he implores, his eyes soft and filled with worry.

So I do. I tell him everything that happened four years ago and everything that happened today—leaving out the part of us having sex. That's something he doesn't need to know. I explain my hesitancy in wanting to jump into a relationship with him. I tell him about the worry I have of him returning to New York and then having to choose between the Famiglia and his son.

"Not everyone is me, sweetheart," he tells me as he pulls me into his arms. "I fucked up more than I could ever make up for. I hurt my wife—even though I hated her, I hurt her. Every time I would come and see you, she'd die a little more inside. The humiliation, anger, and embarrassment she'd feel, knowing I was happiest when I was with you, was hard for her to bear. I made a mistake in choosing to not harm her more than I had already done. I'm sorry that by doing that, I hurt you."

"I know you're sorry, Dad, and I've forgiven you, but the pain I felt is still with me even to this day. I'm sorry that I keep bringing it up." I feel guilty knowing that every time I speak about the pain I felt, his guilt hits him hard.

His arms tighten around me. "Don't apologize, sweetheart. But I need you to listen to me, okay?"

I nod. He's been a huge support to me over the past five years. He's made amends. He's trying. I'll always love him, no matter what.

"Give Alessio a chance, Gabs. The man looks at you as though the world fucking revolves around you. He's smitten, for sure."

I laugh. "He tells me he's obsessed."

Dad smirks. "He seems it. You need to decide if you'd live happily without giving it a chance. If I were to have a guess, you'd regret it. Giving him a chance doesn't mean that you're jumping into a family, Gabs. It means you're giving you and Anthony the best chance to find out who Alessio is and if a relationship is what you truly want."

I rest my head against his chest. That's exactly what I'm unsure about. Can it be that simple?

"I didn't want to be a part of the mafia world, Dad. I wanted to have a quiet life."

He nods. "I know that, and it's the main reason I kept you hidden. But, sweetheart, sometimes what we want and what happens are two different things. No matter what happens now, you're going to be in this world because Alessio is always going to be in Anthony's life."

He's right. There's no way Alessio is going to walk away from his son. That's not who he is, and I'm truly grateful for that because it would break my heart for him to leave without looking back.

"Trust your heart, Gabs," Dad says as he presses his lips against my head. "It'll steer you right." He releases me and walks out of the kitchen, leaving me to be deep in thought about what it is that I really want to do. I begin to clean every countertop that's in the kitchen.

It's not just about me, but also what is right for Anthony and Alessio. I know that having Alessio here with us will addle my mind. The man makes me weak at the knees, and I forget my own name. Having him here constantly, I'll be flat on my back with him fucking me without a second thought. He has that power over me. He's able to have me worked up that much that I give in to whatever he wants.

I hear the sound of heels clicking against the floor, and I brace, knowing that it's either Makenna or Holly. Probably both knowing my luck.

"What you did was wrong," the Irish accent mixed with American is soft yet filled with anger.

"What I did," I begin, not turning around to look at Makenna, "is what I truly believed to be the best decision. What you're doing now, Makenna, is not helping anyone but yourself. How about you take your boss hat off and see this as what it really is. Nothing is a threat against you or your family. This is about a child, a three-year-old child, who was happily spending time with his father before you descended on his house. My son hasn't gone near Alessio since because there are too many new people he doesn't know."

"You kept a child from Alessio," she hisses, completely missing the point of what I have just said. "Alessio is my brother, Gabriella. He's been through fucking hell, and he's worked his way out of the depths of Hell to be standing beside us, to be where he is today."

I nod as I turn to face her. She's glaring at me, something she's done since the minute she walked into my house.

"I don't doubt that. Alessio is an amazing person. He's a great member of the Famiglia. But he's not that for me, for Anthony. He's the father of my child. A child you haven't even looked at. Why is that?"

"I don't trust you. How the hell are we meant to trust you? Hmm. How do we even know that Anthony is Alessio's son?"

I suck in a deep breath. All the anger I'm feeling whirls around me like a fucking tornado. I want to punch her right now. She's insinuating I'm a whore. Fuck her.

"You want a DNA test? Fine, set it up and we'll do it." I throw the cloth I was using onto the counter and barge past her. I'm beyond pissed. How fucking dare she.

"What's wrong?" Alessio asks as soon as I enter the sitting room. "What's happened?"

"Well, apparently, I'm a whore who can't be trusted. Set up the damn DNA test," I snap. "It's time for you all to leave. I'm done. Set the test up, and we'll talk when the results are in." I walk over to my dad, who's got Anthony on his knee as he talks to Malcolm. "I'm going to give him a bath. Can you see to it that they leave?"

My dad doesn't hesitate. He hands my son to me and gets to his feet, his eyes narrowed and filled with rage. This is what I love about him. When I'm hurting, he hurts, and he's angry right now because I am.

"I'll come with," Ray-Ray says. "Malcolm will help your dad."

She's making it clear that in this situation, she and Malcolm are on my side. I hate this. There shouldn't be sides. We should all be working together to help build relationships. Everyone has forgotten that my son is the priority. The Bianchi's seem to have other things on their mind, and I'm not playing that game.

Call me a whore, fine, but don't expect me to be polite or allow you to be in my home. I would never walk into someone's house and disrespect them. That's fucking bullshit. But somehow, the Bianchi's think they have the right to do it to me? Hell no. It's time for them to leave.

Anthony, Raylee, and I go to the bathroom, where I begin to run him a bath.

"Are you okay?" she asks softly.

I shrug. "I'm angry and hurt, but I'm okay. I always am."

She nods. "Yeah, you are. Once we have Anthony bathed, Mal and I are going to go home. I want to call the kids before they go to sleep. But we'll be back tomorrow. Please don't worry, Gabs. Everything is going to be okay."

I wish I had her optimism. I don't think it will be. Everything seems to have imploded, and I'm unsure if there's a way out.

EIGHTEEN
ALESSIO

I grit my teeth as I watch Gabriella take my son out of the room. She doesn't look back. I'm beyond fucking pissed right now.

"Joe," I say, barely able to keep my composure. I'm about ready to blow. "I'll be back in an hour or so." First, I have the matter of my family to deal with. What happened today was unbelievable, and what Makenna said to Gabriella was out of line.

"Sure," the man says as he glares at my brother and sister-in-law. "You come back, make sure you're alone."

The threat is clear. He's making a stand, letting us know he'll not tolerate what happened here today to transpire again. I don't blame him. The shit that went down was unacceptable.

"It'll just be me," I assure him, and stalk out of the house. I don't wait for my brothers to follow. They have no choice.

I climb into the car and start the engine. Before I'm able to drive out of the driveway, Romero slides into the passenger's seat.

"Now ain't the time," I snarl.

He doesn't say anything, just pulls on his seatbelt. He's silent as I back out of Gabriella's drive. His wife climbs into the car with Dante and Makenna, no doubt Romero keeping her away from me while I'm in this state of anger.

"That was fucked up," he says after a while. "Makenna should have never said anything to Gabriella, but, Ales, you had to have known they wouldn't be happy. You left Hayden's house like a rocket and didn't explain anything to them."

"I needed a fucking explanation, Rome. Me. Not them. Fuck!" I snap as I slam my hand against the steering wheel. "Do you even understand what has just happened?"

His jaw clenches. "She's pissed."

I suck in a sharp breath. Pissed? Fuck no, she's beyond pissed. "I had everything worked out, Rome. Then Makenna stuck her nose in my business, and now I doubt she's going to want to let me through the fucking door."

I grip the wheel tighter, my knuckles turning white. "Gabriella got scared and ran. I get it. Fuck, Rome, I get why she did it. It doesn't excuse her for keeping my son from me, but I get why she ran. The shit Makenna pulled today, she could run again."

The thought of losing her once again has my gut clenching.

"I fucking figured out why it was hard for us to find her. She's not under Sanchez anymore; she's under Ranieri. She changed her fucking name," he spits, angry that we didn't figure this shit out before. "We should have just asked Mal. That fucker would have told us."

I scoff. "You mean the same man who stood against his aunt today?" That shocked the fuck out of me. Usually, the Gallagher's are united, but Makenna chose the wrong person to go against. Gabby and Raylee are close, and in turn, Malcolm is with her too.

"What's with the dude they're talking about—Christian?" Rome questions.

My nostrils flare at the sound of the asshole's name. "He's Malcolm's best friend and right-hand man. Seems as though there was something between him and Gabriella."

"Do you think—" he begins.

"Not a fucking chance," I hiss as I cut him off. I know Anthony is my son. I don't need a DNA test to confirm it. You just have to look at the boy and see he's mine.

"We have to ask," he says quietly.

I don't answer him. Sure, I get that he, along with Dante and Makenna, are worried this could turn bad and Anthony isn't mine, but none of them know

Gabby's not like that. She's fucking innocent and pure. The woman is everything I'm not. She's the one I have wanted, child or not. She was always going to be mine.

I pull up to the rental house and take a couple of steadying breaths. Right now, I feel as though I could take everyone out. They've fucked up today and they need to accept that.

I walk into the house just as Dante pulls up outside. I don't spare him a look. I can't. If I do, I may end up going at him. When they walk in, I'm already pacing the room like a caged animal.

"I get that you're pissed," Dante says.

"Pissed?" I echo. "Do you have any idea what the fuck your wife has done?" I snarl. My anger is now coming out.

"Watch it," Makenna warns.

"You are not my boss," I growl. "You are not the head of the Famiglia. I do not need to watch my tone with my sister-in-law."

Holly takes a seat, her eyes wide and her face pale.

In the years that Dante and Makenna have been married, I have always treated her as the boss. Not once have I made the distinction that they're two separate entities, until today.

"You fucked up," I hiss. "You were a bitch, plain and simple. You knew Gabriella was Joe's daughter, and you still called her a whore. What the fuck is wrong with you?"

I have to know what was going through her mind.

What she really thought she was achieving by doing this.

"I didn't call her a whore," Makenna snaps. "I said how do we know the child is yours. It's a valid question, don't you think? Maybe one you should be asking also."

"Did you look at my son?" I ask her, unable to keep the anger out of my tone. "If you did, you wouldn't be asking me that fucking question."

"Ales, you need to calm the fuck down and watch who you're talking to," Dante snarls as he steps a little in front of Makenna.

I grit my teeth. I need to unleash my anger, but right now, I need to go to Gabriella and fix things between us.

"You've got to see where we're coming from, Alessio," Dante says. The anger has left his eyes as he watches me. "I don't know this woman. This is not an insult to you or her, but how can you be so sure? Before today, we haven't even heard you mention Gabriella, let alone you getting her pregnant."

Makenna steps beside her husband, her hand on his arm. "I saw you with her. You were different. The way you spoke to her was the way Dante speaks to me, and Rome speaks to Holly. She means something to you, and you never told us." I see the hurt flash in Holly's eyes as she nods in agreement with her aunt. "This family has been through Hell and back. And we're protective, and that means we're protective of you."

I shake my head, still so angry. "You have no idea. I wouldn't be here today if it wasn't for Gabriella. I wouldn't be alive. She's the one who saved me in Denver when I got shot. She was the one who made sure I stayed alive."

"So you fucked her as a thank you?" Dante questions.

I don't think; I move toward him and get into his face. The rage I'm feeling is batting against me. I want to kill him.

"Don't fucking say it."

A hand lands on my chest and pushes me away. I have tunnel vision right now.

"Okay, enough," Romero says as he continues to push me back. "Alessio has been trying to find Gabby for the past four years." Silence descends through the room at his words. "He promised her he'd be back in a week, but the shit with the Serbians happened and he couldn't get back to her for a while." Romero releases me. I don't move, my chest heaving, the rage still coursing through me. "By the time he did get back, she was gone, so no, it wasn't a thank you fuck. He's pretty obsessed with Gabby."

I grit my teeth. That's an understatement. Obsessed doesn't even compare to how I feel when it comes to Gabriella.

"You have to come to terms with it. You don't have a choice. There is no way I'm letting my woman walk away from me again, and I'm sure as fuck not losing my son today. You walked into a home uninvited. I fucking told you not to come. I was trying to figure things out with Gabriella. Instead of working things out with my woman and getting to know my son, you fucking showed up, and you brought everyone with you. Not once did any of you actually talk to my son. Not once. Until you can grow the fuck up and realize how disrespectful you were, I don't want you around my child." My chest is heaving, and I turn on my heels and storm out of the house.

The way I'm feeling right now is worse than I have ever felt. My anger pulses through my body, wanting to be unleashed. Usually, I kill someone or fuck someone to unleash it. Neither of those are an option right now. Instead, I'm gonna get into my car and drive to Gabriella's. We need to get this shit sorted because there is no way I'm losing her or Anthony. Not a fucking chance.

NINETEEN
GABRIELLA

I sigh as I sink down onto the sofa with a glass of red wine in my hand. It's been a long fucking day, and I'm exhausted, emotional, and angry.

"Sweetheart," Dad murmurs.

"I'm sorry," I tell him. "I couldn't cope, Dad. I was trying my hardest to keep it together to get home safely with Anthony in the car. I couldn't break down. I couldn't listen to your anger and disappointment on top of everything else."

He shakes his head. "I reacted badly," he says. "You're my daughter, Gabs. I'm always going to be worried wherever you're concerned. It was a shock to say the least, but that man dotes on you. He truly cares about you."

I scoff. "Dad, Alessio and I had a few nights together. That was it."

He looks at me, his brow raised, and I inwardly cringe. "Trust me, Gabs, that man is besotted with you. He was furious today. He couldn't go against them, not in front of me. But I have no doubt he's giving them what for right now. You cannot blame him for what his family thinks."

He's right. I know he is. "I reacted with my anger, Dad. I shouldn't have kicked Alessio out, but I do think getting Anthony DNA tested against Alessio will stop all the doubts."

"I agree, but not because some people think you're a jezebel, but because it will help you and Alessio forge forward together. When you get hurt, your instinct is to run, and sweetheart, you can't do that any longer. You have Anthony to think of now as well."

I take a large sip of wine, wishing it was something harder. Then again, if I did that, I'd be a hormonal wreck. "I know. I react instead of taking a couple of moments to collect myself."

It's a trait that I took from my mum. She was so passionate about everything, but the moment she was hurt or angry, she reacted quicker than blinking. The woman would never let anyone hurt her, not after my father did.

"What do I do?" I ask, needing someone to help give me some clarity. I have so many swirling emotions going through me right now that I doubt I can get through tonight without breaking down. I've cried enough today. Of course that's how Alessio found me, in my most vulnerable state. I still have no idea how he managed to enter my house without me hearing.

"That, Gabs, is something only you can decide." His voice is soft and filled with understanding. "But you don't have to decide right now. Take it day by day."

I take another sip of my wine. "Any idea how I go about setting up a DNA test?"

He chuckles. "I'll organize it all for you. Don't worry, sweetheart, everything will work out in the end."

Oh, how I wish that were true. But we both know there's no such thing as a perfect or happy ending that will come naturally. For that, we have to work hard at fighting for it, but at the moment, I have no idea what I'm fighting for.

He gets to his feet. "I'll be back tomorrow. Maybe you'll have some answers. Maybe you won't. But a new day brings new hope, Gabs."

Ugh, why is he always so damn philosophic. "New hope? I doubt that. But whatever happens, I will ensure Anthony and his dad have a relationship."

He smiles brightly at me. "You're your mother's daughter, Gabs. She could have hated me for what I did."

I scoff. "Could have?"

His lips turn up at the corners. "Okay, she did hate me, but she never once kept me from seeing you."

I bite back my retort—that it was the other woman in his life who did that.

"She was essentially a single mother. Of course I paid for anything either of you may have needed, but money isn't the be all to end all. She raised you alone, and Gabby, I'm very proud of the woman you have become. You own up to your mistakes, and that takes a hell of a lot of guts. But you do and you try to rectify those mistakes."

I shrug. "I think keeping Anthony from Alessio is something I'll never be able to rectify. My son lost three years with his father, and Alessio missed out on watching his son grow up. If the tables were turned, I'd be furious. I don't understand why Alessio was so forgiving."

It's something I can't wrap my head around. Alessio, from the moment he found out, has been supportive. He could have called me every name under the sun and tried to fight me for custody, something I would have hated, but he didn't. Instead, he's been amazing, understanding, and supportive. I don't get it. I'm waiting for the other shoe to drop.

"Alessio wants you, sweetheart. That's clear for everyone to see. He wants you and your son. That man intends to lay down roots, and Gabs, I don't think you'd mind so much if he did."

I sigh. He's right. If Alessio wanted us with him, I'd be happy, because I know that it would make my son happy, but I'm not sure how viaible that is. I have a business, one that I love and is thriving. It's taken me a long time to get it where it is. Alessio and I live in different states, and I'm not sure if we'll be able to come to a compromise about what will happen.

"Remember what I said," Dad says, as he presses a kiss against my cheek. "You do not have to make any decisions right now. Just get through today and see what tonight brings." He has a secretive smirk, and I don't like it. What is he planning? "Don't get up, sweetheart. I'll see myself out. But I'll be back in the morning."

"I'll make breakfast," I tell him, knowing he'll be here first thing. He'll want to ensure I'm okay and spend some time with Anthony before he travels back to Kentucky.

"I look forward to it," he says.

"Dad," I call out before he reaches the door. "How has Christina taken the news that you'll be getting a divorce?"

His lips thin as he looks at me. "She's fighting it. She's spitting mad, and I honestly can't blame her, Gabs, but enough is enough." His eyes darken, and I have a feeling something has happened between the two of them. Whatever the hell it is, Dad's furious.

"Is Hazel safe?" I ask, knowing the connections Christina has. Her father has a lot of power—not as much as Dad, but more than others. She could do something both stupid and reckless.

"She is. I have men on her at all times. Do not worry, Gabs, once the divorce is finalized, we'll all be happier."

I smile at him, hoping he's right. I hate that Christina got hurt, but hers and my father's marriage was toxic at best. They both hurt the other, Dad more so than her, but either way, divorce is the best option for them both.

"Go," I tell him. "Have a great night, and I'll see you bright and early for breakfast."

He grins at me. "You too, sweetheart. Try not to drink the entire bottle," he says with raised eyebrows.

I lift my glass to my lips and take a bigger sip than I normally would. My father's chuckle is deep and throaty, and I can hear it even as he closes the front door behind him.

I'm happy he's moving on and has finally found someone he loves. I just can't help but think Christina isn't going to walk away without a fight. That woman has taken a lot of my father's shit over the past two decades, and now he wants a divorce. No, I don't see her going quietly. A woman scorned…

The house is quiet now that my father's gone. Anthony's fast asleep, and when he sleeps, he does so deeply. Trying to wake him is like trying to wake the dead. I put on a movie, needing something funny to watch. I can't deal with romance right now. Hell, I haven't been able to watch any Rom Coms in years. I stumble across a movie I like the sound of and get it set up. I make some popcorn, gather some snacks, and refill my drink. Once I'm ready, I hit play and sit back and enjoy. Sometimes, you just need a good laugh, otherwise you'll end up crying, and that's not something I want to do again today.

An hour into the movie, there's a knock at the door. I hit pause and go check out who it could be. My heart batters against my chest when I see Alessio standing outside, waiting for me to let him in. God, he came back.

I open the door. "Hmm, you do know how to knock," I say with a smile and a raised brow.

His smirk hits me in the stomach and makes my knees weak. "I thought this time, I'd be polite. Didn't think just letting myself in would go down too well."

I roll my eyes. He's full of shit. I open the door wider and let him in.

"There's beer in the fridge and also wine. I don't have anything stronger. Help yourself," I say as I walk back into the sitting room and get myself comfortable once again.

I hear him closing the door and flicking the locks closed. I smile to myself, knowing that if he knew I didn't do it myself, he'd lose his mind. I hit play on the movie and reach for the popcorn.

The couch dips beside me, and I turn to glare at him. "There's another couch. Hell, there's even an armchair."

He shrugs as he throws an arm over the back of the couch. "You're here, so I'm here. Watch your movie, Mama. When it's over, we'll talk."

There he goes again, calling me Mama. Damn

him. God. Heat pools between my thighs, and I squirm on the sofa.

"Good to know," he says quietly.

I turn and glare at him. He can't do this to me. I can't cope with him so close to me. He makes me lose my mind, and I need to be fully functioning.

"Do you mind?" I hiss, trying to cover my reaction.

He shakes his head. "Not at all. But you want to talk, Mama, we can talk now."

I sigh. Do I want to talk, or do I want to watch the movie?

"You pick the movie, Gabby, then we'll talk after."

I grit my teeth and switch the movie off.

"We'll get this over and done with." I reach for my glass, and after three big mouthfuls, it's gone.

Alessio smiles at me. "Sit tight, baby," he says as he places his beer on the table and reaches for my glass. "I'll get you another. Trust me, Gabriella, this talk isn't going to make you mad, nor will it make you want to kill me."

I laugh, despite the wariness I feel. "That's reassuring."

He gets to his feet and moves effortlessly toward the kitchen. I happily ogle his ass as he does so. The man has a phenomenal body. He looks good no matter what he wears. He's tanned, with dark hair, and he has the most amazing amber eyes I have ever seen. He's sexy without ever trying.

"Finished staring?" he says when he returns moments later.

I bite my lip and run my gaze down the front of his body, licking my lips when my eyes get to crotch level.

"There's only so much restraint I have," he growls as he sinks onto the couch next to me. "Keep it up, Mama, and I'll fuck you so hard you'll be crying out my name."

My cheeks heat at his words. I reach for the wine glass.

"Stop it," I snap. Because he'll get what he wants, and that's me back in his bed, when we have other, more important things to talk about.

"Talk to me, Gabby, what's on your mind?" he asks, and the sincerity in his voice has my throat clogging up.

"I'm sorry," I say. "There's so much to apologize for, and I know there are no words that can ever make up for me keeping Anthony from you. But I truly am sorry."

He reaches out for me, and his thumb caresses my cheek. "I know. Trust me, I understand. I forgive you. But it's going to take a while for the anger to go."

"I don't deserve your forgiveness," I whisper. My heart hurts. I should have listened to my father from the beginning. He wanted me to be honest with Anthony's father, but I was wrapped up in my own hurt and feelings to listen.

"You're safe, our son is safe, and you're here.

That's all I give a fuck about. Now, what Makenna said—"

"She was right," I say, cutting him off. "Not by implying that I'm a whore, but she's right to worry and care for you. If it were me, I'd want the same thing. So, Dad's organizing the DNA test. I need to get this done, not only for me and you, but if the rumors spread that Anthony may not be yours, that could hurt him, Alessio, so we'll get it done."

He nods, his eyes darkening. "I hate this, but you're right. We both know what the test will show."

I smile. "I do all the hard work and he comes out looking like you."

His grin is infectious. "He's amazing."

I nod. He really is. I take a sip of my wine and decide it's time to get down to the hard stuff. "What's going to happen now? I live here, our lives are here, and yours is in New York."

"We'll make it work. It'll be a lot of traveling at the beginning, but once you're comfortable and we're at a place to move forward, we'll come back to this conversation."

I sink into him, glad that he seems to have everything sorted out.

"Now, Mama," he growls. "The question I have for you is: what happens between us?"

My breathing deepens and my cheeks flame. I squirm on the sofa as his gaze intensifies. "I'm not sure," I lie.

He nods as he reaches for my glass. "Are you sure about that?"

I hate that he can see through me. "What do you want?" I question, needing to deflect.

His lips go to my ear. "I want you. I've always wanted you."

I swallow hard. God, when he says that, it makes me wonder if being with him would be worth it.

"Right now, though, I'm wondering if Anthony will wake up?"

I shake my head. "He's a heavy sleeper. He'll be asleep until morning."

The grin he gives me is wicked. His eyes are bright with lust. "That's good then, Mama, because it gives me time to eat that pretty pussy of yours."

I tremble as he moves. His fingers go to my legs, and he pulls them up onto the sofa. He makes quick work of my panties and pushes the hem of my dress up to my hips.

"Look at you," he growls. "Soaking wet for me."

I gasp when his tongue sweeps across my folds. My fingers clench around the couch beneath me as he does it over and over again. My body hums as pleasure takes over. I'm grinding down against his mouth, trying to reach my peak.

He tongue-fucks me, leaving me panting, clawing at the couch. He sweeps it across my little nub, the nerve endings sending me into a frenzy. His mouth closes around my clit, and he sucks, while adding a finger inside of me. It's too much. I'm barely able to breathe. He's got me right where he wants me, and I'm unable to think, let alone speak.

My body begins to shake as he finger-fucks me, his mouth on my clit sucking hard. He's pushing me to the edge.

Sensory overload.

My orgasm builds until it reaches boiling point, my body on fire from his touch. The moment he adds another finger inside of my pussy, stretching me, I come, shouting his name as my body quakes with the force of the orgasm.

He doesn't stop. In fact, he replaces his fingers with his mouth, sucking and slurping at my pussy as I come.

"You taste amazing, Mama," he growls.

My pussy shakes with the aftermath. "It's too much," I gasp, but he doesn't stop. His finger goes to my clit, and he sets about making me come for a second time. His tongue swipes at my folds.

My body, still not recovered from the first, starts to climb, this time higher than it ever has. But I want more. I grind down on his mouth, seeking the pleasure, needing to come even though the aftermath of my first orgasm hasn't finished.

Fighting it is pointless. There's no way in Hell I'd be able to do that. Alessio's too talented to let it work. His magical fingers and skillful mouth are too much, and I detonate, completely shattering at his hands. My pussy floods his mouth as I tremble. Once again,

Alessio's name spills from my lips as my orgasm washes over me.

He pulls me to him, and his mouth slants against mine. I moan against him as our tongues caress each other. I taste myself on him, and it sends me into a frenzy. I wrap my arms around his neck and press closer to him.

I hear the sound of his zipper, and excitement rushes through me. I need to have him inside of me. There's no better feeling than having Alessio stretching me. He pulls me over his lap, his cock thick against my pussy.

"Told you, Mama," he growls as he positions his cock at my entrance. "I'm going to breed you." He thrusts deep inside of me.

I cry out. The thickness of him, along with the brutal thrust, has me clinging to him.

"Alessio," I gasp as he grips my hips and slides into me.

"I want you to dance for me, Gabby."

I throw my head back, my hands gripping his shoulders, and begin to move. He thrusts deep as I bounce on his cock, grinding down on him as I do. I'm mewling like a cat at the brutal way he fucks me. I can't deny there's no one like Alessio. He's everything I have always wanted but guarded myself against.

His thrusts are punishing but send my pleasure skyrocketing.

"God," I cry out as his mouth closes around my nipple.

"Not God, Mama," he growls. His tongue circles my nipple, and I close my eyes as I slow down my movements, wanting to savor this, wanting to remember this forever. Alessio seems to realize what I'm doing, because he pistons his hips in a slow but brutal thrust.

"Yes," I cry. "Alessio," I whimper as my pleasure begins to climb.

"Come for me, Gabby. I want to feel you come on my cock."

His hands grip my hips, and he takes over, lifting my body off his cock until the mushroomed head is at my entrance. He pushes back in with a slam.

"Yes," I cry out, my fingers clawing at his shoulders. "Again," I beg.

He doesn't disappoint. He fucks me hard and fast. I'm merely clinging on for the ride.

"Come for me, Mama," he snarls, his hands tightening on my hips. His thrusts are harder, faster, and more brutal than before.

I shatter. I come undone. I cry out his name as I throw my head back in pleasure.

He thrusts once more inside of me, burying himself to the hilt before his cock pulses and he unloads stream after stream of cum inside of me.

TWENTY
ALESSIO

Two weeks later

I grit my teeth as I look around the charred remains of what was once Granny Jones. The restaurant is owned by the Irish Mafia. It was the most popular hangout for the men in the Clann. Now it's burnt to the ground.

It's been two weeks since I had to leave Indianapolis; leave behind my son and woman. But thankfully, Gabby understands that I have to work and is always available whenever I call. She's been fucking amazing throughout the shit storm that brought me back to New York.

The apartment complex Dante owns was the first of our properties to go up in flames, along with three of our men. While we were on the plane arriving home, another property that belongs to us was also set alight. The fuckers were really trying to get our attention, and it worked. However, we've yet to uncover who the bastard behind it all was. Our men managed to track down the assholes who set the fires —both of whom were tortured for information and died without giving up whose orders they were under. Every Famiglia and Clann member is working to find out what cunt did this.

"Ales," Dante calls out.

I turn and see he's standing with my sister-in-law and brother. I grit my teeth. Fuck. I haven't spoken to any of them other than Dante since they were in Gabriella's house. I don't have any intent on doing so either. The way they treated both Gabriella and Anthony is not something I'm willing to sweep under the carpet.

"I want all the security footage from the surrounding buildings," Makenna starts barking orders.

I look at my brother, the only one I have spoken to in the past two weeks, and that's only because he's my boss. "What do you need from me, boss?"

My sister-in-law's eyes flash with anger at the blatant disrespect.

"Ales," Dante says sharply. "Want to watch—"

"I'll do it. I'll call Finn and fill him in also," Romero says, his gaze solely on me.

He's called about a hundred times since we got back from Indianapolis. He's even had his wife call me. I don't pick up. They have nothing I want to hear. And if I were to pick up, they wouldn't like what I have to say. He's not the only one who's called. Dante and Makenna have also, but unlike Rome, Holly, and Makenna, when the boss calls, you have to answer. Any time he wants to talk about anything other than Famiglia business, I end the call. You can't disrespect the boss.

"Ales," Makenna says quietly as members of the Clann start to sift through the rubble, trying to find survivors. "We can't go on like this."

"Makenna," I hiss. "Right now, I have shit to do, and then I'm going to see my son and woman," I say through clenched teeth. I turn to my brother. "Unless you have a problem with that?"

"Alessio," Dante growls as he steps to me. "This shit stops now. She was just looking out for you."

"No, she was looking out for herself," I snap. Knowing Makenna has trouble accepting new people to the family, and having Gabriella part of it now, adds someone she'll have to trust, and that's something that doesn't come easy for her. "Because of her unwillingness to be able to see past her own insecurities, she almost cost me my woman and child."

"Ales—" Rome urges, his voice filled with worry and caution.

"She did the DNA test," I tell them, something they had no idea about. "Anthony's my child, something you'd have known had you actually taken the time to look at him."

Their faces go slack with the announcement.

"Fuck," Romero growls. "You've got to understand—"

I shake my head. "I don't have to understand anything. You knew, Rome, and you fucked up. Now," I say, looking back at Dante, "do you need anything from me?"

"Tomorrow, there'll be a meeting," he tells me. "I need you at my side."

I nod. "I'll be there. Anything else?"

"There's nothing we can do here but wait. With Rome and Finn looking for the security footage, it could take all night. Go get Gabby and Anthony," he tells me.

His tune has changed. I guess finding out you have a nephew will do that.

"Talk to you later," I tell him and move away.

I hear footsteps behind me and brace myself. They're light, but at the same time on the heavier side, which means it's one of my brothers.

"Ales," Dante calls once I reach my car. "How long is this shit going to last?"

I turn and face the man I respect. "If the tables were reversed, Dante, what would you say?"

He runs his hand over his jaw. "Things with me and Makenna are different—"

I laugh. God, this shit. It's always different with them. "Yeah, I knew Gabby years ago, Dante. It wasn't some quick fuck like you'd like to think. That woman means something to me." Dante is the only one I'd be this open with. He has my respect, he is the boss, he deserves the truth. "Growing up, I had no one. You were being groomed into becoming the boss, and Rome did whatever the fuck he wanted. I was left alone to be that cunt's punching bag," I begin.

Dante's eyes darken with anger. This is something we don't talk about. Our father was a son of a bitch. He was a ruthless fucker, but he was also a coward. He targeted those who were weaker than he was.

"Mom was so caught up in her own pain and shit that she never gave a fuck about any of us," I continue. The woman was never motherly to us. She did her own thing and that was that. "Gabriella..." I say. That one word holds so much respect and reverence. "She cared for me when she didn't have to. She stayed with me and cared for me. Do you know what that's like?"

He stares blankly at me.

"She's so fucking pure that she makes me want to be a better man." I laugh at the notion. There's no way I could be anyone but who I am, and yet Gabby makes me believe I could be. "She's so pure that she took a man she knew killed three people and nursed him back to health. She's amazing, Dante, and she's mine. You have no idea what that is, to hold something so fucking pure in your arms, and then watch as it shrinks into itself. That's what you, Makenna, Holly, and Romero did to her. You made her feel so uncomfortable in her own home, she retreated into herself."

"You really care for her?" he asks, somewhat bewildered by the concept.

"Yes. She's mine, Dante. I'd do anything to keep her. I'd kill any man, woman, or child who would try to take her from me. She's mine."

He nods. "Then I owe her an apology."

It's as simple as that.

"You do. You all fucking do. But right now, I'm not feeling too comfortable with the rest of them talking to her. Until that time, they stay the fuck away."

His eyes narrow, and the corners of his mouth tighten. "It can't go on forever like this."

"My woman was called a whore, my child was ignored, and you think I should go on as normal?"

He sighs, his hands going into his pocket. "Who'd have thought you'd be the most protective out of the three of us?"

"Someone has to be," I say as I turn on my heel and open my car door. "I mean it, Dante, they don't come anywhere near my apartment."

He nods. "I'll ensure they don't. Maybe answer their calls and they can apologize?"

I don't answer him. Instead, I climb into my vehicle and start the engine. It's time to go and get my woman and son.

THE WIND WRAPS around me as I wait for her to exit the airport. Two weeks has been too fucking long. Never again. I need her ass to move here. I know it'll mean uprooting her life and leaving behind her thriving gallery. I'll buy her a new property here in New York if it means keeping her with me.

"Daddy," I hear Anthony's shrill shriek.

I smile at the sound. Fuck. It feels so good to hear him call me that. I never thought I'd want kids, but the moment I saw Gabriella with Anthony, it made me a changed man. Now I'm going to spend all my spare time fucking Gabby raw, and I'm going to knock her up. I want to see her round with my child.

Anthony pulls away from his mother and rushes toward me, a bright smile on his face. I'm unable to keep myself from smiling back at him. Gabriella thinks Anthony is my double, but she has no clue that our son is just as sweet and caring as she is. Over time, he'll learn to hide that side to him because people use it against you. But as a child, his innocence will remain until he's inducted into the Famiglia.

I scoop him up into my arms, and he wraps his arms around my neck, his face buried into mine and he presses a kiss against my cheek. My gaze goes to my woman, who's looking sexy as fuck, wearing a white blouse that has the top three buttons undone, giving me a peek of her cleavage. Her pants are molded perfectly to her body. She looks phenomenal.

She's smiling happily as she snaps pictures of Anthony and me.

"Mama, get your ass over here," I growl, wanting her in my arms.

"Oh-oh, Daddy, you said a bad word. Momma's going to be mad," my little boy says with wide eyes.

"Alessio Bianchi, do not curse in front of your son," she snaps. "He's already picking it up from Dad."

I can only grin at her. There's no way I'm curtailing my language. Not at fucking all.

"Here, Mama," I growl, and her eyes flash with want and need. Within seconds, she's in my arms and my lips are on hers. Fuck, this is what I've wanted.

"Hey," she says when I pull back.

"Hey, baby, have a good flight?"

She nods as I take her hand, keeping Anthony in my arms. "Yeah, it was touch and go. I had a meeting with my financial manager, and I thought we'd miss it."

"Everything okay?"

She nods. "Yeah, I was just seeing how much a property here in New York would be. Since you've been gone, Anthony has been asking constantly when you're coming back. It's not fair on either of you to be apart."

I smile. Fuck. She's amazing. "You think I'm going to have your ass anywhere but with me?" I ask. She's deluded if she thinks otherwise.

"Well, I was kind of hoping you'd say that, but I'd

also need to look into properties for the gallery. I need to work and—"

"And art is your passion," I finish for her, letting her know I've listened to everything she's said to me on our calls while I've been away from them.

Her smile is blinding, and she sinks into my body as we walk toward my car.

"Ales," she whispers. "What are you doing to me?"

"You like this?" I ask cockily. "Wait until we get home."

Her cheeks heat, and I know she's looking forward to it just as much as I am. I've never wanted or needed anyone as much as I do Gabriella. This is where she belongs, where they both do. With me.

TWENTY-ONE
GABRIELLA

He moves toward me, naked, his cock thick and full. I swallow hard as I watch him. His confidence is a huge turn-on. God, everything about him is a turn on.

I need to taste him. That's all I can think of.

I get to my knees and crawl to the edge of the bed. His eyes darken with lust as he watches me. The second he's in front of me, I take his thick length into my mouth, my tongue swirling around the purple mushroom head.

A low, deep moan falls from his lips, spurring me on.

"Fuck, Mama," he snarls as his hands tangle into my hair. "I'm going to fuck your face, and then I'm going to fuck you."

I'm panting, my pussy soaking wet at his words. His hands tighten in my hair, and he thrusts deep into my mouth. The tip of his cock hits the back of my throat, and I relax my jaw, breathe deeply, and let him do what he needs to.

His gaze is on me as he fucks my mouth. I keep the connection, loving watching every emotion pass through his gorgeous honey eyes.

I reach for his cock, my fingers brushing his balls as I do. His eyes heat at the barest touch. I wrap my hand around the base of his cock and begin to pump in rhythm to his fucking. I'm going to pleasure him just as he does for me.

He closes his eyes. "That's it, Mama, make me come," he growls.

Shivers run down my spine. I'm soaked, I'm horny, and I'm in search of release, but first, he needs to come. While I pump and suck, my other hand reaches for his balls. I roll them between my fingers as I take him deeper into my mouth.

"Fuck," he snarls, his thrusts becoming harder and faster. He's on the edge.

I twist his balls as I tighten my grip on the base of his cock. He's unable to hold back. His hand tightens painfully in my hair as he slams his cock into my mouth. He lets out a low groan as he releases his cum into the back of my throat.

I take down every single drop, ensuring not to miss a thing.

His eyes narrow. He knows I'm tormenting him, but I love the wildness in his eyes. It's something I haven't seen before, and definitely something I want to see again.

"On your back, Gabriella," he instructs.

Goosebumps break out over my body at his command. I scurry back up the bed and lie down. I, too, am completely naked.

His gaze roams over my body, and the appreciation in his eyes makes me blush. He likes what he sees.

"Look at you," he says. "All primed and ready for me."

I breathe harshly, my breasts rising and falling as I stare at him. His cock is still thick and hard. He's ready to go again. How is he able?

He positions himself at my entrance, leaning forward until his lips crash against mine. I give him everything, taking it back in return. I'm falling for him. It's so stupid—we barely know each other—but I am.

He slides into me, and I gasp. It's been two weeks since we've been together, and it only ever gets better.

"Bella," he grunts. His movements are precise. He's fucking me hard, fast, and deep.

With every thrust, I give a little more of myself to him. I never expected to ever fall for someone, let alone someone in the criminal world. It was everything I didn't want, everything my father tried to shield me from, and here I am, falling deeper and deeper for him as the days pass.

I moan, my pleasure building. His pace is relentless. He captures my mouth and kisses me, and I moan in the back of my throat and cling to him. I can feel my pleasure rising.

He twist his hips, making him hit deeper with every thrust. God, it feels so good.

"Ales," I cry, my orgasm teetering on the edge.

"Come for me, baby," he grunts, his thrusts increasing, the rhythm no longer in sync. He's frantic. He's close too.

My orgasm hits me like a tsunami. My body trembles, my eyes close, and my body bows. God, he owns my body. He's giving me everything I could want. I cry out, his name spilling from my lips.

"Fuck, Mama," he grunts as his pace becomes relentless. "You're mine, Gabby, all fucking mine."

"Yours," I agree, because there's no one in this world like Alessio.

He thrusts deep into me, his cock pulsing as he spills his cum inside of me.

"You're staying here with me," he growls. "I'm not letting you go."

I look into his bright honey eyes. "I'm falling for you, Ales," I confess.

His grin is filled with triumph. "Good, Mama, because I'm beyond fallen." He pulls out of me, and I wince. He sits back, his eyes on me, his gaze intense.

That's when I realize he's staring at my thighs, at where his cum is leaking down them.

"Can't have that," he says, scooping his cum up with his fingers and pushing it back into my pussy.

"Ales," I cry out, my body too sensitive for him to finger me.

"Take it," he growls. "Told you, baby, I want you pregnant."

He pushes his cum back into me, and when he's finished, he holds my legs vertically in the air.

"Have you been researching ways to make me pregnant?" I ask, wondering how he knows about the leg thing.

He gives me a cheeky grin, and I know that's exactly what he's done.

Five minutes later, he pulls me into his body as we lie in bed. "Whatever you need, Gabby, tell me. I need you to be happy here with me."

"We will be, Ales. You're here," I say simply. That's all we need.

He holds me close. *"Tu sei il mio sogno, bello. Niente è meglio di te. Sono caduto duro."* (*You are my dream, beautiful. Nothing is better than you. I have fallen hard.*)

Hearing him speak Italian is beautiful. His voice thick and rich with the accent. It's something I'd love him to teach Anthony, and something I would love to hear more of. I have no idea what he's saying, but my heart warms at his words. I press a kiss against his chest and close my eyes. It doesn't take long until I'm fast asleep.

I TURN in the bed and frown when I'm met by empty air. Where's Alessio?

I glance at the clock and see it's almost ten in the morning. I sit up, shocked that it's late. I can't remember the last time that I was able to sleep this long. I climb from the bed and quickly pull on my pajamas.

The second I open the bedroom door, I hear Anthony's small, muffled giggle. My heart warms as it's followed by his father's much deeper one. There's nothing better than hearing them laugh together. It's the one thing I have grown to love: the two of them smiling, laughing, and having fun.

When Alessio came back into our lives, Anthony took to him instantly. He looks up to Alessio with big eyes, kind of like he's starstruck. I love the look of pure love and happiness that Anthony has every time he looks at his father. To think that I was okay with keeping them apart. I hate that Alessio missed the first three years of Anthony's life. I wish I could turn back the clock and make things right, but I can't.

I creep toward the noise, not wanting to disturb the two of them. My heart melts when I see Alessio has built a fort for Anthony. It's big enough for them both to fit in.

Who'd have thought that a man as deadly as Alessio would have a soft heart and be so loving?

Anthony giggles once again, and I smile. My baby is happy.

I take this opportunity to shower and get ready

for the day, knowing Alessio has him and that he's safe in his hands.

"You good, Mama?" Alessio asks me almost two hours later.

I nod as I step into his embrace. "Yes, how about you?"

His eyes darken. "I know you were watching us earlier," he tells me, and presses a kiss against my head. "Thank you for giving us that time."

I smile at him. "He loves you. He's happy being around you. That's not something I'm willing to separate, so we'll stay here until you've had enough of us."

It's something that I came to decide two days after Alessio left. Anthony was miserable and so was I. After speaking with my dad, Raylee, and Ade, I knew that the only decision was to come to New York and give them the opportunity to grow their relationship. Alessio wouldn't be able to leave the Famiglia. There's just no way that could happen.

"I appreciate what you've given up."

I shrug. "Anthony is the most important person in my life, Ales. He means the world to me, and his happiness is what matters most. That means us working together—whether we're together or not—to do everything to have this work smoothly."

Co-parenting can be hard. I watched my mother and father do it. Although, that was mainly my dad demanding when to see me, and my mum wanting to do anything possible to make me happy, so she allowed it.

He looks at me with a furrow between his brow.

"What's wrong?" I ask, hating that look of confusion on his face.

"Fuck, Gabby, I have no idea what the fuck I'm doing."

I press my hand against his chest, my heart clenching at the sound of distress in his voice. "About what?" I whisper.

"How to be a parent. Mine were fucking awful, Gabby. If they were alive, I'd kill them before I let them anywhere near our son."

I swallow hard at his words. "Oh, Ales."

His jaw clenches. "My dad was a mean son of a bitch, Gabs," he growls.

"I heard your dad was awful, Ales. Did he hurt you?" I ask, hoping he didn't.

But Alessio nods, and tears spring to my eyes.

"I was the easy target," he begins. "I was small, until I hit the age of fifteen. In Matteo's mind, I was the one he'd be able to control. I'd come to heel. But my father's brutality made my mother into a shell of a woman who didn't give a fuck about anyone. I watched the shit he'd do to her and other women. Baby, I saw the most nefarious shit anyone can do to another human. I watched my father rape and slaughter women for fun."

I'm sobbing, unable to believe that any parent would ever do that or allow their child to see that.

My heart hurts for the young Alessio, who was subjected to so much pain and trauma. He was tortured mercilessly by his own father just for sheer fun of it.

"You're not him," I say, my hands clenching into fists in his tee. "You're not him, Alessio. You care. You would never harm me, nor would you harm Anthony."

His eyes widen at my words. "No," he says, shaking his head. "Never."

"You could have, though, Ales. If you were like him, you could have hurt me when you discovered our son."

His lips curl into a snarl. "Never even crossed my mind."

I smile at him. "You are not him. Matteo Bianchi is dead and buried, Ales. He can't hurt you. But you sure as hell can live your life knowing that your father would be disappointed that he couldn't make a mini him. Unlike you; you've made a perfect replica of you."

He crushes me to his body. "He'd be turning in his grave knowing that none of us followed in his footsteps, that we'd rather cut off our hands than harm those we love. He'd see that as a weakness."

God, the man was a fucking dick. "Love is our greatest strength."

"Momma, Daddy," Anthony calls, and I giggle. Perfect timing.

"Tonight," he says as he slants his lips against

mine. "I'm going to fuck you until you're unable to walk."

My breath hitches at his words. "Later," I promise him.

"You bet your ass, later, Mama."

He kisses me once again before walking out of the kitchen and going to our son.

Never, not ever, have I been as happy as I am right now. I couldn't imagine my life without Alessio.

I hope this feeling stays like this.

TWENTY-TWO
GABRIELLA

"When are you coming out here?" Raylee asks. "I miss you and so do the kids. You can even bring Alessio with you."

I roll my eyes. That's my best friend's not so subtle way of trying to pry at what's happening between me and Ales. I've been here in New York for a week, and I haven't told her or Ade what's going on between Alessio and I. They're constantly asking, but the truth of the matter is, I have no idea what's going on. All I do know is that I love him, and I have let my guard down. Two things I never thought possible.

"I'll organize something. It may not be before Ade's due date, which means you'll be here before I get out there."

I hear her heavy sigh. "I hate that we're so far apart."

"I do too." Ray-Ray and I have always been close.

When I lived in Manchester, she did too. It's where we met, and since that first day, we've been best friends. It didn't take more than a week after Raylee and her mum moved to Spain before me and Mum followed behind, thanks to Dad wanting us somewhere no one would think to look for us. Moving to the States years ago was one of the hardest things I have ever done. Leaving Ray-Ray was awful, but thankfully, our friendship can stand the distance, and we're still as close as ever.

"I'd better go. It's late here and no doubt one, or even all my children will be up early, and with Malcolm working late, I'll be the one to wake with them."

I smile as I glance at the clock. It's a little before eight in the evening here, which means it's close to two am where Raylee is. The woman does indeed need to get some sleep. "Go. I'll speak to you tomorrow. Love you."

"Love you too, Gabs," she says, and the call ends.

I get up off the couch, my cell in hand, and get ready to check in on Anthony. Alessio called an hour ago. Something came up and he wanted to say goodnight to Anthony. I love that he takes that time to speak to our son, even when he's busy at work. Ales is unlike both of our fathers. He's making his son a priority, and I love him even more for doing so.

Tires squeal outside, and I frown. This is a residential apartment complex, mainly lived in by the members of the Famiglia. My gaze moves to the window, and I see two cars parked haphazardly out front. I swallow hard when I see multiple men exit the vehicles with their faces covered in balaclavas and guns in their hands.

Oh God. What the hell is going on?

I move through the apartment, unsure of what's happening, but my instincts are telling me to protect my son. My hands tremble with fear as I can hear loud voices move through the stairwell outside of the apartment.

The men are coming.

My heart races, my stomach clenches, and I feel nausea roll through my body. Once I'm in Anthony's room, I call Alessio.

The call rings and rings and rings. It feels like an eternity.

"Mama, I'm going to have to call you back—"

I hear the front door splintering, followed by loud shouts and curses.

"Ales," I breathe.

They're here.

"Baby, talk to me." The urgency in his voice is clear to hear, but I'm so focused on the footsteps that are growing ever so closer that I'm paralyzed with fear.

The door to Anthony's bedroom opens, and within seconds, I'm surrounded by seven men. All I can see is the whites of their eyes. They're angry, and they're speaking in another language, one I'm unsure of but think is Eastern European.

"Move bitch," one of the men snarls.

I shake my head. No. I will not let them take my baby.

"Leave," I yell, hoping and praying that someone is in the apartment complex and they'll hear me. "Leave now."

A dark laughter chills me to the bone.

"Not going to happen," the smaller of the men says as he steps forward and viciously punches me in the stomach.

I lurch forward, dropping my cell as the breath is taken from me and pain erupts from my belly. Tears tumble down my face.

"No," I gasp, as I surge forward, trying to get the man to stop moving toward Anthony. It's no use though. I'm savagely punched in the face. Blood spurts from my nose and lip, and I crumble to the floor from the sheer force of it. My eyes begin to blur from the blow, but I'm able to see the man reach for my baby.

"No!" I scream once again.

"Momma," Anthony yells, fear and worry in his voice.

My heart breaks at hearing his fear. I need to get to him.

God, Alessio, please come home.

A foot connects with my leg, and the sound of bone breaking fills the air, along with my scream of pain. I try to push through it. I twist my body, my hands clawing at the floor, and I try to pull myself along, needing to get to Anthony. But the man who's got him is already walking out of the door. I'm not going to make it to him in time.

A hand fists in my hair, dragging me backward. My back arches at the sheer brutality. I struggle against the hold but it's useless. He's too strong. I fight as hard as I can, clawing at him, kicking at him. It's no use. He's bigger and stronger than I am. My efforts are futile.

He throws me to the floor once again, delivering a swift kick to my stomach that has me rolling onto my back. Within seconds, his weight is on top of me, his fists punching at my face. I claw at him, pulling and scratching at his face, clothes, and neck. I'll be damned if I let this bastard get away unscathed.

I need to do all I can to prolong this torture so Ales can get here. He'll be able to see who took our son and then get him back.

I hear laughter and glance around the room, and see there are three men still here.

I swallow hard. God, please don't hurt me anymore. I can't bear to think what they may actually do to me.

"Tell that Italian bastard his time as boss is coming to an end, as is his whore of a wife's."

I'm once again delivered a punch to my face, just as the other men close in on me. My eyes close from the pain and from the dizziness I feel. I swallow back the bile that rises once again. I need to get Anthony. I need my baby.

I lie on the floor, unable to move, but that doesn't stop these assholes. They kick, punch, and beat me. The pain I feel is unlike anything I've ever felt.

"You're going to die," I croak when they finally stop. I'm in way too much pain. I'm floating on the edge of consciousness. "You're going to die painfully."

Whether it be at my father's or Alessio's hands, these men are going to die, that much I know for sure. I'm a lover, not a fighter, but these men deserve everything they're going to get. They've taken my son, and I have no idea if he's okay. I can't get to him. I'm stuck here on this floor, tears streaming down my face, as I stare at the man who's beaten me the most.

The spider tattoo has a jagged scar running through it that I'm able to see partially on his shoulder. It's the only thing I'm able to identify.

"No," he snarls as he moves into my space once again. "They're going to die." He lifts his foot, and I know I'm not going to survive this. I just pray that Alessio finds our boy.

His foot connects with my face, and darkness takes over.

TWENTY-THREE
ALESSIO

I lift my chin in greeting to Stefan and move through the club toward the back. It's early yet, and the staff are getting ready to open in a few hours. But Dante called me twenty minutes ago and told me I had to get my ass here. He sounded urgent. When the boss calls, I go wherever he needs me to.

I was supposed to read Anthony a story this evening. He already picked his favorite and wanted me to read it to him. But when Dante rang, that plan went out the window. Thankfully, both Anthony and Gabriella understood, and I'll be home whenever I can be.

Our talk last week brought us a fuck of a lot closer. Gabby knows about my childhood—well, the bare bones of it. I will not subject her to any more of it. Matteo Bianchi is dead. The fucker is six feet under and no longer in control of anyone. But she was right, we aren't our parents, and I'm sure as fuck not Matteo. My kid means more to me than anything. I'd fucking die to protect him, to protect Gabby. My father would have pushed us in front of a bullet if it meant saving his own fucking life.

I know more about what Gabriella went through with Joe being her father and allowing that bitch of a wife of his to dictate how and when he got to spend time with his daughter. That's beyond fucked up, and I'm glad the man finally had enough and forged a relationship with his daughter. One I know has grown in strength since she moved here from Spain. I also know the pain she went through while losing her mother. Something I can't relate to. When my parents died, it only brought relief that I'd no longer have to put up with their bullshit.

Gabby is the only person in my life who has cared for me without having to. She's the one person who looks at me like I'm not a fuck up. I've made plenty of mistakes in my life, but Gabriella doesn't see me as that person.

I push the door open to Dante's office and come to a halt. My eyes darken, and rage takes over.

"Alessio," the bastard says. His heavily Russian-accented voice just further pisses me off.

"What the fuck are you doing here?" I snarl.

"Alessio, sit down," Dante says. "Nikolai is here as he needs our help."

I shoot my brother a dark look. He can't be fucking serious?

"Maksim has been kidnapped. We have no idea

who or why he's been snatched. Lena is ready to tear the world down to find her grandfather," he growls. "You are the only ones Lena trusts to help us."

I scoff. "Why's that?"

He shrugs, seemingly not happy that his wife puts trust in us. "She said you are good men. You could have killed her after what I did, but you didn't. I must admit, I reacted out of anger and paid the price by losing my men."

"You're lucky that's all you lost," I growl. There's no fucking way he gets to waltz in here and ask for our help. No fucking way.

"Okay," Dante begins, his eyes narrowed slightly. "Today we push aside what happened to deal with this. What do you know?" he questions Nikolai.

"Maksim's car was attacked. His men were killed, and he's been taken," Nikolai explains. "By the time we discovered this, he was gone for over an hour."

Dante's face is grim. "Which means they've already killed him, or they've got him holed up somewhere."

I shake my head. This is a clusterfuck. The last thing I want to do is work with Nikolai, but Maksim is a fair man. He's always been welcoming, and I owe the man to try and help find him. "If they wanted him dead, they'd have done so when they attacked the car. No, they've got him stashed somewhere. Question is: why?"

"Money or power," Dante says.

It always comes down to those two things.

"So we need to find out who wants Maksim's power or money," I sigh. "I'd put my money on it being whoever the fuck tried to set Maksim up for the shootout in Dynamite."

My cell rings, and I pull it from my pocket. Gabriella's name flashes on the screen.

"Mama, I'm going to have to call you back—" I say, but I stop speaking when I hear a loud crash. My gaze goes to my brother, and the hairs on the back of my neck stand up.

"Ales," she says quietly, almost as if she's afraid to speak.

Fuck. What the fuck is going on?

I'm up on my feet, Dante doing the same.

"Baby, talk to me." I'm fucking terrified right now. Is she okay? What's happening?

"Move, bitch," I hear someone snarl.

The cell is snatched from my hand.

"Gabby?" Dante says, but whatever he hears has his eyes darkening with anger. His footsteps are purposeful as he moves out of his office and out the backdoor. It takes us less than a minute until we're climbing into his car.

He hits speakerphone, and my gut clenches. My hands ball into fists as I listen to the call.

"No," Gabby screams her voice is hoarse. She sounds like she's in pain

"Momma," Anthony yells. The fear in his voice has my eyes closing as pain spreads across my chest.

They've got my boy.

I hear movement and a low grunt. My breath is taken from me as I hear Gabby's pained cries. Over and over again they beat her, and I listen to every hit, every cry. I take it all in. My heart is pounding with anger, rage, and pain. God, Gabby... I can't lose her. I can't lose either of them.

"Tell that Italian bastard his time as boss is coming to an end, as is his whore of a wife's."

I freeze at the words, my gaze moving to Dante. This is about him and Makenna. This is those fuckers who have been after us. They've now gone after my family.

Dante drives like a mad man to my apartment.

I thought they were safe there. I thought they'd be protected there.

I was wrong.

I hear her cry out again and grit my teeth. Fuck. I can't bear to hear the pained cries, along with those animals beating on her.

"You're going to die," she says, her voice low and groggy. She doesn't sound like herself. But fuck I'm proud of her for telling those bastards that. "You're going to die painfully."

I crack my knuckles. Too fucking right they are. When I get my hands on them, I'm going to kill each and every fucking one of them.

Footsteps sound, and it's as though those cunts are leaving. Soon, there's nothing but silence.

"Gabby?" I say loudly, so that I can be heard. My voice is hoarse. Fuck. I can't do this shit. I can't lose her. My heart feels as though it's about to burst.

"Alessio," Nikolai says. "We will find out who did this to your woman."

"How?" I snarl at Dante. "How the fuck did they know about her?" I kept her hidden while she was in New York. Her and Anthony have been mostly at home. They've gone out a few times but not with me. How did these animals know she was mine?

Dante shakes his head. "We'll find out. We're going to find out who these fuckers are."

"They are Russian," Nikolai tells us. "From the East of the country. I can't pinpoint who they are, but one sounds familiar. But I cannot be sure."

I grit my teeth and nod, appreciating that he's given us that information.

It takes us another ten minutes before we reach my apartment. I don't wait for Dante to put the car in park; I'm already out of the car and sprinting toward the entrance. I take the stairs two at a time, noting that not only is Dante behind me, but also Nikolai.

"Boss," I hear Angelo says. He's a relatively new recruit. He's good, and I like him. "I've called an ambulance. Roberto is with her." His face is grim, but I don't stop to chat. I need to get to Gabriella.

I rush into my apartment, the men crowding the entrance to Anthony's room, I push past them, needing to see where my woman and son are.

I almost drop to my knees when I see her. She's lying on the floor, and her blood coats the carpet, walls, and the bed. But it's seeing Gabby that has me wanting to turn around and kill someone.

She's lying there, her face battered and bruised, her leg twisted in an odd angle. I can't breathe. I can't fucking move. I'm stuck staring at the lifeless woman I love.

"She's breathing," I hear one of the men tell me. "She's taken a beating, but she's alive. She's in need of medical treatment."

A commotion sounds behind me, and then Dante's at my side. "EMT's are here, Ales. She's going to be okay."

I swallow hard. "Have you seen her?" I ask, wondering if he's actually taken a look. I'm unable to take my eyes off her. It fucking kills me to see her like this.

"I did," he growls. "We're going to find out who did this, and then we'll kill them."

I shake my head. "I'll kill them. Dante, I want my son."

The EMT's carefully lift Gabby onto a gurney.

"We're going to get him back," he promises me. "We'll burn this fucking world to ashes if we have to."

"I failed her," I tell him, hating that I haven't been able to protect her.

"No," Nikolai says vehemently. "They would have waited until you were gone. They would have been watching. There was nothing you could have done, Alessio. They were going to come when you were gone."

I pin the man with a glare. "Awfully convenient that you're in town when it happens."

The fucker smirks. "You're right to be distrustful, Alessio, but I did not do this. I'm not the man to lie about this. Had I done it, I'd tell you."

He's right. The man's a fucking asshole on the best days, but he'd claim the assholeness.

"Then who the fuck did?" I need to know who the fuck harmed my woman and stole my child.

"We're going to the hospital," Dante says as he grips my shoulder. "I want everyone out on the street. Find out whatever the fuck you can. This is a priority. I don't care what you do, or how you do it, I want Anthony found, and the cunts who did this, dead."

TWENTY-FOUR
GABRIELLA

I wake up to a beeping sound. It's constant and terrifying. My entire body feels as though it's been hit by a semi. I'm in pain everywhere.

I swallow and instantly regret it. Doing so feels like shards of glass are stabbing my throat.

Opening my eyes is difficult, painful, and one doesn't budge. I grit my teeth and sit up. I'm confused, dizzy, and disorientated. I glance around the room I'm in and see that I'm in a hospital. I suck in a sharp breath and wince as everything comes rushing back to me. The pain is from the men who broke into Alessio's apartment; the heaviness on my chest is from the worry I have about my son.

Anthony. God, I need to find him.

I gingerly get to my feet. I can't be here. I need to find my baby. I sway once I'm standing, but I lock my knees and keep upright. I can't drop. I don't have time. I need to find Anthony. I take a step toward the door, gritting my teeth as pain ricochets through my foot.

How long was I out for? My foot has been put in a cast. I knew it was broken but fuck, I've been asleep too long. Where's Alessio?

The beeping sound gets faster and louder, making my head pound. Something tugs at my arms, and I realize I'm hooked to machines. No, I can't be. I need to leave. I need to find my baby. I reach for the tubes and pull, uncaring about the extra pain it brings, nor do I care about the blood that pours from the wounds.

I move toward the door and push past the pain and the dizziness. I focus on what I need to do. If I don't, I'm going to be on the floor crying with how sore I am.

"Miss," I hear cried. "You cannot be out of bed." The nurse hurries toward me and causes a commotion the moment I step out of the room.

"Don't," I grit, trembling with pain. "I am not staying here. Give me whatever the hell I need to sign. I need to go."

"Ma'am," someone else says, their voice closer to me. They're on my left side, I'm unable to see them, because of my eye. "Please, Ma'am, let me help you back into bed." They put their hand on me, and I recoil from their touch.

"Don't touch me," I yell, unable to have anyone touch me right now. I just want Alessio and Anthony. "I need to go."

"Ma'am, you're in no fit state to go anywhere." They try to get me to see reason, but I'm not listening. I push forward once again, determined to get the hell out of here.

"Someone call the doctor," the first nurse shouts as she gets closer to me. "Please, Ms. Sanchez, you're in a really bad way. You need to be in bed."

I look at the woman, and through the blurriness of my eyes, I see the worriedness in her own.

"I can't," I plead with her to understand. "I need to find my baby. Please don't make me stay."

"You can't leave," she says.

Someone grabs my arm, trying to pull me back to the room.

"Get off me," I scream as I shrug them off. "Don't touch me."

"Get the fuck off her," I hear growled deep but clear.

My heart soars at the sound. Alessio.

"Unless you want to lose them, take your fucking hands off my woman."

I'm released, almost as though I've burned them. I stumble forward but manage to reach out and grab hold of the wall.

Within seconds, Alessio's in front of me, his hands gentle as he frames my face.

"Mama," he murmurs, his eyes burning with pain and anger. "Please, baby, I need you to get back into that bed and let them take care of you."

I shake my head. "Anthony," I croak. "I have to

find him."

"I'm going to," he promises me.

"I'm so sorry," I whisper. "I tried to stop them, but I wasn't strong enough."

He rests his forehead against mine. "You did good, Mama. You tried your hardest. You protected him with everything you have. Now it's my turn to do the same for you both."

Hearing his words and knowing he doesn't blame me for our son's disappearance, I crash into his body, the pain taking over and consuming me. My sobs wrack through my body. "They took him."

I'm lifted into his arms. I'm safe when I'm with Ales. I know that no matter what, he'll protect me. He carries me back to the room and I close my eyes. The pain is too much. I can feel my body start to sink again, but I fight it. I need to fight it.

"Are you okay?" he asks once I'm lying down on the bed again. The nurses and doctors start to put the tubes back into my arms. "This shouldn't have happened, baby. I promise you, this will never happen again."

It was everything I never wanted. Everything I was afraid of happening. Never in a million years did I think their enemies would take my son.

"I just want Anthony back," I croak. "He's going to be so scared."

Ales nods, his eyes closed as he brushes my hair from my face. The doctors and nurses move away from me, asking that I please stay in bed.

"She will," he assures them, before turning back to me. "I'm going to find him," he promises me. "I'll not stop until our son is in our arms."

I nod, believing he'll do everything in his power to do so.

"I fucking love you, Gabriella," he tells me, and the sincerity in his voice has tears springing to my eyes once again. "I've never loved anyone but you."

I swallow hard. "I love you too. The only one." I could never give anyone what I give to Alessio. He's my everything. "Be safe, and find our boy."

He presses a chaste kiss against my lips. "I will. I'm going to call your dad, then I'm going to get our boy."

I smile at him, glad that he's not staying, although I can see the war in him. He wants to be here with me, but he needs to be out with his brothers and men, finding our son.

I watch as he exits my room, and the fear and pain come back in full force. Alessio beats them back for me, but without him, I'm a scared wreck.

The abyss is calling me again.

This time, I don't fight it. Alessio is doing what I'm unable to, and that's all I can ask.

"HEY." I hear the soft Irish-American accent. "That's it, open those eyes for me, Gabriella."

I turn my head toward the sound and open my eye. The left is still having trouble opening.

"Makenna," I sigh, glad she's okay but confused as to why she's here.

"Fuck, Gabby, I'm so sorry," she tells me.

I shake my head, wincing as I do. "It wasn't your fault." It really wasn't. Whoever did this hates her and Dante. It doesn't mean any of us deserved what happened.

"Dante, Alessio, Romero, and the other men are out looking for Anthony. I'm going to stay with you," she tells me.

I frown. "Why?" I don't understand. She's the boss. Surely she'd be with them?

"I fucked up," she says. "It's not something I admit very often, but with you and Alessio, I fucked up. I had no idea about your history, and I'm extremely protective of my family, Gabby. I needed to be sure Anthony was Ales'."

I nod, completely understanding her reasons. "That day was emotional for me in more ways than one. I got angry and reacted. That's something I do a lot. You were looking out for your family. No one can fault that."

She smiles at me. "Thank you."

I give her a soft smile in return.

"Can you tell me about the men? Any identifying marks?"

I close my eyes and think back, swallowing as bile rises up my throat.

"They were prepared," I tell her. "They all wore balaclavas over their faces, hiding their identities." I curl my fingers. "I fought one of them," I say quietly. "I tried to fight to get more time, hoping that the noise would draw attention. But I managed to claw and tear the man's shirt. He had a spider tattoo on his shoulder. It has a jagged scar running through it."

"You did great, Gabby. Not many people would be able to fight off an attacker, let alone get some information on their looks. You put up a hell of a fight."

"I had to do it. I needed to protect Anthony." I shake my head. "A lot of good that did. They took him anyway."

She reaches for my hand. "You did everything you could have done. Listen to me, Gabby. You were amazing. You fought hard and you tried to protect your boy. He'll be back with you soon. Alessio isn't going to sit on his ass. He's going to find out who did this."

I squeeze her fingers. "Thank you," I say softly. "I really appreciate you sitting with me."

"You're family, Gabby," she says simply.

Tears silently fall down my face, but once again, the darkness closes in.

"Sleep," she tells me. "I'll be here when you wake up."

That's all I need to hear. I succumb to the darkness and let sleep take me once again.

TWENTY-FIVE
ALESSIO

"Alessio?" Joe answers. He's on alert.

"Anthony's been taken and Gabby's in hospital," I tell him, my stomach clenching with my words.

Fuck. Watching my woman try and fight her way out of that hospital will be with me forever. Beaten, broken, and fucking bloody, she didn't care. She stood among the nurses who tried to get her back to bed and wouldn't budge, all so she could find our son.

I love everything about her. She's mine, and I'm going to enjoy killing everyone who hurt her.

"Is she alive?" he asks after a moment of silence.

"Yes. She's bloody and beaten, but she's alive. She wants to leave and find Anthony. We're trying to find out who did this. We know they're Russian, but that's all we have to work off."

"It has to be someone you know," he says after I tell him about the shit that's happened over the past few years. "They've targeted your family, Alessio.

They told my daughter that they want Dante and Makenna dead. This isn't a hidden enemy, but a seen one, or someone who knows you."

I tell him about what brought Nikolai to New York. "We're at square one," I tell him. Our number one suspect is also missing.

"So someone who wants to take over everyone. That's a greedy asshole, Alessio. Someone that fucked up isn't doing it alone. They'd have spilled to someone. We need to find out who."

"That, Joe, is what we're trying to uncover." It's fucking frustrating. We have nothing to go off of.

My anger is rising with every second I'm away from Gabriella and Anthony. I'm going to enjoy making those Russian fucks die.

"I'm on my way," he tells me. "It should take around two hours. Take care of my girl, Alessio."

"With my life. I'll call with any updates," I say and end the call.

I turn to Dante. The man's been watching me with caution. Is he wondering if I'll go off the deep end? I probably will whenever I get my hands on the fuckers who beat my woman and took my child.

"Any update from the men?" I ask, needing someone to give me fucking something. We're back in my apartment, trying to find a clue, anything that'll lead us to these fucks.

He shakes his head. "Nothing. Romero is on his way, and Nikolai is talking to Yelena."

I bow my head. This isn't fucking good. It's been

an hour since we left the hospital, an hour, and no one has any information. My chest tightens at the thought of not seeing Anthony again.

Dante's cell rings and hope sparks.

"Makenna," he tells me and answers it.

"Ales," Rome calls out as he steps into the apartment. "Fuck, Ales," he says, his gaze doing a sweep around the broken door.

"Don't go into the bedroom," I snarl. "You don't want to see that shit."

Of course he doesn't fucking listen and moves through the apartment. I don't watch as he goes to my son's room. That shit is fucking more than enough to give me nightmares for the rest of my life. Gabriella and Anthony should have never been touched.

"Fuck, Ales, is Gabby okay?"

My family are supporting me. It's a vast change to how things started, but fuck, there's no more time for anger. Not when Anthony is missing.

"No. She's been beaten and her leg's broken. Fuck knows what else."

"The woman wanted to leave the hospital," Dante says as he joins us. "She'll be okay once Ales and Anthony are back with her. Makenna was talking with her, and she gave us something we didn't have before."

Nikolai steps back into the room, his gaze on us.

"One of the men who attacked her had a spider tattoo on his shoulder."

"It's the sign of a thief who has been in prison," Nikolai supplies for us. "Whoever it is, has spent some time inside."

"Gabby also said he's got a jagged scar down the tattoo. That's got to give us something. Someone has to know."

"I'll call Lena," Nikolai says. "He's Russian. She'll be able to help us find him quicker than anyone."

"Why is he here?" Romero asks, his eyes narrowed on Nikolai's back. "I don't trust that fucking asshole. Not after what he did to Ales."

"He's helping us. We're keeping him close," Dante snarls. "If he's involved in this, he's not escaping from our clutches."

Hmm. Keep your friends close and enemies closer. Seems as though Dante isn't messing around.

"So," Nikolai says as he returns to us. "Lena thinks she knows who it is."

"Don't fucking leave us hanging," I growl. "Who?"

"Taras," he says as though that's supposed to mean something to us. "He's married to Yelena's cousin."

I smile. Finally, fucking finally we have some actual information.

"Ah, yes, Annika. The bitch's husband couldn't keep the contempt out of his eyes at the last sit down we had with Maksim," I inform Dante.

Dante nods. "Then we go and pay Taras a visit."

Hell fucking yes, we do. It's time to ensure these fuckers realize just what they've done.

"ALESSIO," Annika greets with disdain. "It's been a while."

The restaurant is empty. It's just past closing, and Annika is the only one left in the building. Stupid fuckers. They should have known we'd come for her.

Joe is on his way. I'm hoping to have Anthony back before his flight touches down. He's working on having his people find any properties these fuckers may have. We'll have these cunts cornered sooner or later.

She glances behind me, her eyes narrowing when she sees my brothers. Both of them are hiding Nikolai from view. "Spit it out, Alessio, I've got shit to do."

Oh, this bitch is going to be in a world of hurt. "Annika, where's your husband?"

She rolls her eyes and goes back to counting the money in the register. "What's it to you?"

"Well," I snarl as I move forward and rip the money from her hands. "Your husband has something that belongs to me, and I want it back."

The smirk on her face tells me she knows exactly who he has. "Aww, that whore of yours had a baby?"

I grip her neck and push her back against the wall, my fingers digging into the skin.

"You think anyone is going to save you from me?" I growl, loving the fear that emits from her. "Your cunt of a husband took my son, and he beat my woman. Can you imagine what I'm going to do to you?"

She swallows hard. "You won't hurt me."

A dark, bitter laughter sounds from behind me, and Annika's eyes widen with even more fear.

"Nikolai?" she gasps.

"You should really listen to him, Annika. The man is going to hurt you no matter what. You want to survive this ordeal, tell him where Taras is. Otherwise, you're going to be sobbing on the floor while he brutally murders you."

"You're family," she says.

He shrugs. "Lena is my family. You," he snarls, "are nothing but a whore. You do not deserve to be Lena's family."

Ah, I guess he knows all about this bitch's jealousy when it comes to Yelena.

"How does it feel, Annika, knowing you'll never be as beautiful, smart, or as powerful as Yelena? You had to marry a man no one respected just to be seen."

"Bastard," she cries, but I dig my fingers deeper into her neck.

"Where is your husband?" I ask once more.

She doesn't answer. Instead, her gaze moves to her cell that's sitting on the counter. Hmm, I guess calling the fucker would work. If he wants his wife safe, he'll give me my son. I drop the bitch to the ground and reach for her cell.

"What are his plans?"

She grasps her neck as she sucks in some much-needed oxygen.

"I bet these two fucking assholes have had enough of being overshadowed. With Yelena marrying Nikolai, Maksim must be basking in happiness, knowing his empire will be in the safe hands of his favorite granddaughter's husband," Dante says boredly as he leans against the countertop. "So, you and your useless husband hatched a plan to take over. But you got greedy, and instead of becoming the head of the Bratva, you tried to take us out also. Your pathetic attempts have failed completely."

The bitch smiles. "We have his son, and we have Maksim. I wouldn't say we failed."

I can't hold back the swift anger that hits me. I lift my foot and kick the bitch in her midsection, smiling as she splutters with pain and shock.

Once I unlock her cell—the woman didn't even have a passcode on it—I call her husband.

"Annika?" he answers instantly. "Are you finished?"

"I'm not Annika," I reply, putting the call on speakerphone.

Silence.

"Where's my wife?"

"She's alive," I begin. "For now. Where's my son?"

"He's here. How's the whore of yours, Alessio? I bet she's a fucking great fuck. She looks wild."

I grit my teeth. That's something he'll never find out. "Better than your cold as fuck wife, that's for sure. Now, you're going to tell me where the fuck my son is, or your wife is going to be in a world of pain."

His laughter only adds fuel to my anger.

"You're not going to hurt her," he chuckles. "Your father, now he would hurt her. But you Bianchi men don't hurt women."

I glance around at my brothers. Both of them have smiles on their faces. Oh, how wrong he fucking is. For my family, I'd do anything. Including killing this bitch.

I pass the cell to Dante and reach for my knife. This bitch doesn't deserve me to hold back. Hell fucking no. She knew exactly what her husband was going to do, and she allowed it to happen. For that, she's going to die slowly.

I unsheathe my knife, and her eyes go wide.

"No, Alessio, please," she begs.

I chuckle. "This is going to be fun," I say as I twirl the blade in my hand. "I've not even started yet, and you're already begging me."

"Leave her alone," Taras shouts, but I ignore him.

Men like him only want one thing, and that's power. He has a lot in common with Makenna's brother, Patrick—stupidity leads them to do things they otherwise wouldn't do, like going after family in order to become the boss. Something he'd never become because he doesn't have the manpower behind him. If Maksim died, the Bratva would be handed either to Nikolai, the husband of his granddaughter, who's active in the Bratva, or to Maksim's right-hand man. Taras is neither, meaning this has all been for nothing.

Greed fucks with people. Taras sees an opening and has tried to take it. No doubt he believes that he'd be the one to take over from Maksim. That's the greed blinding him. He's smart, he's managed to get men onboard his fucked up plan, he's managed to build a small army.

Those men are going to die and for what? Nothing, they'll die in vain and it's all down to Taras and his stupidity.

I kick out my foot and connect with Annika's side. She cries out and drops to the ground, on her stomach. I have no qualms in hurting her. Hell, I have no qualms in hurting anyone. I know the line, and I very rarely cross it. Dante has rebuilt the Famigila on principle and honor. He protects the communities, just like my grandfather did, something that was lost on our father. Dante ensures that women and children aren't harmed, and no innocent man is either. I toe the line Dante has set, and I do what is asked of me. But that doesn't mean I'm incapable of harming innocents. It's in my blood to kill. Usually, I kill only people Dante approves. But today... no, today, I'm taking out everyone who had a part in harming my family. I don't give a fuck if my brother approves or not. I'll do whatever the hell it takes to get revenge.

I begin to slice through her ring finger, just above the knuckle. Her screams are music to my ears. I smirk as she bucks against the grip I have on her.

"You brought this," I hiss. "You went after my family. There's no escape for you."

"Please," she whimpers. "Oh God, please stop."

Never. I'm not going to stop until I get the information I need. I want to find out where my son is.

I add a little more pressure and finish slicing through her finger.

Her screams are shrill, fearful, and filled with pain.

I chuckle. "Now, Taras, this is only the beginning."

Annika whimpers. "No, please," she screams.

"Where the fuck is my son?"

"Leave her alone," he snarls. "You can't hurt her."

Dante's the one to chuckle now. "You don't give a shit about her. You're worried that if we kill her, you'll lose the only line to the empire. No one will want to appoint you when you're no longer a member of the family. It doesn't matter; Yelena will always be next in line."

"That fucking stupid bitch, Adele," Taras mutters. "It was simple. All she had to do was get the Croats to kill her, then this would have all been mine."

"Taras," Nikolai growls, his voice deep and filled with hate and anger.

Adele Taylor was Yelena's mother. That bitch set her own daughter up to be killed. What the fuck is wrong with her?

The man is going to want to tear Taras apart, but he's mine to kill. He may have set up Nikolai's wife to be killed, but he beat my woman until she was unconscious, and took my son. There's no coming back for him. Not fucking ever.

"Nikolai," Taras stutters. "What are you doing there?'

"What I do is none of your business, but thank you for the information that you set my wife up to be killed."

"She's still alive, isn't she? She's even more powerful than ever. How does she sleep at night, Nikolai? Hmm? I mean, you were married to her mom when she fucked you. She got pregnant, and now Adele's dead and Yelena's living the life that should have been her mothers."

I glance at my brothers in shock. That was something we didn't know. Hell, they kept that in house and didn't let it get out. Not that I blame them. Yelena looks happy and Nikolai is protective of her, that's all that matters. They're together, and what they do is no one's business but their own.

"Now, Taras," I say, pulling his attention away from Nikolai, who currently looks homicidal. "Where is my son?"

Silence. The man really doesn't like his wife, does he?

"Fine," I laugh. "You can listen to her screams."

I reach for her other hand and give it the exact same treatment I gave to the first. She's a fucking wreck, her body shaking with both fear and sobs. She's got her eyes closed tight, so she doesn't have to look at her dismembered hands.

"Remember, Annika, this could have been avoided had your husband given a fuck about you," I taunt her.

"He loves me," she sobs.

I chuckle. "No, the man loves the power he thinks you'll give him. He doesn't love you. If he did, he'd have told me where my son is."

She twists her head to look at me, and the anger and hatred in her eyes is clear to see. It's mixed with fear and pain. "This is on you," she spits. "This is your fault. You've done this to me."

"I wonder," Dante muses aloud. "Who thought it would be a bright idea to target not only the Italians and Irish, but also Joe Ranieri?"

"What?" Taras growls. "What does that maniac have to do with this?"

It's Nikolai who answers. "You should really do your research, Taras. Had you done, then you'd have known that the woman you beat to a bloody pulp is the daughter of the so-called maniac."

TWENTY-SIX
ALESSIO

"No," Taras snarls. "There's no way."

"My son," I hiss. "Where is he?"

"Oh, so that means," Dante taunts, "my nephew is also Joe's grandchild. You're more than fucked, Taras. When we find you, you're going to be in for a world of hurt. You have a choice: tell us where you are and die easy, or don't, and when we find you—because we will—you'll be in unimaginable pain."

"Dante, you should know better than to think I'll give up where we are."

"Ales," Dante grins. "You know what to do."

I smirk. Hell fucking yes. Now it's time to play with this bitch. She wanted to be involved in this shit, now she'll pay for it. "Tell me, Annika, just how much pain can you handle?"

"Your whore cried a lot, Alessio," Taras tells me with glee. "She was sobbing and crying. The sweetest part was her standing in front of your son, trying to protect him."

I grip Annika's hair and pull her into a standing position.

"That cunt needs to keep his mouth shut," I hiss at her so only she can hear me. "All he's doing is making me angrier, and Annika, it's you who's going to feel the brunt of that anger."

Her eyes flash with fear, but her bravado sinks in. "Fuck you."

"Not even in your wildest dreams, bitch," I snarl as I sink my knife into her side.

She gasps, her eyes widen, and she looks shocked. I fucking warned her.

A cell rings, and within seconds, I hear Dante speaking.

I sink my knife into Annika over and over again. Her body trembles. She's no longer full of herself. She's scared. She's finally realized she's going to die.

"Last chance, Taras. Where is my nephew?" Dante growls.

Taras just chuckles.

"I'd say goodbye to your wife, if I were you."

"You fucking wouldn't—" Taras shouts, but Dante ends the call. "Joe called," he announces, pushing my cell away from him. "We have three locations as to where that fucker could be hiding Anthony. The boxing club, the strip club, or the Midnight Lounge."

When Dante says the Midnight Lounge, Annika

whimpers. She's just given us the location of where her husband is.

"Don't worry," I tell her. "He'll join you in Hell soon enough."

"What?" she gasps, not realizing what I'm saying.

This time when I slide my knife into her, I purposefully tilt the blade, pushing it up into her lung and piercing it.

"Hurts?" I laugh as she whimpers. "Good. I hope to fuck it does."

I release her and she crumbles to the floor, gasping for breath. She'll be dead in minutes. There's no one that's going to save her. Not today.

By the time we reach the exit of the restaurant, Annika's no longer breathing. One down, one more asshole to go.

TWENTY MINUTES later and we're in the parking lot out front of the Midnight Lounge. The darkness is keeping us hidden from view. This is the bar the Russians own, and by the looks of it, the cunts who helped Taras get my child. Anyone who stands in my way is going to die.

"You know the plan," Dante says as he looks at his men.

"Fuck the plan," Joe snarls. "These fuckers have gone too far, Dante. It's not going to be plain sailing. We take out anyone who's in our way."

I nod in complete agreement. It's time to end this fucking shit.

"We will, but we also need to ensure no one escapes. It's all well and good taking as many of them out as possible, but what happens if Taras escapes?"

Joe doesn't answer him. Instead, he turns to me, and Dante continues talking to the men, making sure they understand the plan and stick to it.

"My daughter loves you, Alessio. She's never had that before, and I'm grateful that it's you."

I raise my brow in surprise. I never expected to hear that from his mouth.

He grins. "You'll burn the fucking world down to protect her. How many other men would do that? Not many." He turns to gaze at the bar. "You know that I'm going straight?"

I nod. Gabriella told me. She wants to believe he will, but she's not sure.

"I want you to take over from me. I want someone I can trust, and that's not many people. By birth, it should be Gabby's, but she's not going to want to it You, on the other hand… You'll be a great leader. You can join my men to the Famiglia. They'll come because of who you are to me and my daughter. When the time comes, Alessio, I want you to give Anthony the business."

I stare at the man in complete shock. What the fuck? Surely he's not being serious.

"You will lead my men, Alessio. I have no doubt about that. The question is, do you want it?"

I grit my teeth. Do I want to lead my own men? Yes. But I have a loyalty to Dante, and this is already a life Gabby doesn't want. "I need to talk to my family."

The fucker smiles. "Excellent answer."

I step away from him. This isn't the time to have this conversation. My focus needs to be on my boy. I need to protect him, to get him home where he belongs.

"Everyone ready?" Stefan asks.

I stretch my neck, gun in hand. I'm more than fucking ready. "Let's do this."

Half of the men, followed by Stefan and Joe, move around the back of the building, keeping to the edge of the darkness. The rest of the men and Nikolai, along with Dante, Romero, and I, move toward the front. The second Stefan gives Dante his signal, we step into the light.

It takes the men at the doors a few seconds to realize we're not here for the show. Two of the guys raise their guns, while another speaks on his mic, no doubt alerting the men inside that we're here.

Our men have taken out the two men who had their guns raised. They never got a chance to fire a bullet. The moment they raised their guns, they were dead. By the time we reach the entrance of the bar, more of the Bratva traitors have surfaced.

I'm a step behind Dante, but when I see that motherfucking Russian bastard's hand move as he gets closer, the flash of steel, I pick up speed. My fingers close around the cunt's wrist, and I savagely twist, hearing the pop and groan of pain. Fucking bastard. No one tries to take out my brother—the boss. I fire my gun into the cunt's chest and release him. He falls to the ground, dead before he even hits it.

I'm surprised at how many of the men are turning against their boss. This is what happens when people are fed up with the lies and bullshit told by a greedy motherfucker. They believe said lies and end up looking like schmucks. Now look at them. Most of them are lying on the ground with bullet holes in their bodies.

I step over the dead and into the bar. It's silent. Not a fucking sound to be heard. Everyone is cowering under tables, clutching each other. They're trying to stay out of sight. They want to survive, and the only way to do that is not get in our way.

"Boss," Stefan says, his eyes dark and his lips pulled into a harsh line. "We've cleared the back rooms. No one is here. There's only upstairs left."

I don't wait around to see what's going to be said next. I turn on my heel and head for the stairs. I know the layout of this place like the back of my hand. When I was working to get close to Maksim for my father, I spent the majority of my time around the Russians, and this was one of the places I frequented a lot. They haven't done any updates since then.

I'm careful not to put to much pressure on my foot as I make my way up the staircase. I put my gun away and reach for my knife. I'm even more deadly with this than I am with a gun. It's always better to kill up close and personal. There's only one person in the hall, standing guard. He's not doing a good enough job, since there's only one exit and I'm using it, yet he's watching the doors behind him.

I creep up on him. The fucker has no idea I'm here. I slide my knife into his side, much like I did with Annika. He's dead before I pull it back out.

"Which door?" Romero asks as he comes to stand beside me. There are four rooms.

"We take one each. That way, no one gets past us," Nikolai says. "Whoever finds the boy is to protect him with their life."

I nod, grateful the man is here, despite all the shit that's happened between us. He's been a fucking huge help in us getting to this point. If it wasn't for him and Yelena, we'd still be thinking this had something to do with Maksim, or even wondering who the fuck it was. But because of them, we were able to get the information we needed quicker than even I could have expected.

On the count of three, we burst through the doors. I grit my teeth when I see Taras standing in the middle of the room, a beaten Maksim standing against him with a gun pointed at his head. I hear grunts and curses coming from the other rooms, and I shake my head.

The fucker set this up. No matter what room anyone entered, they'd have been ambushed.

"Alessio," Taras greets with a smile.

Before I'm able to say anything, a man comes at me. From recollection, I remember the guy as being one of Maksim's men. Daniel. Someone who was one of his better fighters. The man has been with the Bratva for years. He seemed loyal, but obviously not.

He comes at me hard and fast, landing a wicked punch to my side. It takes the breath from me. But I was trained. I'm ready for this. I shake it off quickly, and knife still in hand, I slice through his jugular with a brutal swipe.

I don't have time to recover, because yet another fucker comes at me. He's stronger and faster than Daniel. He's been trained by the best, and it shows. I dodge punch after punch, jab after jab. He's vicious with his pacing, but I'm determined. I need to get to my son, and he's the only thing that stands in the way of me and Taras. I will not fail.

He throws another jab, one which I duck, stabbing my knife into his thigh before righting myself. He howls in pain, his hand slapping against the wound. It gives me the perfect opportunity to aim for his chest. It's quick and easy. I thrust my hand forward, pushing the knife deep into his chest.

Taras throws his head back and laughs. "Well done!" He grins. "You have exceeded my expectations. Over the past five years, you have grown in strength. I'm impressed."

I pull the knife out of the fucker's chest and move forward. "I'm afraid I can't say the same about you,

Taras. You got greedy. Five years ago, you were just a guy who was hanging on the outskirts of the bratva. You did well getting Annika to marry you."

He shrugs. "That woman was begging for love. She was jealous of her cousin. It was easy to get her to do as I wanted."

"Then you fucked up. You came after my family." I shake my head and tut. "Had you left us alone, you'd have probably taken over as the Pakhan, but now you're going to die." I throw my knife at him and reach for my gun. My blade lands in his shoulder, causing him to release Maksim and howl in pain.

"You're going to die," Taras growls as he steps forward. I fire the gun twice. One hits his chest, the other his forehead.

"He's dead, Ales," Rome says as he lays a hand on my shoulder.

"Too fucking easy," I say as I turn on my heel and make my way out of the room. I need to find my son.

That bastard got an easy death. If I didn't have Anthony and Gabriella to worry about, I'd have taken the cunt somewhere and tortured him mercilessly. Instead, he's gotten away with a couple of bullets.

Fuck.

"True, but he's gone and can no longer hurt Gabby or Anthony again," Rome says. "That's something that'll make you sleep easy."

I nod, knowing he's right.

"Ales." Dante's voice is tight and filled with rage. "Nikolai and Anthony are outside in the ambulance."

I blink. What the fuck?

"He's unconscious. I believe he's been drugged. He's breathing, but we're going to have him checked out. Joe's sitting with him right now."

Relief washes through me. Thank fuck for that.

"Nikolai was stabbed," Dante says as we make our way down the stairs. "He walked into that room and was ambushed. The knife sliced along his arm. He's bleeding heavily but he's okay. He killed the fucker and then took Anthony to safety."

I owe the man. He's the reason my son is safe. I'll never be able to repay him for what he's done.

"So," Rome asks once we're outside. "What did Joe want?"

Nosey fuckers. No doubt they heard what we were talking about. I stride toward the ambulance. "He wants me to take over from him in Denver. He's going straight."

I smile as both men are silent. I guess that shocked them just as much as Joe asking me shocked me.

I climb up into the rig and pull my son into my arms. Other than a few bruises, he's relatively unharmed.

"We gotta talk," Joe says in a low voice, his jaw clenched and his eyes burning with anger.

I lift my chin, letting him know that he can talk. I

keep Anthony in my arms and watch the man in front of me try to compose himself.

"Christina," he growls. "The bitch, she told Taras that Gabby was yours." He shakes his head. "Taras' cousin was awfully chatty. Christina told him that she was staying with you, the cunt was sleeping with him. Pillow talk," he grits out. "The fucking whore knew what she was doing." He runs a shaky hand through his hair. "She's always hated my Gabby, always hated that I had a child. I never thought she'd do this."

I work my jaw, careful not to tighten my grip on my son. But fuck, my anger is rising once again. "How did she know Gabby was with me?"

"She followed her one day. The bitch didn't tell Taras that she was my daughter."

The fucking ex-wife of his is going to die. "It wasn't your fault, Joe, don't take that blame. None of us had any clue that she was gunning for Gabby."

Had we known, the bitch would already be six-feet under.

Silence spreads between us and I leave him be. He's reeling. The woman was in his bed for years, someone he married. No matter how fucked up their relationship was, this shit wasn't okay. She's going to get what's coming to her.

Anthony moves in my arms and I look down at his sleeping form. Fuck. Nothing feels better than having him here. Now it's time to take him back to his mom.

TWENTY-SEVEN
GABRIELLA

"Those meds the doctors give you seem to be helping," Makenna says.

The woman hasn't left my side since Alessio left. When I first met her and saw how bitchy she was, I honestly thought she'd be someone I wouldn't get along with, but I was wrong to judge her, just as she was with me. Makenna is actually a badass bitch who cares a hell of a lot for her family. I respect that about her. She didn't need to stay here with me, but she did. She's been my voice of reason and support while Alessio has been gone.

"Yeah, I'm able to stay awake now, which is good. I just wish I was able to see out of this bloody eye. It's pissing me off."

Her laughter is soft. "Give it time to heal, Gabs. You took one hell of a beating."

"I know. I'm just not very patient." It's probably

one of my worst qualities. I'm snappy, impatient, and damn right rude sometimes.

"Eh, you have every right not to be. You went through a tough time today. But Alessio and the others will be back soon with Anthony. Just have faith."

"I trust Alessio with my life," I tell her honestly.

She looks at me with curiosity. "You love him, don't you?"

"With everything that I am. If truth be told, I fell in love with him four years ago. It hurt that he didn't come back."

Since I woke up after falling asleep when she first arrived, we've spoken about everything, including my reasonings for keeping Anthony a secret. She may not like what I did—hell, she may not even think my reasons are valid—but she sat beside me and listened without judging—out loud anyway. She's been a huge support, something I hadn't imagined.

"He loves you too," she says. "These Bianchi men had a hard time growing up, Gabs. They didn't feel love until they met their wives, or in Alessio's case, you. Just give him time."

"I know. Alessio's told me all about his childhood." Her eyes widen in shock at my words. "Alessio was hurt deeply as a child. He felt alone, abandoned, and ashamed. In his eyes, no one has cared for him just because. He told me about what happened at your wedding, and how you cared for him. He believes that you did that for Dante, because he's family."

Her lips part, and she makes the letter 'O'.

"In his eyes, you all see him as the one who messed up, when technically he didn't. He was working a job for his father, one he wanted to see out to the end. In his eyes, he was still working for the Famiglia. He wanted Dante to have a full report on what was going on when he took over. But instead of letting him explain, and understanding what he was doing, you treated him like the enemy."

"He was in enemy territory, Gabs."

"But did he know that it was enemy territory, or did he think he was still doing a job for the Famiglia?"

Her silence is enough of an answer for me. It's something Alessio has moved on from, but he still feels the abandonment from it. "Alessio is more than a man who made a mistake. He's your brother, an uncle to your children. He's the man who will put his life on the line to save yours, and yet he has no clue that you value him as more than family. It hurts that he feels that." My eyes fill with tears. I know that many families aren't all about love and affection, but I want Alessio to know that no one sees him as this burden they have to watch out for.

"He loves you because of how purely you love him," she muses. "I get it now. You're good for him, Gabby. Probably the best thing that has ever happened to him. Welcome to the family."

I smile. God, it feels so good to hear that.

The door opens, and my heart stutters to a stop when I see Alessio walk in with a sleepy Anthony in his arms. I can't stop the onslaught of tears. I reach out my arms, pushing past the pain, wanting to hold the two of them, wanting to shower them with love.

Alessio doesn't miss a beat. He steps over to me and presses his face into my neck. "He's here, Mama," he says softly. "He's right here."

"I love you," I whisper as I press a kiss against my baby's head. "God, Alessio, I love you."

"Always, baby," he promises me.

"Is he okay?" I ask as he gently rises and holds Anthony to me.

"He was drugged, but the doctors have checked him over. He's recovering well and they'll be getting a bed for him in here so we can both be with him."

I nod, happy he's organized that.

"What happened?" I ask, realizing we're alone. Makenna's gone.

Alessio tells me everything that went down, including Nikolai saving him. The same man who tried to have him killed. I'm so very grateful to all the men who helped bring my son home to us safely.

"There's no way I could ever repay them for what they have done for us, Ales."

He presses a kiss against my head. "No, Mama, there isn't. But they know the gratitude we have for them."

The door opens once again, and a bed for

Anthony is pushed into the room, followed by a multitude of doctors and nurses, all of whom want to check on both me and my son.

"Okay, baby, we have to talk," Ales says once we're alone again. Anthony is sleeping soundly in his bed, hooked up to a drip, but other than that, he's doing okay. "Your dad wants me to take over Denver. He wants me to be the head of the Ranieri empire and promise him that when the time is right, to have Anthony take over."

I swallow hard. God, Dad. I get why he's done it. He'll value and trust Alessio to be head, but that means having Anthony and I in the limelight. Is it something I want? No, but it's Anthony's birthright. It's not something I can deny him.

"If it's what you want, Ales, then I'm behind you." I love Alessio despite the fact he's a cold-blooded killer. I'm willing to do anything in my power to be with him, and for our family to be together, so if it means moving back to Denver, then so be it.

He smiles. "You're fucking amazing, Mama. You know that?"

My cheeks heat at his words.

"Also, Gabs, I've got one more thing to tell you. Anthony being taken was Christina's fault. She worked with the Russians to have him taken. I don't know the full ins and outs as of yet, but your father's leaving to fly to Denver in an hour—" He pauses, almost as though he's trying to find the right words.

"You want to be on that plane," I finish for him.

He grits his teeth, his jaw hard. "Yes, but I don't want to leave either of you."

I press a kiss against his lips. "If this is what you need to do, then do it. We're safe here, Ales. We're going to be okay. Just come back as soon as you can."

He gets to his feet and gives me a deep, hard kiss. "I'll be back as quick as I can. The Famiglia men will be on guard. Stefan will be in this room with you."

As much as I want to roll my eyes at his overprotectiveness, I don't. He's worried and wants us protected. I can live with that.

"Okay, be safe," I whisper, hating that he's leaving again but knowing this is what he needs to do.

"Love you Mama," he tells me as he rounds the bed to Anthony and presses a kiss against his tiny head. "Be safe, and I'll be back soon."

"Love you," I say, and watch as he leaves the room.

I feel relief. That's all that I feel at knowing he's taking care of us and ensuring no one else can hurt us again.

God, he's amazing, and I'm never going to stop loving him.

TWENTY-EIGHT
ALESSIO

"Holly's on her way," Makenna tells me as I exit Gabriella's hospital room. "Raylee and Malcolm will be here tomorrow."

I nod. "Thank you," I say, knowing she's been here the entire time. "Will you stay with her?"

She smiles. "Finn and Destiny are watching the kids. They're even taking care of Molly," she says with a smile. Molly is my niece. She's Holly and Romero's daughter. "I want to apologize, Ales. I know I hurt Gabby with what I said, but I didn't mean to offend. I was just looking out for you."

"I understand, it's all good," I assure her. "Watch over them for me," I ask.

"With my life. Stefan and I have them, and Holly will help keep them entertained."

I smile. Small talk is not Makenna's forte. "Thank you."

Walking out of the hospital is hard. All I want to

do is turn back and go be with Gabby and Anthony, but I need to do this. I need to get rid of the last remaining threat they have. Christina. Going to Denver isn't what I wanted, but it's sure as fuck where I'm going.

"We're coming with," Dante tells me. "You don't need us, but we're coming."

I nod, knowing that as the boss, he'll want to be there.

"You should take the offer," Romero says once we're in the car. "It makes sense. Being here with us is the thing we all dreamed about, but Ales, you have what it takes to be the boss. You've proven that over the years. Everyone can see it."

"Take it," Dante agrees. "It will help us expand throughout the US, making us more powerful than ever."

"But I'm your Consigliere."

Dante nods. "You were, but now you're going to be a boss. Stefan will make a great Consigliere."

My chest feels tight, but I manage to nod my gratitude. Fuck. Never did I think I could be the boss. I was always destined to be the younger brother. Now I have the time to prove that I'm more than that. More than the youngest Bianchi sibling and a hell of a lot more than the fuck up.

"Have you spoken to Gabby about this?" Rome asks me.

"Yeah. She's never wanted to be a part of this life. For her, she's always wanted a quiet life," I tell them, letting them know just how much she's giving up for me. "But she'll be wherever I am."

She's always given a fuck. That's one of the many things that drew me to her. She cared even when she shouldn't have. The woman is an anomaly, and I'm a lucky bastard that she's all mine.

The rest of the car ride is silent. My anger is still simmering. I'm fucking pissed. I didn't get to quench my bloodlust. Everyone died way too easily. I would have loved to prolong the pain; kept the cunt alive for weeks—hell, even months, and made sure he understood what happens to those who come for my family. Instead, I'm going to have to make peace with the fact the asshole doesn't get to feel that. He'll never feel the pain he put my woman through.

"I take it you've spoken to my daughter," Joe says in lieu of a greeting when we enter the private jet.

I nod stoically, grateful to have this opportunity but still unsure about it. It means being away from my brothers, something I never thought possible.

"Good. Once Gabby and Anthony are fighting fit, we'll get you introduced to the men. Within a year, you'll be taking over."

"Sounds great," I reply, and move toward the back of the plane and take a seat. I pull out my cell and call Makenna.

"They're fine, Ales. Anthony is still sleeping, and Holly is talking Gabby's ear off. You know what Hol's like when she gets going."

I chuckle. Holly loves to talk. She's sweet and

different from her aunt, but she'll hover over Gabby until she's released from the hospital. "Thanks. I'll call you when we land."

"Make that bitch pay," she spits.

I smile. She's no doubt jealous she can't be in on the action. "Oh, she'll be in a world of hurt, Kenna, don't you worry."

"I know. We've got Gabby and Anthony, Ales. We'll make sure they're safe."

"I ow—"

"Don't fucking say it," she snaps. "You're family. This is what we do."

I say goodbye and end the call. Dante, Romero, and Joe are sitting together talking. I leave them be. I'm in no mood to make small talk.

I close my eyes and listen to their voices. The sooner we get to Denver, the better.

"SHE'S INSIDE, BOSS," one of Joe's men says with a smirk. "The bitch has no idea what's about to happen."

"Stupid," Joe hisses as he leads us into the house. "Why would she stay here? She'd have known this would be the first place I'd come looking."

"Joe?" Christina says, her face paling and her eyes wide. "What are you doing here?"

'You seriously didn't think you'd get away with this, did you?" Joe snarls at his soon-to-be-ex-wife.

"My child, Christina, you went after my daughter and grandson."

The woman's eyes flash with shock, but she quickly recovers.

"What did you expect? You weren't being careful, Joe. Everyone knew that the bitch was your child. If that wasn't bad, you got that whore of yours knocked up. Christ," she spits. "Do you not know how to keep your fucking dick in your pants? Thirty years, Joe. I gave you thirty fucking years, and this is how you repay me."

Joe laughs in her face. "You have always been a bitch, Chris. The moment you found out about Gabby, you hated her. You wanted me away from her. Why? Jealousy?"

"You never loved me. You always were looking for something else. Of course I was jealous. I'm the reason you got this powerful. I stayed by your side as you built this empire, but the second your floozy gets pregnant, you divorce me."

"The moment you pushed my grandson away, Chris, that was the day you sealed your fate."

Her eyes flash with anger and her cheeks redden. "That fucking child. He's your pride and joy. No one will ever compete with that bitch and brat."

"It was never a competition, bitch. You were never in their league. Instead of accepting that we were done, you went into bed with the fucking Russians?"

She shrugs, unaffected by what she's done. "I saw

that bitch in New York," she snarls. "Living it up like she's something. I followed her and found her shacked up with none other than Alessio Bianchi. Imagine my surprise when I go to dinner and overhear the Russians talking about how much they despise the Bianchis. It was fate."

"You cunt," I snarl, and she laughs. "Do you know what they did?"

"I don't care. By the looks of you being here, I'd say they did a good job. Did they die?"

I step forward and watch her swallow hard. "The Russians did die. Fuck, they didn't die as I wanted, but they're now no longer breathing. As for my woman and child, they're safe, and you're going to pay for what you've done."

She crosses her arms over her chest. "My dad will have something to say about this."

Joe laughs. "No, he won't. I've already spoken to him. He had a choice. He either lost you or he lost his empire. I guess no one ever loved you, Chris."

"You always were a bastard, Joe."

He smirks at her. "You're going to die, Chris, and it's going to be painful. I've been thinking a fuck of a lot since finding out you had a hand in this. I wanted to find the best way to kill you, and everything I thought of wasn't enough. But then it came to me. You made my daughter live her worst nightmare by having her son taken from her. Now you get to live out your own."

The woman's eyes get wide with fear, and she starts to step backward.

"No," she whispers, and the horrified sound makes me smile. Oh, he's got her rattled. "Please, Joe, don't do this." She's hyperventilating, her face red and splotchy, her hands shaking as she continues to take steps backward.

"It's done, Chris, but I'm going to enjoy you begging for your life." He nods to the men behind her, and instantly, they reach for her.

"No!" she screams, kicking her legs and bucking against their hold. "Don't do this."

The men carry her out of the room, and we follow behind them. I'm more than intrigued about what's going to happen. Judging by the frightened look on her face, it's going to be fun to watch.

We step out into the backyard, and that's when I see some of his men standing over a fucking hole.

"Joe, don't do this," she yells, her screams renting the air, her voice filled with fear.

The man's not listening to her. Hell, after what she's done, she deserves everything she gets.

His men unceremoniously throw the bitch into the shallow grave they've built.

"Gentleman," Joe says as his men start to shovel the dirt back into the hole. "Chris here is terrified of being buried alive. She was locked in a closet by accident when she was a girl, and since then, she's been terrified of it happening again. She's going to die, terrified out of her mind."

Fucking hell.

"Why not carve the bitch up?" Romero asks with knitted brows.

"Because, she'd have died in pain. This way she's going to be in pain and frightened. The bitch is going to piss and shit herself. She'll be so scared, she won't be able to control it."

I chuckle. It's ruthless and less messy than I'd have liked but fuck if it doesn't quell my need for revenge. This bitch is getting her just desserts, and I'm glad to stand back and watch this play out.

"Joe!" Her scream is muffled by the dirt that now covers her. "Please don't do this. I beg you. I'll do anything, please."

Her pleas go unanswered. No one here gives a fuck about what she wants or needs. She's going to die whether she likes it or not. No amount of crying and screaming is going to stop this.

Her breathing starts to deepen as her panic grows higher. God, what I'd give to be able to see what's going on down there. The sounds are fucking music to my ears.

I've heard people plead for their lives. I've heard the cries of pain and sorrow. Hell, I've even heard people be scared. But this. Fuck, her screams are hoarse and filled with so much fear and pain that if it were anyone but this bitch, I'd feel sorry for them.

Everyone in the backyard is silent, listening to Christina's painful shallow breaths. There's no way in Hell she'll be able to survive this any longer.

Funnily enough, I've never heard someone be scared to death, so this is a first for me, and it's a sweet as fuck first.

The breathing is either too low or stopped all together, and I take a deep breath and release it. Dead. The bitch is fucking gone, and there's no one left to come at my family. Anyone tries in the future, and I may just take a leaf out of Joe's book and find their fear. Kill the asses that way.

"Alright, son," Joe says with a smug grin. "The wicked witch is dead, my daughter is safe, and it's time for us to go home to her. Our job here is done."

I smile. He's right. Now I need to focus on ensuring that both Anthony and Gabby heal.

"Dante, have Makenna look for a home for us. I want us to be moved in before Gabby and Anthony even leave the hospital." I won't have them returning to the apartment. I want to rid the memories for them.

Dante chuckles as he types out a message. "She's going to love this."

He throws his head back and laughs, handing his cell for me to read the message.

Makenna: Challenge accepted.

I smile. Fuck. It feels good to breathe freely. No more enemies hiding in the shadows. It should be plain sailing from here on out. Now to go back to my woman and son.

TWENTY-NINE
GABRIELLA

Ten weeks later

I sit on the couch, the TV on in the background, but I'm not watching or listening. I'm numb. I swallow hard, trying to come to terms with the news I've just gotten.

I should have been more careful. I should have realized the pain medication would have made my pill be wonky, not to mention the days I spent in the hospital.

Pregnant.

Damn. After the awful birth I had with Anthony, I never really thought much more about having another. But whilst in the throes of passion with Ales, I agreed to letting him impregnate me. The last thing I want is a repeat of what I went through—this time I may not survive. My heart won't stop pounding, my palms are sweaty, and I'm trembling.

After what happened in New York, it took a while for me to heal. Alessio was with me every step of the way, holding my hand through the pain. He didn't bring us back to the apartment. Instead, he rented out a house for us to stay in, knowing that being in the apartment would be too much.

Thankfully, Anthony doesn't have any nightmares or lasting effects from being kidnapped. I can only hope that he was too young to understand what truly happened. As for me, I'm slowly being able to close my eyes and not think of that day. It's going to take time until I can do it without seeing that man take Anthony, but I know I'll get there eventually.

I know Alessio has been wanting this. He set out from the beginning to get me knocked up and I laughed it off, but now that it's happened, I'm struck with paralyzing fear of what could happen. I can't help but feel raw and numb at the prospect of my child and me dying during childbirth, leaving Anthony and Alessio alone. That thought alone has me hyperventilating.

I'm losing it. God, most people when finding out they are pregnant are overjoyed and cry happy tears. I'm sitting here sobbing with fear.

"Mama?" Alessio's voice is deep but silky. I love the way he calls me Mama. It sends shivers throughout my body. "Baby, what's happened?"

I suck in a sharp breath as he crouches down in front of me, his calloused hands framing my face. "Ales," I breathe, unable to stop the panic.

"Breathe for me, Mama. Come on, you've got this." I listen to his voice, focusing on it, using it as a channel to guide me to the present. "That's it, baby, breathe."

It takes us a while, but he gets me to a place where I can think and breathe. I'm able to focus clearly on him. My breathing, although a little erratic, becomes steadier.

"Talk to me," he urges.

I take a steadying breath, looking at him, watching him, wanting to see his face when I tell him my news. I'm scared. Beyond that. I'm terrified.

"I'm pregnant," I whisper, that fear grasping my heart with an ice-cold hand. "I'm so fucking scared, Ales." I swallow back the rising bile. "When I went into labor with Anthony, it was awful. We both almost died."

His beautiful honey eyes flash with fear, worry, and confusion. "What happened?"

I recount one of the worst days of my life. I tell him about the pain and heartache at the thought I was losing our baby. I walk him through everything that happened: the confusion, pain, and fear I felt at not really knowing what was going on, and then ultimately the emergency cesarean that was our only option. I was hemorrhaging. If they didn't get the bleeding under control, they would have had to give me a hysterectomy. God, even thinking back to that day, hurts.

"Why didn't you tell me?" he asks softly.

Over the past ten weeks, things between us have been amazing. We're settling back in Denver. To my shock, Alessio purchased my old home, a place I loved and that gave me some of the best memories. It's where I met Ales, where Anthony was conceived. To have us living here together was the best present I could have ever been given. Only to find out that Ales purchased it not long after I fled Denver. I love him more with every passing day. Being here, away from New York, I have watched him grow in his new position as second-in-command to my father. The men love him and have accepted him with open arms. I believe that's down to Ales and I having Anthony, but I'm so proud of how he's adapted to being away from his family.

"I didn't realize I'd be this afraid, Ales," I tell him, taking another steadying breath. "I knew you wanted another baby; I just didn't expect it to come with this debilitating fear."

He pulls me into his arms and carries me to our bed, not once saying a word. My heart is in my throat. Is this a deal breaker? What if I can't get past the fear? Will this be the end of us?

He lies me on the bed and looms over me, his fists either side of my face. "Mama, I couldn't give a fuck if you never got pregnant again. While I'd love to watch your amazing body change as you grow our baby, I'm not putting you through that if you don't want it," he tells me as he leans in closer to me. "You want to go to the clinic and terminate, I'll be right at your side."

I stare up at him. "Really?"

"Mama, you are all I have wanted for the past four years. You think I'm going to throw us away because of something that could kill you? Fuck no. No matter what happens, you're mine, and I fucking love you."

I sob. This man is amazing, and I'm so glad he's in my life.

"Don't cry, Mama. No matter what, we're going to be okay."

I smile up at him. "I love you," I tell him, needing him to know just how much.

His grin makes my heart melt. God, I love that cheeky grin he has. "I fucking love you, Gabriella Sanchez. Will you do the honor of marrying me?"

I blink, completely shocked by his words. We've never discussed this before. Hell he's never even let me think this has been on his radar.

"You're killing me, Mama. Are you going to marry me or what?" He reaches into his pocket and pulls out a teal blue box. My heart stops as I stare at it. What the hell? "You've been mine since the night you saved me, Gabby. You had no idea that you'd done more than just have me patched up. Without you, I'm nothing."

"Yes," I whisper, my tears flowing freely. "You

are the only man I will ever love, Alessio. You made me believe in trust."

He slams his lips down on mine, his tongue sliding into my mouth, and I release a moan in the back of my throat. His hand dives into my hair, and he tilts my head, giving him better access. God, I love how he gets me so worked up with just a kiss. I'm soaking wet. I need him.

His cock thickens against my stomach, and I grind against it, loving the friction, needing to feel him inside of me. He breaks the kiss, and I feel the loss of it. I whimper, wanting him back. But I smile when he reaches for my clothes and starts to pull them off my body. I reach for him and help him out of his slacks and shirt. God, I love his body. Toned and muscular. Everything about him is like he just walked out of a GQ shoot.

He slides his hand around my nape and pulls me in for another kiss. I moan against his lips as I cling to his shoulders and wrap my legs around his waist. His cock butts against the entrance of my pussy.

He slowly pushes into me, and I groan as he inches inside of me, the thickness of him pulling at my pussy. It feels as though he's splitting me in two. I love it.

"Fuck, Mama, nothing is better than being inside of you. Nothing is better than this." He takes my mouth once again, and I'm lost in him. Lost in everything that is us.

He slowly pulls out of me. "God, Ales, I love you," I cry out as he thrusts deep inside of me, his thickness stretching my tight walls. "More," I whimper, needing him to give me everything.

He grins, knowing exactly what I love. Ales is more than capable of taking me to the highest of heights.

He quickens his pace, and his thrusts become hard, heavy, and brutal, but so damn good. I'm so lost in him, us. He's right, nothing is better than him being inside of me. I love our connection.

I fuck him back, meeting him thrust for thrust. I preen as he releases a guttural growl. He's close to the edge, the place where he loses it and takes me hard, fast, and fucking amazingly. I need him to get to that place.

I press my lips against his neck and nip at the skin. And that's all it takes. He pistons his hips, his cock pushing into me over and over again.

"I'm going to come," I gasp, my pleasure rising.

"Come for me," he grunts. "Mama, come," he demands, his voice thick and gritty.

My orgasm hits me like a freight train, and I cry out, unable to hold it in.

"Fuck yes," he snarls, his hips pushing harder and faster. "Mine, Mama, all fucking mine."

He thrusts once—twice—thrice, his hands tighten on my hips, and he releases a long, ragged groan as he comes inside of me.

We're both breathless as he collapses onto the bed beside me. "Never doubt it, baby, you're all I fucking want. We have our family: you, me, and Anthony. We don't need anyone else."

I press against him. "I love you."

He kisses the top of my head. "I love you too, Mama." He reaches down for the sheets and throws them over us. "Are you ready for the trip tomorrow?"

I smile. "Yes," I breathe. I'm so excited to go visit Indianapolis. Ade and Hayden welcomed their baby five days ago, and they want us to come out and meet her. I can't wait.

"I know that you miss her and Raylee," he says quietly.

"I have everything I need right here in this home, Ales. My girls are always a call away."

He crushes me to his body, and I snake my arm around his waist. It doesn't take long until I'm falling asleep, the lull of Alessio's heartbeat hypnotic.

"I'M SO happy to see you," Adelina says as I take a seat next to her. She passes me beautiful Vivi-Anna and I cuddle the little girl close. "How are you feeling?"

Not only did Raylee arrive the day after the attack, but Adelina did also. Both women spent the majority of time in my hospital room with me. They were worried, and I love that they love me, but I didn't want them to be worried, especially with Ade being pregnant.

"I'm okay. We're all getting there. Healing takes time, but we're okay."

She pushes my shoulder with her own. "You're not alone," she whispers. "No matter what, you have us, whenever you need a shoulder to cry on. Not to mention that man of yours loves you something fierce and will do anything you ask."

I swallow hard at her words. He really would do anything I ask, including giving up his dream of wanting another child. Being pregnant has thrown my emotions off kilter, and I'm so confused as to what I want to happen. I woke up this morning unsure of what to do. I change my mind at least twice an hour. I think it's best to think on it for a while. I still have time to decide without rushing into it.

"I thought Chloe was coming?" Holly says as she comes to sit with us. "Da says she was joining us." Chloe is Holly's eighteen-year-old sister, she's Denis' daughter, and Makenna's niece.

I glance at Ade, who's got a furrow between her brows. "She should have been here by now," she whispers. "Hay," she calls out, and the room goes silent. "Wasn't Chloe supposed to be here by now?"

The air in the room goes static at her words. "I'll call Elio," Rocco says, in regards to his brother.

"I'll call Chloe," Jade mutters as she reaches for her cell.

"I'll call Denis," Makenna sighs.

We wait on bated breath for everyone to finish their calls.

"No answer," Jade says as she hits something on her cell and puts it to her ear again.

"Denis said that Elio and Chloe left almost three hours ago. They should have been here by now," Makenna tells us.

Rocco enters the room again, his eyes dark with anger.

"I got through to Elio's cell," he begins, and my heart batters against my chest. God, this doesn't sound good. "He didn't answer, but a cop did. Elio's car was struck by a semi. There were signs of a struggle, and the passenger's side door was left open. Chloe's gone."

Movement happens at once. Every member of the Gallagher family is heading toward the door, not a word said between them. Hayden moves to Ade.

"I'll call once I have news," he tells her. "Alessio, are you staying here?"

Alessio isn't far from my side these days. Unless he's at work, and even then he has more men surrounding the house than what's needed, but I know it gives him peace of mind, so I don't complain. The day that I was beaten and Anthony was taken, there were no guards on us and that's what's shaken him to his core. "I'm staying. I'll guard Ade and Vivi-Anna with my life."

Hayden nods, presses a kiss against Ade's head,

and does the same to his daughter's before he follows his family out the door.

"They'll find her," Alessio assures Ade. "The Gallaghers are a force to be reckoned with. Pissing them off is never a good idea. Whoever took Chloe will be punished," he announces, before going in search of our son.

"I just hope they find her before she's hurt," Ade whispers, and the pain in her voice makes my heart clench.

"I do too," I reply.

God, how much heartache does one family have to have?

SEVEN MONTHS LATER, I gave birth to a beautiful baby girl, who looks just like me. Gracie Josephine Bianchi is the apple of her father's eye and the pride of her big brother.

My family is complete, and I couldn't be happier.

The End.

This may be the end of the Made Series but it's far from the end of these families.

Chloe's story is up next in a Fury Vipers and Made

Series crossover - https://books2read.com/FuryVipersPyro

Elio's story is coming soon in a new series called the Gallo Famiglia- https://books2read.com/RuthlessArrangement

HAVE YOU MET THE KINGPIN?
THE KINGPIN SERIES IS OUT NOW

Chapter One
Mia

"Mia!" Sarah cries and I quickly pull on my strappy heels, throwing open the bathroom door I narrow my eyes as she claps her hands like a seal. "You look hot!" She smiles widely, "Are you planning on handing in your V-card tonight?"

I roll my eyes, that's all she's focused on. "No plans to." This has been a constant discussion between us in the last month, I haven't found anyone who I'm attracted to and I'm worried that there's something wrong with me.

She huffs at me as she flicks her blond hair over her shoulder, "Mia, you're going to college, no one goes to college as a virgin anymore."

"Shut up." I say as I throw my bag on the floor, "I'm ready whenever you are." My nerves are setting in, I've never done anything like this before, if Mom knew what Sarah and I have planned she'd go crazy, she believes that I'm staying at Sarah's and Sarah's mom thinks she's staying with me tonight.

She claps her hands together and grins, "Let's go, I'm so excited. Tonight is going to be epic." She links her arm through mine and we walk out of the motel room and towards the BART station, four stops and we'll be in San Fran. My excitement is building as the adrenaline courses through my body.

Walking up to the club, there's a long line and I sigh, the longer we wait the more nervous I'm going to get, but Sarah grabs my hand and practically drags me toward the front of the line, causing a lot of groans from the people in the queue as we pass them and I instantly feel bad. I'd be pissed too if someone was cutting the line. "Hey Jagger." Sarah purrs as we come to a stop.

Jagger's at least six foot seven along with having tattoos snaking across his neck and when combined with his shaven head, gives him a menacing aura. He takes a sweeping glance at both Sarah and I, a smile spreading across his face. "Damn Sarah, looking good." He winks as he holds out his hands and we both pass him the fake IDs Sarah's brother Frankie got for us. He doesn't really pay much attention to them as his gaze is directed on Sarah's chest, he just hands them back to us, "Have a wonderful night ladies." He nods his head indicating for us to go on ahead.

Both Sarah and I casually stroll into the club, while inside I'm squealing. I can't believe we managed to get in. "Look a table, Mia, grab it and I'll get us some drinks." She instructs. My feet move toward the empty table and I take a sweeping glance around the club. It's crazy busy already, there's people talking and having fun while others are on the dance floor, the one thing they all have in common, is their bright smiles.

"Let's toast!" Sarah says loudly trying to be heard over the music as she hands me a drink. "To us, may we achieve everything we set our minds to. May we be happy wherever in this world we may end up, and lastly, may we forever be friends!" I raise my hand and our glasses clink against one another. "Mia, we've been friends since first grade, we've been through a lot and made it out the other end. Thank you for being here with me tonight."

Sarah and I have been friends since first grade, we along with six other girls had been inseparable since then. We'd do anything and everything together. We all had our weddings planned out, with the other seven girls being bridesmaids. That was up until two months ago when Sarah slept with Riley just after he had broken up with Lola. Yes, Sarah went against girl code but she didn't deserve the brutal shunning that all the girls gave her, I wouldn't be a part of that and I too was shunned. It showed me that they were never truly my friends if they could turn against me that quickly.

I give Sarah a warm smile, "I'm so glad that we came, I already feel lighter." I've been so stressed about going to college, it's going to be the furthest I've ever been away from home and I'm not sure if I'll be able to do it.

"Let's enjoy our last night together. Tomorrow is a new chapter." Sarah tells me. I'm going to miss her like crazy, she's going to New York to try and pursue a career in fashion. She wants to be anywhere but Oakland. She's happy to get away from the crap she's been dealing with.

"You want to dance?" She asks and I shake my head, I'm not in the mood yet. I'm not a great dancer and it takes it a while to gather the courage to let loose. "Suit yourself." She winks at me and leaves me at the table as she saunters off to the dance floor. Within seconds she's dancing with a guy, a beautiful smile on her face, she's so happy, it's good to see especially after her feeling down the past couple of months.

I stand here and watch silently as I sip on my drink. I can feel eyes on me, the heat from their gaze makes the hair on the back of my neck stand up. Turning around I can't see anyone in particular who's making me feel this way. Shaking my head I turn back to the dance floor. Sarah's having so much fun, she's really letting her hair down and relaxing. She smiles and waves over at me as the song changes and her eyes light up, its Cardi B's *Bodak Yellow* that fills the club, "Mia," She calls as she raises her arms in the air and her body begins to sway.

Downing the drink, I place the glass on the table and make my way over to Sarah, my hips swaying as I do so. Sarah reaches her hands out as I get closer to her and she pulls me toward her, both of us getting lost in the music and dancing away. Tonight, neither of us have any problems, we're living in the moment.

I manage to stay out dancing for six songs before I need a rest. Walking over to the bar, I order us Margaritas, I manage to get the table we were at when we first came in and place the two drinks down. Peering up at Sarah who's dancing alone, I've not seen her this happy for a long time, even before she slept with Riley.

A shadow falls over the table and I look up, and my breath catches as a gorgeous man stands before me. Jet black hair, piercing brown eyes and a smirk that screams bad boy, not to mention the tattoo that's peeking out from his shirt collar. "You alone?" His deep and gravely tone sends tingles down my spine. I instinctively know that he was the one who was staring at me earlier, the person who made the hair on my neck stand up.

My tongue sweeps across my bottom lip as I stare, mesmerized by him. I shake my head, "No, I'm here with a friend."

His eyebrow raises in question, "Friend?"

"Yeah, friend." I tell him and I glance over at

Sarah, she's now dancing with the guy she had danced with earlier.

His lips twitch, "That's good."

"Oh and why is that?" I ask, my voice husky. I can't believe that I'm flirting with this guy. I've never flirted with anyone, I'm usually the shy one, the girl that gets overlooked because my friends are amazing.

"Because you're coming home with me tonight and I'd hate to break up a relationship."

I splutter, "I'm sorry, says who?" How dare he?

"Says me." He smiles and God, he's beautiful.

"I'll think about it." I don't know what the hell has gotten into me tonight but I'm tempted to go home with him.

His smile widens, "You do that." He slowly walks away, his eyes boring into me as he does so. I can't take my eyes off of him.

"Who's the hunk?" I spin on my seat, my heart beating fast as I come face to face with Sarah, her eyes on the crowd that the guy just disappeared into.

Taking a sip of my drink, trying to steady the rhythm of my pulse. The tequila is strong but the lime takes the edge off of it. "I don't know."

"So, are you going home with him?"

I gape at her, "How the hell did you hear that?"

She shrugs, "I didn't, I can lip read. You should totally do it."

"I don't know, I don't even know his name. Hell he just asked if I was alone and then told me that I was going home with him." What the hell has gotten into me? I would think that was an ultimate turnoff and yet, I find it sexy as hell.

Her eyes widen and a slow smirk forms on her lips, "That is hot! Look, see how you feel by the end of the night. You can go with him and see where it takes you. No one is pressuring you to do anything, if they do, I'll kick their ass." She winks at me as she picks the Margarita up and takes a sip, "He really is hot."

I nod, "Yeah he is." He's freaking gorgeous. "What about you? You going home with that guy?"

She waves her hand dismissively, "I'm not sure, we're just dancing at the moment. I'd love to go home with Jagger, but I don't see that happening."

"Why?"

She tips her chin behind me and I turn and see Jagger standing by the door, his arm around some girl's waist as they talk. "That's why. She's Carina, she's his on and off again girlfriend. The last I heard they were off permanently. Guess that's no longer the case."

Shit, gone is her happiness and in its place is the usual defeated, sad Sarah that I'm used to seeing. "His loss, come on, let's go and dance again."

We both finish our drinks and she smiles, "You're right. It's his loss. Besides, it's not as though I'm going to see him again after tomorrow so what's the point?"

Linking my arm through hers we make our way to the dance floor, the hairs on the back of my neck stand up once again, turning I see the dark-haired sexy God standing at the back of the club with his arms crossed looking at Sarah and I. My heart begins to race as his eyes rake over my body.

"Mia, I've never seen you so flustered before." Sarah says as we dance, "You keep glancing at the back of the club, is he there?"

"Yes, he hasn't taken his eyes off of us."

She scoffs, "Oh Mia, my sweet, sweet Mia. His eyes are not on me."

"What am I going to do Sarah?" This is all so new to me, I've no idea what to do, and I don't even know what to say or how to act. I should forget it and go back to the motel with Sarah.

"Mia, that's something I can't tell you. What does your head tell you?"

I laugh, "To run back to the motel."

She smiles, "And your heart?"

I throw my head back and groan, "My heart wants to go and see what happens."

She pulls me into her arms, "Your head wants to protect your heart, and you have to decide which one you want to follow."

I nod, "I guess it's going to be a decision I make when the time comes."

"That time is going to come sooner than you realize." She laughs, "Mia, it's almost closing."

Glancing around the club, the throbbing crowd from earlier is thinning, I catch sight of a guy holding his girl's shoes as they leave the club hand in hand. A cheer rings out, turning, I see a guy downing his beer being egged on by his friends. Damn, she's right. "One more drink?" It may help me make a decision.

She shrugs, "Yeah sure, we are celebrating after all."

Fifteen minutes later and the club is closing, I glance around and see that the mystery man is gone. That makes up my mind anyway. Sarah isn't leaving with anyone either. I'm not upset; I've actually had an amazing night.

"Ladies." A deep voice says as we reach the door.

I turn around and see Jagger standing there waiting for us, "Hey," I say softly, but he doesn't respond, his eyes darkening as they take in Sarah.

"Hey Jagger, did you have a good night?" She asks softly, a flirty smile on her lips.

His tongue darts out and swipes at his bottom lip. "I'm hoping it's about to get a hell of a lot better, sweetness. You want to come back to my place?"

Sarah instantly nods, and I suck in a sharp breath. Damn, what is with these men and the way they can make us lose our minds? "Jag," Sarah says turning to face him, her brow furrowed, "Do you know her mystery man?"

A cocky grin appears on his face, "Describe him. I know a lot of people."

"Tall, jet black hair, piercing brown eyes." Heat rises in my cheeks as I describe him. "He has a tattoo on his neck."

"Sugar," He says a bright smile on his face, "take a seat and wait a moment, your man's coming for you." The last couple of party goers leave, making us the only ones left here. Sarah walks up to Jagger, and he wastes no time in wrapping his arms around her. I have to look away as they make gooey eyes at each other. "He's a good man, he'll treat you right." He tells me, and I feel a little less anxious about staying here.

Sarah rushes over to me, "Remember what I said, do whatever you want, today is our last day here Mia, I want it to be one we remember. Meet me back at the motel at six, that way we'll be home and no one will notice."

"Okay, have fun," I whisper to her, nerves and excitement starting to settle in me. He didn't leave, he's still here. I'm really tempted to go back with him and see where this goes.

Her smile is infectious, "Oh, trust me, I will." Jagger pulls his keys out of his pocket and takes a step toward the exit. Sarah looks back at me, hesitates and places a hand on Jagger's chest to stop him. "Do you want us to wait with you?"

I shake my head, "No, you two go and have fun."

"I'll see you tomorrow," Sarah calls out as they leave, Jagger locking up behind him, leaving me alone in this club.

I take out my cell from the hidden pocket in my dress; there are no missed calls or texts. I'm not sure why I thought there would be, Mom has no reason to believe I'm not at Sarah's house. I've been there a million times before.

I quickly send a message to Sarah's brother, Frankie. He's like my brother too; he's been a part of my life for a long time. I've not seen much of him since he joined the Military. He's a SEAL, and a good one at that.

> Be safe out there and come home to us.

I'm going to miss him, but I'm proud of him, he's doing what he's wanted to do since he was a teenager. He replies instantly.

> You know me, nothing can bring me down.

I shake my head, he's such an ass.

> Frankie I'm being serious. Be safe.

His reply makes me sad as I don't know when the next time we'll see each other will be.

> Always Mia, look after yourself and I'll see you soon.

Putting my cell back in my pocket, I glance around the club, it's completely empty and looks so different than when it's open. The bar is black and when the main lights are on it looks fluorescent. It's such a cool feature, but makes it look ordinary once the lights aren't on.

Hands run down my arms, leaving goosebumps

in their wake. "Sorry for the delay." His deep voice settles over me, making my heart race. "Thank you for waiting."

I turn to face him. It's weird being the only ones left in the club. "No worries," I reply softly, unsure of myself and what I'm doing here.

His hand comes up to my chin, and his fingers tilt my face up so that I'm looking into those gorgeous brown eyes of his, I could get lost in them, "Do you want to come with me?"

My tongue darts out and licks my bottom lip, I'm nervous, and it's showing. "Yes. I want to come with you."

He leans down, and his mouth captures mine. This isn't soft and sweet like I thought it would be, it's hard and consuming. Our lips are closed, but it doesn't matter. It's still the best kiss I've ever had and if this is a preview of what's to come then sign me up. "Ready?" He asks as he pulls away from me.

I nod, I'm unable to talk, he's left me breathless.

"Good." He smirks and helps me to my feet. His hand on the base of my back, he leads us to the door which he unlocks and then leads me out of the club. The fresh air fills my lungs as I wait for him to lock the club up, when he's finished he leads me into a waiting car. Shit, he has a chauffeur. Climbing into the back, he gets in beside me, and his hand grips my thigh. His fingers begin to slowly caress my leg. Heat rises throughout my body, and I squeeze my legs together as liquid pools there. Shit, I've never been so turned on from someone touching me before. Leaning closer, his lips graze the outer shell of my ear. "I can't wait to get you inside my house. I can't wait to finally have you, watching you all night has been driving me crazy." He whispers, and I whimper. "We're going to have fun tonight."

I don't know how much time passes before we reach his house, but it only seems like minutes. He's been driving me crazy the entire drive, his fingers caressing my skin, going higher and higher up my leg but never going anywhere near my panties. His breath hot against my ear as he whispered what he wanted to do to me when he got me inside. He helps me out of the car, placing his hand on the base of my back. I'm hot and bothered, I need him, and I have no idea how or why, but I know that I do.

As soon as we enter the house, he's on me. His mouth fusing against mine, his tongue sweeping into my mouth and our teeth clashing. It's hot, wild, and brutal. It's amazing. My hands go to his shirt, wanting, no *needing* to touch him. "The first time is going to be quick. I hope you didn't plan on getting any sleep tonight. I have plans for you." He growls as he pulls my dress over my head, leaving me standing in my panties and heels. His eyes darken as he rakes over my body. "I'm going to have so much fun with you."

BOOKS BY BROOKE:

The Kingpin Series:

Forbidden Lust

Dangerous Secrets

Forever Love

The Made Series:

Bloody Union

Unexpected Union

Fragile Union

Shattered Union

Hateful Union

Vengeful Union

Explosive Union

Cherished Union

Obsessive Union

Gallo Famiglia:

Ruthless Arrangement

The Fury Vipers MC Series:

Stag

Mayhem

Digger

Ace

Pyro

Shadow

Standalones:

Saving Reli

Taken By Nikolai

A Love So Wrong

Other pen names

Stella Bella

(A forbidden Steamy Pen name)

Taboo Temptations:

Wicked With the Professor

Snowed in with Daddy

Wooed by Daddy

Loving Daddy's Best Friend

Brother's Glory

Daddy's Curvy Girl

Daddy's Intern

His Curvy Brat

Taboo Teachings:

Royally Taught

Extra Curricular with Mr. Abbot

Private Seduction:

Seduced by Daddy's Best Friend

Stepbrother Seduction

His Curvy Seduction

ABOUT BROOKE SUMMERS:

USA Today Bestselling Author Brooke Summers is a Mafia Romance author and is best known for her Made Series.

Brooke Summers was born and raised in South London. She lives with her daughter and hubby.

Brooke has been an avid read for many years. She's a huge fan of Colleen Hoover and Kristen Ashley.

Brooke has been dreaming of writing for such a long time. When she was little, she would make up stories just for fun. Seems as though she was destined to become an author.

WANT TO KNOW MORE ABOUT BROOKE SUMMERS?

Check out her website:
www.brookesummersbooks.com

Subscribe to her newsletter: www.brookesummersbooks.com/newsletter

Made in the USA
Las Vegas, NV
29 January 2025